RULES OF
ATTRACTION

ALSO BY SIMONE ELKELES
Perfect Chemistry

RULES OF ATTRACTION

SIMONE ELKELES

SIMON AND SCHUSTER

First published in Great Britain in 2011 by Simon and Schuster UK Ltd
A CBS COMPANY
Originally published in the United States of America in 2010 by
Walker Publishing Company, Inc.

Copyright © Simone Elkeles 2010

Simon & Schuster UK Ltd
1st Floor, 222 Gray's Inn Road,
London WC1X 8HB

A CIP catalogue record for this book is
available from the British Library.

ISBN 978-0-85707-043-2

1 3 5 7 9 10 8 6 4 2

Printed in the UK by CPI Cox & Wyman, Reading, Berkshire RG1 8EX

www.simonandschuster.co.uk

To Karen Harris, an incredible friend, mentor, critique partner, writer, and so much more. I would have been lost without your guidance and friendship these past seven years. Thank you a million times over for sharing this journey with me.

1

CARLOS

I want to live life on my own terms. But I'm Mexican, so *mi familia* is always there to guide me in everything I do, whether I want them to or not. Well, "guide" is too weak a word. "Dictate" is more like it.

Mi'amá didn't ask if I wanted to leave Mexico and move to Colorado to live with my brother Alex for my senior year of high school. She made the decision to send me back to America "for my own good"— her words, not mine. When the rest of *mi familia* backed her up, it was a done deal.

Do they really think sending me back to the U.S. will prevent me from ending up six feet under or in jail? Ever since I got fired from the sugar mill two months ago, I've lived *la vida loca*. Nothing is ever gonna change that.

I look out the small window as the plane soars above the snow-capped Rockies. I'm definitely not in Atencingo anymore . . . and I'm not in the suburbs of Chicago, either, where I lived my entire life before *mi'amá* made us pack up and move to Mexico during my sophomore year.

When the plane lands, I watch other passengers scramble to get off. I hold back and let this whole situation sink in. I'm about to see my brother for the first time in almost two years. Hell, I'm not even sure I want to see him.

The plane is almost empty, so I can't stall anymore. I grab my backpack and follow the signs for the baggage claim area. As I exit the terminal, I see my brother Alex waiting for me beyond the barricade. I thought I might not recognize him, or feel like we were strangers instead of family. But there's no mistaking my big brother . . . his face is as familiar to me as my own. I get a little satisfaction that I'm taller than him now, and I don't look anything like that scrawny kid he left behind.

"*Ya estás en* Colorado," he says as he pulls me into a hug.

When he releases me, I notice faint scars above his eyebrows and by his ears that weren't there the last time I saw him. He looks older, but he's missing that guarded look he always carried around with him like a shield. I think I inherited that shield.

"*Gracias*," I say flatly. He knows I don't want to be here. Uncle Julio stayed at my side until he forced me on the plane. And then threatened to stay at the airport until he knew my ass was off the ground.

"You remember how to speak English?" my brother asks as we walk to the baggage claim.

I roll my eyes. "We only lived in Mexico two years, Alex. Or should I say, me, *Mamá*, and Luis moved to Mexico. You ditched us."

"I didn't ditch you. I'm goin' to college so I can actually do somethin' productive with my life. You should try it sometime."

"No, thanks. I like my unproductive life just fine."

I grab my duffel off the carousel and follow Alex out of the airport.

"Why are you wearin' that around your neck?" my brother asks me.

"It's a rosary," I answer, fingering the black-and-white beaded cross. "I turned religious since I saw you last."

"Religious, my ass. I know it's a gang symbol," he says as we reach a silver Beemer convertible. My brother couldn't afford a bangin' car like that; he must have borrowed it from his girlfriend, Brittany.

"So what if it is?" Alex was in a gang back in Chicago. *Mi papá* was a gang member before him. Whether Alex wants to admit it or not, being a badass is my legacy. I tried living by the rules. I never complained when I made less than fifty *pesos* a day and worked like a dog after school. After I got canned and started running with the *Guerreros del barrio*, I made over a thousand *pesos* in one day. It might have been dirty money, but it kept food on our table.

"Didn't you learn anything from my mistakes?" he asks.

Shit, when Alex was in the Latino Blood back in Chicago I worshipped him. "You don't want to hear my answer to that."

Shaking his head in frustration, Alex grabs my duffel out of my hand and tosses it in the back of the car. So what if he got jumped out of the Latino Blood? He'll wear his tattoos the rest of his life. Whether he wants to believe it or not, he'll always be associated with the LB whether he's active in the gang or not.

I take a long look at my brother. He's definitely changed; I sensed it from the minute I saw him. He might look like Alex Fuentes, but I can tell he's lost that fighting spirit he once possessed. Now that he's in college, he thinks he can play by the rules and make the world a shinier place to live. It's amazing how quickly he's forgotten that not too long ago we lived in the slums of the Chicago suburbs. Some parts of the world can't shine, no matter how much you try and polish off the dirt.

"¿Y Mamá?" Alex asks.

"She's fine."

"And Luis?"

"The same. Our little brother is almost as smart as you, Alex. He thinks he's gonna be an astronaut like José Hernández."

Alex nods like a proud papa, and I think he really does believe Luis can live his dream. The two of them are delusional . . . both my brothers are dreamers. Alex thinks he can save the world by creating cures for diseases and Luis thinks he can leave the world to explore new ones.

As we turn onto the highway, I see a wall of mountains in the far distance. It reminds me of the rough terrain in Mexico.

"It's called the Front Range," Alex tells me. "The university is at the base of the mountains." He points off to the left. "Those are the Flatirons, 'cause the rocks are flat like ironing boards. I'll take you there sometime. Brit and I take walks there when we want to get away from campus."

When he glances at me, I'm looking at my brother like he's got two heads.

"What?" he asks.

Is he kidding?—*¿Me está tomando los pelos?* "I'm just wondering who you are and what the hell you did with my brother. My brother Alex used to be a rebel, and now he's talkin' about mountains, ironin' boards, and takin' walks with his girlfriend."

"You'd rather I talked about getting drunk and fucked up?"

"Yes!" I say, acting like I'm excited. "And then you can tell me where I can get drunk and fucked up, 'cause I won't last long if I don't get some kind of illegal substance in my system," I lie. *Mi'amá* probably told him she suspects I'm into drugs, so I might as well play the part.

"Yeah, right. Save the bullshit for *Mamá*, Carlos. I don't fall for it any more than you do."

I put my feet up on the dash. "You have no clue."

Alex shoves them down. "Do you mind? It's Brittany's car."

"You are seriously whipped, man. When are you gonna dump that *gringa* and start bein' a normal college guy who hooks up with a bunch of girls?" I ask him.

"Brittany and I don't date other people."

"Why not?"

"It's called being boyfriend and girlfriend."

"It's called bein' a *panocha*. It's not natural for a guy to be with one girl, Alex. I'm a free agent and I plan to stay one forever."

"Just so we're clear, *Señor Free Agent*, you're not screwin' anyone in my apartment."

He might be my older brother, but our father has been dead and buried a long time. I don't want or need his bullshit rules. It's time I set some of my own. "Just so you're clear, I plan on doin' whatever the fuck I want while I'm here."

"Just do us both a favor and listen to me. You might actually learn somethin'."

I give a short laugh. Yeah, right. What am I gonna learn from him, how to fill out college applications? Do thermal chemistry experiments? I don't plan on doing either of those.

We're both silent as we drive for another forty-five minutes, the mountains getting closer and closer with each mile. We pass right through the University of Colorado at Boulder campus. Redbrick buildings jut out of the landscape and college students with backpacks are scattered everywhere. Does Alex think he can beat the odds and actually find a high-paying job so he won't be poor the rest of his life? Fat chance of that happening. People will take one look at him and his tattoos and throw his ass out the door.

"I've got to be at work in an hour, but I'll get you settled in first," he says as he pulls into a parking space.

I know he got a job working at some auto-body shop to help him pay off a shitload of school and government loans.

"This is it," he says as he points to the building in front of us. *"Tu casa."*

This round eight-story eyesore of a building resembling a giant corncob is the farthest thing from being a home, but whatever. I pull my duffel out of the trunk and follow Alex inside.

"I hope this is the poor side of town, Alex," I say. " 'Cause I get hives around rich people."

"I'm not livin' in luxury, if that's what you mean. It's subsidized student apartments."

We ride the elevator to the fourth floor. The hallway smells like stale pizza, and a bunch of stains are scattered across the carpet. Two hot girls in workout clothes pass us. Alex smiles at them. From their dreamy reaction I wouldn't be surprised if they suddenly kneeled down and kissed the ground he walks on.

"Mandi and Jessica, this is my brother Carlos."

"Hel-*lo*, Carlos . . ." Jessica scans me up and down—I have definitely reached horny college central. And I'm definitely feelin' it. "Why didn't you tell us he was a hottie?"

"He's in high school," Alex warns them.

What is he, my cock-blocker? "A senior," I blurt out, hoping that'll lessen the blow that I'm not a college guy. "I'll be eighteen in a couple months."

"We'll throw you a birthday party," Mandi says.

"Cool," I say. "Can I have you two as my presents?"

"If Alex doesn't mind," Mandi says.

Alex walks away and weaves a hand through his hair. "I'm gonna get myself in trouble if I get into this discussion."

This time, the girls laugh. Then they jog down the hall, but not before looking back and waving bye.

We go in Alex's apartment. He's definitely not living in the lap of luxury. A twin bed with a thin black fleece blanket is off to the side of the room, a table and four chairs are on the right, and a kitchen so small that two people would have a hard time fitting in together is by the front door. This isn't even a one-bedroom apartment. It's a studio. A *small* studio.

Alex points to a door next to his bed. "There's the bathroom. You can put your stuff in the closet across from the kitchen."

I toss my duffel in the closet and walk farther into the apartment. "Um, Alex . . . where do you expect me to sleep?"

"I borrowed a blow-up bed from Mandi."

"*Está buena*—she's cute." I check out the room again. In our house back in Chicago I shared a much smaller room with Alex and Luis. "Where's the TV?" I ask.

"Don't have one."

Shit. That's not good. "What the hell am I supposed to do when I'm bored?"

"Read a book."

"*Estás chiflado*, you're crazy. I don't read."

"Startin' tomorrow you do," he says as he opens the window to let in some fresh air. "I've already had your transcripts sent. They're expectin' you at Flatiron High tomorrow."

School? *My brother is talkin' about school?* Man, that's the last thing a seventeen-year-old guy wants to think about. I thought he'd at least give me a week to adjust to living in the U.S. again. Time to change course. "Where do you stash your weed?" I say, knowing I'm pushing his patience to the limit. "You should prob'ly tell me now so I don't have to go rummagin' through your place tryin' to find it."

"Don't have any."

"Okay. Then who's your dealer?"

"You don't get it, Carlos. I don't do that shit anymore."

"You said you work. Don't you make money?"

"Yeah, so I can afford to eat, go to college, and send whatever's left to *Mamá*."

Just as that news is sinking in, the apartment door opens. I recognize my brother's blond girlfriend immediately, her keys to his apartment and her purse in one hand and a big brown paper bag in the other. She looks like a Barbie doll come to life. My brother takes the bag and kisses her. They might as well be married. "Carlos, you remember Brittany."

She opens her arms out wide and pulls me close. "Carlos, it's so great to have you here!" Brittany says in a cheery voice. I almost forgot she used to be a cheerleader back in high school, but as soon as she opens her mouth I can't help but remember.

"For who?" I say stiffly.

She pulls back. "For you. And for Alex. He misses having his family around."

"I bet."

She clears her throat and looks a little uneasy. "Umm . . . okay, well, I brought you guys some Chinese food for lunch. I hope you're hungry."

"We're Mexican," I tell her. "Why didn't you get Mexican food?"

Brittany's perfectly shaped eyebrows furrow. "That was a joke, right?"

"Not really."

She turns toward the kitchen. "Alex, want to help me out here?"

Alex appears with paper plates and plastic utensils in his hands. "Carlos, what's your problem?"

I shrug. "No problem. I was just askin' your girlfriend why she didn't get Mexican food. She's the one who got all defensive."

"Have some manners and say 'thank you' instead of makin' her feel like crap."

It's crystal clear whose side my brother is on. At one time Alex said he joined the Latino Blood to protect our family, so Luis and I didn't have to join. But I can see now that family means crap to him.

Brittany holds her hands up. "I don't want you two getting in a fight because of me." She pushes her purse farther on her shoulder and sighs. "I think I better go and let you two get reacquainted."

"Don't go," Alex says.

Dios mío, I think my brother lost his balls somewhere between here and Mexico. Or maybe Brittany has them zipped inside that fancy purse. "Alex, let her go if she wants." It's time to break the leash she's got him on.

"It's okay. Really," she says, then kisses my brother. "Enjoy the lunch. I'll see you tomorrow. Bye, Carlos."

"Uh-huh." As soon as she's gone, I grab the brown bag off the kitchen counter and bring it to the table. I read the labels on each container. Chicken chow mein . . . beef chow fun . . . pu-pu platter. "Pu-pu platter?"

"It's a bunch of appetizers," Alex explains.

I'm not goin' near anything with the word "pu-pu" in it. I'm annoyed that my brother even knows what a pu-pu platter is. I leave that container alone as I scoop myself a plateful of the identifiable Chinese food and start chowing down. "Aren't you gonna eat?" I ask Alex.

He's looking at me as if I'm some stranger.

"*¿Qué pasa?*" I ask.

"Brittany's not goin' anywhere, you know."

"That's the problem. Can't you see it?"

"No. What I see is my seventeen-year-old brother actin' like he's five. It's time to grow up, *mocoso*."

"So I can be as borin' as shit like you? No thanks."

Alex grabs his keys.

"Where you goin'?"

"To apologize to my girlfriend, then head to work. Make yourself at home," he says, tossing me a key to the apartment. "And stay out of trouble."

"As long as you're talkin' to Brittany," I say as I bite off the end of an egg roll, "why don't you ask her for your *huevos* back."

2

Kiara

"Kiara, I can't believe he text-dumped you," my best friend, Tuck, says, reading the three sentences on my cell phone screen as he sits at the desk in my room. *"It's nt wrkg out. Sry. Don't h8 me."* He tosses the phone back to me. "The least he could have done is spell it out. *Don't h8 me?* The guy's a joke. Of course you're gonna hate him."

I lie back on my bed and stare at the ceiling, remembering the first time Michael and I kissed. It was at the outdoor summer concert in Niwot behind the ice cream vendor. "I liked him."

"Yeah, well I never did. Don't trust someone you meet in the waiting room at your therapist's office."

I flip onto my stomach and sit up on my elbows. "It was *speech* therapy. And he just drove his brother for sessions."

Tuck, who has never liked a guy I've dated, pulls out a pink skull-and-crossbones notebook from my desk drawer. He shakes his index finger at me. "Never trust a guy who tells you he loves you on the second date. Happened to me once. It was a total joke."

"Why? Don't you believe in love at first sight?"

"No. I believe in *lust* at first sight. And attraction. But not love. Michael told you he loved you just so he could get into your pants."

"How do you know?"

"I'm a guy, that's how I know." Tuck frowns. "You didn't do *it* with him, did you?"

"No," I say, shaking my head to emphasize my answer. We fooled around, but I didn't want to take it to the next level. I just, I don't know . . . I wasn't ready.

I haven't seen or talked to Michael since school started two weeks ago. Sure, we texted a few times, but he always said he was busy and would call when he got a minute. He's a senior in Longmont twenty minutes away and I go to school in Boulder, so I just thought he was busy with school stuff. But now I know the reason we haven't talked wasn't because he was busy. It was because he wanted to break up.

Was it because of another girl?

Was it because I wasn't pretty enough?

Was it because I wouldn't have sex with him?

It can't be because I stutter. I've been working on my speech all summer and haven't stuttered once since June. Every week I went to speech therapy, every day I practice speaking in front of a mirror, every minute I'm conscious of the words that come out of my mouth. Before now I always had to worry when I spoke, waiting for that confused look people got and then that "Oh, I understand—she's got a *problem*" revelation. Then came the look of pity. And then the "she must be stupid" assumption. Or, in the case of some of the girls in my school, my stuttering was the source of amusement.

But I don't stutter anymore.

Tuck knows this is the year I'm determined to show my confident side—the side I've never shown the kids at school. I've been shy and introverted my first three years of high school, because I've had an intense fear of people making fun of me stuttering. From now on instead of Kiara Westford being remembered for being shy, they're going to remember me as the one who wasn't afraid to speak up.

I didn't count on Michael breaking up with me. I thought we'd go to Homecoming together, and prom . . .

"Stop thinking about Michael," Tuck orders.

"He was cute."

"So is a hairy ferret, but I wouldn't want to date one. You could do better than him. Don't sell yourself short."

"Look at me," I tell him. "Face reality, Tuck. I'm no Madison Stone."

"Thank God for that. I hate Madison Stone."

Madison raises the term "mean girls" to an entirely new level. The girl is good at everything she tries and could be easily crowned the most popular girl in school. Every girl wants to be friends with her so they can hang with the cool crowd. Madison Stone *creates* the cool crowd. "Everyone likes her."

"That's because they're afraid of her. Secretly everyone hates her." Tuck starts scribbling words in my notebook, then hands it to me. "Here," he says, then tosses me a pen.

I stare at the page. RULES OF ATTRACTION is written on top, and a big line is drawn down the center of the page.

"What is this?"

"In the left column write down all the great things about you."

Is he kidding? "No."

"Come on, start writing. Consider this a self-help exercise, and a way for you to realize that girls like Madison Stone aren't even attractive. Finish the sentence *I, Kiara Westford, am great because . . .*"

I know Tuck isn't going to let up, so I write something stupid and hand it back to him.

He reads my words and cringes. "*I, Kiara, am great because* . . . I know how to throw a football, change the oil in my car, and hike a four-teener. Ugh, guys don't care about this stuff." He grabs the pen from me, sits on the edge of my bed, and starts writing furiously. "Let's get the basics down. You've got to measure attractiveness in three parts to get the full result."

"Who made up those rules?"

"Me. These are Tuck Reese's Rules of Attraction. First, we start with personality. You're smart, funny, and sarcastic," he says, listing each one in the notebook.

"I'm not sure all of those are good things."

"Trust me, they are. But wait, I'm not done. You're also a loyal friend, you love a challenge more than most guys I know, and you're a great sister to Brandon." He looks up when he's done writing. "The second part is your skills. You know about fixing cars, you're athletic, and you know when to shut up."

"That last one isn't a skill."

"Honey, trust me. It's a skill."

"You forgot my special spinach and walnut salad." I can't cook, but that salad is an all-time favorite.

"You do make a killer salad," he says, adding that to the list. "Okay, on to the last part—physical traits." Tuck looks me up and down, assessing me.

I moan, wondering when this humiliation will end. "I feel like I'm a cow about to be auctioned."

"Yeah, yeah, whatever. You've got flawless skin and a perky nose to match your tits. If I wasn't gay I might be tempted to—"

"Eww." I slap his hand away from the paper. "Tuck, can you please not say or write that word?"

He shakes his long hair out of his eyes. "What, *tits*?"

"Ugh. Yes, that one. Just say boobs or breasts, please. The 't' word just sounds so . . . vulgar."

Tuck snorts and rolls his eyes. "Okay, perky . . . *breasts*." He laughs, totally amused. "I'm sorry, Kiara, that just sounds like something you're gonna barbeque for lunch or order off a menu." He pretends my notebook is a menu as he recites in a fake English accent, "Yes, waiter, I'd like the barbequed perky breasts with a side of coleslaw."

I throw Mojo, my big blue teddy bear, at Tuck's head. "Just call 'em privates and move on."

Mojo bounces right off him and lands on the floor. My best friend doesn't miss a beat. "Perky tits, scratch. Perky breasts, scratch." He makes a big deal of crossing both those out. "Replace with . . . perky privates," he says, writing each word down as he says it. "Long legs, and long eyelashes." He eyes my hands and wrinkles his nose. "No offense, but you could use a manicure."

"Is that it?" I ask.

"I don't know. Can you think of anything else?"

I shake my head.

"Okay, so now that we know how fabulous you are, we need to make a list of what kind of guy you want. We'll write this on the right side of the page. Let's start with personality. You want a guy who is . . . fill in the blank."

"I want a guy who's confident. Really confident."

"Good," he says, writing it down.

"I want a guy who's nice to me."

Tuck continues writing. "Nice guy."

"I'd like a guy who's smart," I add.

"Street smarts or book smarts?"

"Both?" I question, not knowing if it's the right or wrong answer.

He pats me on the head like I'm a little kid. "Good. Let's move on to skills." He shushes me, stopping me from contributing. Fine by me. "I'll write this part down for you. You want a guy who has the same skills as you have, and then some. Someone who likes sports, someone who can at least appreciate your interest in fixing up that stupid old car of yours, and—"

"Shoot." I jump off my bed. "I almost forgot. I need to go into town and pick up something from the auto-body shop."

"Please don't tell me it's fuzzy dice to hang on your rearview mirror."

"It's not fuzzy dice. It's a radio. A vintage one."

"Oh, goodie! A vintage one, to match your vintage car!" Tuck says sarcastically, then claps a bunch of times in fake excitement.

I roll my eyes at him. "Wanna come with?"

"No." He closes my notebook and shoves it back in my desk. "The last thing I want to do is hang around and listen to you talk about cars with people who actually care."

After I drop off Tuck at his house, it takes me fifteen minutes to get to McConnell's Auto Body. I pull my car into the shop and find Alex, one of the mechanics, bent over the engine of a VW Beetle. Alex was one of my dad's students. Last year, after a study session, my dad found out that Alex works on cars. He told Alex about the 1972 Monte Carlo I've been restoring, and Alex has been helping me get parts for it ever since.

"Hey, Kiara." He wipes his hands on a shop cloth, and asks me to wait while he gets my radio. "Here it is," he says, opening the box. He pulls out the radio and removes it from the bubble wrap. Wires are sticking out of the back like spindly legs, but it's just perfect. I know I shouldn't be so excited about a radio, but the dash wouldn't be complete without it. The one that came with my car never worked and the front plastic was cracked, so Alex has been looking online to find me an authentic replacement.

"I didn't get a chance to test it, though," he says as he wiggles each wire to make sure the connections are solid. "I had to pick up my brother at the airport, so I couldn't come in early."

"Is he visiting from Mexico?" I ask.

"He's not visitin'. He'll be a senior at Flatiron startin' tomorrow," he says as he fills out an invoice. "You go there, right?"

I nod.

He puts the radio back in the box. "Do you need help installin' it?"

I didn't think so before I saw it up close, but now I'm not so sure. "Maybe," I tell him. "Last time I soldered wires, I messed them up."

"Then don't pay for it now," he says. "If you've got time tomorrow after school, stop by and I'll put it in. That'll give me time to test the thing."

"Thanks, Alex."

He looks up from the invoice and taps his pen on the counter. "I know this is gonna sound *loco*, but can you help show my brother around school? He doesn't know anyone."

"We have a peer outreach program at school," I say, proud that I can help. "I can meet you in the principal's office in the morning and sign up to be his peer guide." The old Kiara would have been too shy and would never have offered, but not the new Kiara.

"I've got to warn you . . ."

"About what?"

"My brother can be tough to deal with."

My lips turn into a wide grin, because as Tuck pointed out . . . "I love a good challenge."

3

CARLOS

"I don't need a peer guide."

Those are the first words out of my mouth as Mr. House, the Flatiron High School principal, introduces me to Kiara Westford.

"We pride ourselves on our peer outreach programs," Mr. House says to Alex. "They help ensure a smooth transition."

My brother nods. "No problem with me. I'm sold on the idea."

"I'm not," I mumble. I don't need a damn peer guide because (1) it's obvious from the way Alex greeted Kiara a few minutes ago that he knows her, and (2) the girl is not hot; she has her hair up in a ponytail, is wearing leather hiking boots with three-quarter stretch pants with an Under Armour logo peeking out the bottom, and is covered from neck to knee by an oversized T-shirt with the word MOUNTAINEER written on it, and (3) I don't need a babysitter, especially one that my brother arranged.

Mr. House sits in his big, brown leather chair and hands Kiara a copy of my schedule. Great, so now the girl knows where I'm supposed to be every second of the day. If this situation weren't so humiliatin', it'd be hilarious.

"This is a big school, Carlos," House says as if I can't figure out the map on my own. "Kiara is an exemplary student. She'll show you to your locker and escort you to each class for your first week here."

"You ready?" the girl asks with a big grin. "The first-period late bell already rang."

Can I request another peer guide, one who isn't so happy to be at school at seven thirty a.m.?

Alex waves me off, and I'm tempted to flip him the finger but I'm not sure the principal would appreciate it.

I follow the *exemplary student* out into the empty hallway and I think I've entered hell. Lockers line the hallways and signs are taped to the walls. One says YES WE KAHN!—VOTE FOR MEGAN KAHN FOR STU-DENT PRESIDENT and another reads JASON TU—YOUR "GO-TU GUY" FOR STUDENT COUNCIL TREASURER! are displayed along with the rest of the signs from people who actually want to MAKE HEALTHIER STU-DENT LUNCHES THE NORM!—VOTE FOR NORM REDDING.

Healthier student lunches?

Hell, back in Mexico you ate what you brought from home or whatever crap they put in front of you. There weren't choices. Where I lived in Mexico you ate to survive, without worrying about counting calories or carbs. That's not to say that some people don't live like kings in Mexico. Like in America, there are definitely the rich areas in every one of the thirty-one Mexican states . . . but my family just didn't live in any of 'em.

I don't belong at Flatiron High, and I sure as hell don't want to follow this girl around all week. I wonder how much the *exemplary student* can take before she gives up and quits.

She directs me to my locker and I shove my stuff inside. "My locker is two away from yours," she announces, as if that's actually a good thing. When I'm ready, she studies my schedule and walks down the hall at the same time. "Mr. Hennesey's class is one flight up."

"*¿Dónde está el servicio?*" I ask her.

"Huh? I don't take Spanish. *Je parle français*—I speak French."

"Why? Do a lot of French people live in Colorado?"

"No, but I want to do a semester abroad in France my sophomore year of college like my mom did."

My mom didn't even finish high school. She got pregnant with Alex and married my dad.

"You're learnin' a language that you'll use for one semester? Sounds stupid to me." I stop when we reach a door with a male stick figure painted on it. With my thumb, I point to the door. "*Servicio* is bathroom . . . I asked where the bathroom is."

"Oh." She looks a little confused, as if not exactly knowing how to handle deviations from the schedule. "Well, I guess I'll just wait out here for you."

Time to have a little fun by screwin' with my peer guide. "Unless you want to come inside and show me around . . . I mean, I don't know how far you wanna take this whole peer guide thing."

"Not *that* far." She purses her lips like she just sucked on a sour lemon and shakes her head. "Go ahead. I'll wait."

In the bathroom, I brace my hands on the sink and take a deep breath. All I can see in the mirror above the sink is a guy whose family thinks he's a total fuckup.

Maybe I should have told *mi'amá* the truth: that I got fired from the mill for protecting little fifteen-year-old Emilie Juarez from being harassed by one of the supervisors. It was bad enough she had to quit school and start working to help her family put food on their table. When our boss thought he could put his filthy hands on her just because he was *el jefe*, I went ballistic. Yeah, it cost me my job . . . but it was worth it and I'd do it again even if it had the same consequences.

A knock on the door brings me back to reality, and the fact that I have to be escorted to class by a girl who dresses like she's goin' mountain climbing. I can't imagine a girl like Kiara ever needing a guy to fight for her, because if any guy threatened her she'd probably suffocate him with her oversized tee.

The door creaks open the slightest bit. "You still in there?" Kiara's voice echoes through the bathroom.

"Yep."

"You almost done?"

I roll my eyes. When I walk out of the bathroom a minute later and head toward the stairs, I notice my escort isn't following. She's standing in the empty hallway, that sour look still plastered on her face. "You didn't even have to go," she says, sounding annoyed. "You were stalling."

"You're a genius," I say flatly, then take the stairs up two at a time.

Score one for Carlos Fuentes.

I hear her footsteps tapping on the floor behind me, trying to catch up. I walk down the second-floor hall, thinking of ways I can ditch her.

"Thanks for making me super late to class for no reason," she says, hurrying up behind me.

"Don't blame me. Wasn't my idea to have a babysitter. And, for the record, I can find my way around just fine on my own."

"Really?" she asks. "Because you just passed Mr. Hennesey's room."

Shit.

One point for the *exemplary student*.

Score is 1–1. Thing is, I don't like ties. I like to win . . . by big margins.

I can't help but be annoyed at the flash of amusement in my peer guide's eyes.

I step closer to her, really close. "Have you ever cut class?" I ask her, mischief and flirting laced in my voice. I'm trying to throw her off so I have the upper hand again.

"No," she says slowly, looking nervous.

Good. I lean in even closer. "We should try it together sometime," I say softly, then open the classroom door.

I hear her suck in a breath. Listen, I didn't ask for a face and body girls find attractive. But thanks to the mixture of my parents' DNA, I've got them, and I'm not ashamed to use 'em. Having a face Adonis would admire is one of the few advantages I've been given in life, and I use it to its fullest potential whether it's for good or evil.

Kiara quickly introduces me to Mr. Hennesey, then just as quickly she's out the door. I hope my flirting has scared her off for good. If not, I might have to try harder next time. I sit in math class and scan the room. All of the kids here look like they come from upper-class homes. This school is nothing like Fairfield, the Chicago suburb I lived in before we moved to Mexico. At Fairfield High, we had rich kids and poor kids. Flatiron High is more like one of those expensive private high schools back in Chicago, where every kid wears designer labels and drives fancy cars.

We used to make fun of those kids. Now I'm surrounded by them.

As soon as math is over, Kiara is waiting outside the classroom. I can't believe it.

"So how was it?" she asks over the noise of everyone else rushing to their next class.

"You don't want me to answer honestly, do you?"

"Probably not. Come on, we only have five minutes." She weaves her way through the students. I follow behind, watching her ponytail sway like a horse's tail with every step she takes. "Alex warned me you were a rebel."

She ain't seen nothin' yet. "How do you know my brother?"

"He was one of my dad's students. And he helps me with the car I'm restoring."

This *chica* is unreal. Restoring a car? "What do you know about cars?"

"More than you," she says over her shoulder.

I laugh. "Wanna bet?"

"Maybe." She stops in front of a classroom. "Here's your bio class."

A hot chick passes us and goes in the room. She's wearing tight jeans and an even tighter shirt. "Whoa, who was that?"

"Madison Stone," Kiara mutters.

"Introduce me to her."

"Why?"

Because I know it'll annoy the shit out of you. "Why not?"

She clutches her books to her chest, almost as if they're a shield of armor. "I can think of five reasons off the top of my head."

I shrug. "Okay. List 'em."

"There's no time, the bell is about to ring. Do you think you can introduce yourself to Mrs. Shevelenko? I just remembered I forgot my French homework in my locker."

"You better hurry." I look at my wrist, which doesn't have a watch wrapped around it, but I don't think she notices. "The bell is about to ring."

"I'll just meet you here after class." She runs down the hall.

In class, I wait for Shevelenko to look up from her desk and acknowledge me. She's on her laptop, sending what looks like personal e-mail.

I clear my throat to get her attention. She glances at me, then changes programs. "Choose any seat. I'll call attendance in a minute."

"I'm new," I tell her. She should have figured that one out on her own because I haven't been in her class the past two weeks, but whatever.

"Are you that exchange student from Mexico?"

Not really. It's called *transfer student*, but I don't think this woman cares about the details. "Yeah."

I can't help but notice the beads of sweat on her peach-fuzz mustache. I'm pretty certain there are, you know, people who can take care of that. My aunt Consuelo had the same problem until my mom got ahold of her and some hot wax and put them in the same room together.

"You speak Spanish or English at home?" Shevelenko asks.

I'm not even sure that's a legal question, but whatever. "Both."

She cranes her neck and scans the rest of the class. "Ramiro, come here."

This Latino kid walks up to her desk. The guy is a taller version of Alex's best friend, Paco. When they were seniors in high school, Alex and Paco got shot, and our entire lives turned upside down. Paco died. I don't know if any of us will ever fully get over what happened. Right after my brother got out of the hospital, we moved to Mexico to stay with family. Since the shooting, nothing's been the same.

"Ramiro, this is . . ." Shevelenko looks up at me. "What's your name?"

"Carlos."

She eyes the Ramiro kid. "He's Mexican, you're Mexican. Make sure you two Spanish speakers pair up."

I follow Ramiro back to one of the lab tables. "Is she for real?" I ask.

"Pretty much. Last year I heard Heavy Shevy called this guy Ivan 'The Russian' for six months before she learned his name."

"Heavy Shevy?" I question.

"Don't look at me," Ramiro says. "I didn't make it up. She's had that nickname for at least twenty years."

The class bell rings, but everybody is still talking. Heavy Shevy is back on her computer, still busy with her e-mail.

"*Me llamo* Ramiro, but it's too beaner so everyone calls me Ram."

My name's beaner, too, but I don't feel the need to dis my heritage and change my name to Carl to fit in. One look at me and you know I'm Latino, so why pretend to be somethin' else? I've always accused Alex of wanting to be white because he refuses to be called by his given name, Alejandro.

"*Me llamo* Carlos. You can call me Carlos."

Now that I'm paying more attention to him, I notice that Ram's wearing some golf shirt with a designer logo. He might have family in Mexico, but I bet *su familia* doesn't live anywhere near mine.

"So what's there to do for fun here?" I ask him.

"The question is what's there *not* to do," Ram says. "Hang out at Pearl Street Mall, go to the movies, hike, snowboard, raft, mountain climb, party with chicks from Niwot and Longmont."

None of those things are my idea of fun, except for the partying part.

Across the table from us is that hot girl Madison. Along with her tight clothes, she's got long, streaked blond hair, a big smile, and even bigger *chichis* that actually rival Brittany's. Not that I'm lookin' at my brother's girlfriend, but they're kinda hard to miss.

Madison leans across the table. "I hear you're the new guy," she says. "I'm Madison. And you are . . ."

"Carlos," Ram blurts out before I can say anythin'.

"I'm sure he can introduce himself, Ram," she hisses, then tucks her hair behind her ear, showing off diamond earrings that might actually blind someone if the sun hit 'em at the right angle. She leans toward me and bites her bottom lip. "You're the new guy from *Meh-hee-co*?"

It's always irritating when the white kids try to sound like they're Mexican. I wonder what else she's heard about me. "*Sí*," I say.

She flashes me a sexy smile and leans closer. "*Estás muy caliente*." I think she just called me hot. That's not the way we say it in *Meh-hee-co*, but I get the idea. "I could use a good Spanish tutor. My last one turned out to be a total loser."

Ram clears his throat. "*¡Qué tipa!* If you haven't guessed, I was her last tutor."

I'm still watching Madison. She's definitely got it goin' on, and obviously has no problem flaunting her assets. While honey-skinned, exotic Mexican *chicas* are my usual type, I suspect no guy can resist Madison. And she knows it.

When a girl calls her over to the next table, I turn to Ram. "Did'ja tutor her, or date her?" I ask him.

"Both. Sometimes simultaneously. We broke up a month ago. Take my advice and stay away. She bites."

"Literally?" I ask, grinning.

"Honestly, you don't want to get close enough to her to find out the answer to that question. Just know that toward the end of our relationship, I became the student and she became the tutor. And I'm not talkin' 'bout Spanish."

"*Está sabrosa.* I'll take my chances."

"Then go for it, man," Ram says with a shrug, just as Heavy Shevy gets up and starts to teach. "But don't say I didn't warn you."

I don't plan on bein' anyone's boyfriend, but I wouldn't mind bringin' a couple of girls from Flatiron High back to Alex's place just to prove I'm the complete opposite of him. I glance back at Madison and she smiles like there's a promise of something more. Yeah, she'd definitely be perfect to bring home to Alex. She's like Brittany, but without the halo over her head.

After suffering through my morning classes, I'm definitely ready for lunch. When the bell rings, I'm glad Kiara's not outside waiting for me like she said she would. I head to my locker to get the lunch I packed from Alex's fridge.

Maybe my peer guide quit. That's cool with me, except it takes me ten minutes to find the cafeteria. When I walk into the lunchroom, I'm ready to sit by myself at one of the round tables until I see Ram waving me over.

"Thanks for ditching me," a voice says from behind me.

I glance back at my peer guide. "I thought you quit."

She shakes her head as if that's the most ridiculous thing she's ever heard. "Of course I didn't quit. I just couldn't get out of class early."

"That's too bad," I say, pretending to be sympathetic. "I would have waited if I knew . . ."

"Yeah, right." She nods at Ram's table. "Go sit with Ram. I saw him waving you over."

I give her a shocked look. "Are you actually givin' me permission to sit with him?"

"You can sit with me," she says, as if that's an option I'd jump at.

"No, thanks."

"That's what I thought."

While Kiara stands in the hot-lunch line, I walk over to Ram's table. I straddle the back of a chair as Ram introduces me to his friends, all white dudes that look like clones of one another. They're talking about girls and sports and their fantasy football teams. I doubt any of them would survive one day at the sugar mill back in Mexico. Some of my friends made less than fifteen dollars a day. These guys' watches probably cost more than some of my friends' yearly salaries.

Madison appears at our table when Ram goes back to the cafeteria line. "Hey, guys," she says. "My parents are going out of town this weekend. I'm having a party on Friday night if y'all want to come. Just don't tell Ram about it."

Madison reaches into her purse and pulls out a tube of lip gloss. She dips the wand in a bunch of times, then puckers up and places it on her lips. Just when I think she's done, her lips form a perfect *O* and she swirls the wand around and around. I check to see if anyone else is following the erotic lip-gloss show. Sure enough, two of Ram's friends have stopped talking and are totally focused on Madison and her special talent. Ram comes back and is totally focused on eating his slice of pepperoni pizza.

The smack of Madison's lips brings my attention back to her. "Carlos, let me write down my info for you," she says, then pulls out a pen and grabs my arm. She starts writing her phone number and address on my forearm above my tats as if she's an artist. When she's done, she waves by wiggling her fingers, then walks away to sit with her friends.

I take a bite of my sandwich and scan the cafeteria, searching for

Kiara, the anti-Madison. She's sitting with a guy with shaggy blond hair that falls in his face. The dude is about my height, my build. Is he her boyfriend? If he is, I feel sorry for him. Kiara is the kind of girl who would expect her boyfriend to be submissive and kiss her ass.

My body and mind aren't wired to be submissive, and you'll find me dead before you find me kissin' anyone's ass.

4

Kiara

"So how was being a peer guide?" my mom asks me at the dinner table. "I know you were looking forward to it this morning."

"Not the best," I answer as I hand my little brother a third napkin because he's got spaghetti sauce all over his face.

I think back to the end of eighth period, when I showed up to Carlos's class only to find he'd already left for the day. "Carlos ditched me twice."

Dad, a psychologist who thinks people are specimens to be analyzed, furrows his brows as he scoops up a second helping of green beans. "Ditch you? Why would he do that?"

Um . . . "Because he thinks he's too cool to be escorted around school."

My mom pats my hand. "Ditching your peer guide is not cool at all, but be patient with him. He's been displaced. It's not easy."

"Your mom's right. Don't be too judgmental, Kiara," my dad says. "He's probably just trying to find out where he fits in. Alex stopped in my office after class and we had a long talk. Poor kid. He's just twenty himself, and now he's responsible for a seventeen-year-old."

"Why don't you invite Carlos over tomorrow after school?" Mom suggests.

Dad points his fork at her. "That's a great idea."

I'm sure the last thing Carlos wants to do is come to my house. He's made it perfectly clear he's just tolerating me this week because he has to. Once my peer guide job is done on Friday, he's probably going to have a party to celebrate. "I don't know."

"Do it," Mom says, ignoring my hesitation. "I'll make cookies from this new orange-marmalade recipe Joanie gave me."

I'm not sure Carlos will appreciate orange-marmalade cookies, but . . . "I'll ask him. But don't be surprised if he says no."

"Don't be surprised if he says yes," Dad says, always the optimist.

The next morning, as I'm escorting Carlos to class between third and fourth period, I finally gather up enough nerve to ask, "Do you want to come over after school?"

His eyebrows go up. "You askin' me out?"

I grit my teeth. "Don't flatter yourself."

"Good, 'cause you're not my type. I like my women sexy and stupid."

"You're not my type, either," I snap back. "I like my guys smart and funny."

"I'm funny."

I shrug. "Maybe I'm just too smart to get your jokes."

"Then why do you want me to come over?"

"My mom . . . made cookies." I cringe after the words leave my mouth. Who invites a guy over *for cookies*? Maybe my brother does, but he's in kindergarten. "It's not like it'll be a date or anything," I blurt out in case he thinks I'm secretly trying to hit on him. "Just . . . cookies."

I wish I could rewind this entire conversation, but there's no going back now.

We reach the door to his classroom, and he still hasn't answered.

"I'll think about it," he says, then leaves me out in the hall by myself.

He'll think about it? As if coming over to my house would be doing me a huge favor instead of the other way around?

At our lockers at the end of the day, when I hope he's forgotten I even asked him over, he leans his weight on one foot and stuffs his hands in his front pockets. "What kind of cookies?"

Out of all the questions in the world, why did he have to ask that one?

"Orange," I say. "Orange marmalade."

He leans closer, as if I didn't say it loud enough or clear enough. "Orange what?"

"Marmalade."

"Huh?"

"Marmalade."

I'm sorry, but there's just no cool way to say the word "marmalade," and all those *m*'s so close together make me sound goofy. At least I didn't stutter.

He nods. I can tell he's trying to keep a straight face, but he can't. He bursts out laughing. "Can you say it one more time?"

"So you can make fun of me?"

"*Sí*. It's become the only thing I look forward to in life. Just so happens you're an easy target."

I slam my locker door shut. "Consider yourself officially uninvited." I walk away, but then remember that I've left all my homework in my locker and have to open it again. I quickly grab the three books I need, shove them in my backpack, and head out.

"If they were double-chocolate chip, I would have come," he calls after me, then laughs.

Tuck is waiting for me in the senior parking lot. "What took you so long?"

"I was arguing with Carlos."

"Again? Listen, Kiara, it's only Tuesday. You've got three more days with him. Why don't you quit being his peer guide and be done with the misery."

"Because that's just what he wants," I say as we get in my car and I drive out of the lot. "I don't want to give him the satisfaction of one-upping me all the time. He's so obnoxious."

"There's got to be something you can do to make him eat his words."

Tuck's words spark the perfect idea. "That's it! Tuck, you're a genius," I say excitedly. I make a sharp U-turn.

"Where are we going?" Tuck asks, then points behind us. "Your house is that way."

"First we're stopping at the grocery store and McGuckin's Hardware. I need the ingredients for double-chocolate chip cookies."

"Since when do you bake," Tuck asks. "And why double-chocolate chip cookies?"

I flash him a mischievous smile. "I'm going to use them to make Carlos eat his words."

5

CARLOS

On Wednesday, I walk out of school and head over to the body shop to meet Alex. Just as I cross the street, a red Mustang pulls up beside me. Madison Stone is driving, her windows wide open. When I get closer she asks where I'm goin'.

"McConnell's—the place where my brother works," I tell her. He said I could help him to make some extra cash.

"Hop in. I'll drive you."

Madison orders her friend Lacey into the backseat and tells me to sit in front, next to her. I've never lived in a place where you're not judged by the color of your skin or your parents' bank accounts, so I'm wary of Madison's immediate interest in me. Hell, I put on the charm for Kiara before Heavy Shevy's class and she didn't even bat an eyelash or attempt to loosen those pursed lips. All I got was a disgusted gasp. Although yesterday she invited me over for cookies. *Orange-marmalade cookies.* Who the hell invites someone over for orange-marmalade cookies? The funniest part about it was that I think she was serious. Today she walked me from class to class without saying a damn word to me. I even tried to goad her into talkin' by making fun of her, but she refused to take the bait.

Madison punches in the address to McConnell's on her GPS.

"So, Carlos," Lacey says, leaning between the seats as Madison starts driving. She taps me on the shoulder as if I didn't hear her. "Is it true you got expelled from your last school for beating someone up?"

I've only been in school three days, and already people are talkin'. "Actually it was three guys and a pit bull," I joke, but I think she takes me seriously because her mouth opens in shock.

"Wow!" She taps me again. "They allow dogs in school in Mexico?"

Lacey is dumber than a beanless burrito. "Oh, yeah. Pit bulls and Chihuahuas only, though."

"Wouldn't it be great if I could bring Puddles to school!" She taps me on the shoulder again. I'm tempted to tap her back a ton of times so she knows how annoying it is. "Puddles is my Labradoodle."

What the hell is a Labradoodle? Whatever it is, I bet my cousin Lana's pit bull could eat Puddles the Labradoodle for lunch.

"So is your brother the guy who brought you to school on Monday when you registered?" Madison asks.

"Yeah," I answer as we pull into the parking lot of the auto body.

"My friend Gina told me she saw the two of you in the office. Were your parents out of town?"

"I live with my brother. The rest of my family is back in Mexico." No need to go into my whole life story about how my father died in a drug deal when I was four and how *mi'amá* practically kicked me out and shipped me here.

Madison looks shocked. "You live with your brother? No parents?"

"No parents."

"You're so lucky," Lacey says. "My parents are around all the time, and my sister is a complete psycho, but I escape to Madison's most days because she's an only child and her p's are never home."

Madison is looking in her rearview mirror. At the mention of her parents, she stills for the slightest moment before smiling again. "They're always traveling," she explains while reapplying more of that shiny lip gloss. "But I like it, because I can do whatever I want with whoever I want without any rules."

Considering my life has been full of people tryin' to rule it, her life sounds *bueno* to me.

"Omigod, you and your brother look like twins," Lacey says as Alex approaches the Mustang.

"I don't see the resemblance," I tell her as I open the door. Madison and Lacey get out, too. Do they expect an introduction? They stand in front of me with their flawless pale skin and their makeup sparkling in the sun. "Thanks for the ride," I say.

They both hug me. Madison gives me an extra-long squeeze. It's definitely a sign that she's interested.

I can tell Alex isn't exactly sure what I'm doin' with these two chicks. I drape my arms around Madison's and Lacey's shoulders. "Hey, Alex, this is Madison and Lacey. The two hottest chicks at Flat-iron High."

Both girls nod at Alex and flash their bright smiles. They like the compliment, although I think they know they're smokin' and don't need to be reminded.

"Thanks for givin' my brother a ride," Alex says, then turns around and heads back inside.

After the girls drive off, I follow him into the shop and find him working on the front bumper cover of an SUV that's obviously been in an accident.

"You the only one here?" I ask.

"Yeah. Help me remove this thing," he says as he tosses me a Phillips.

Alex and I used to work on cars together at my cousin Enrique's auto-body shop. It was one of the few things we did when we were actually tryin' to stay out of trouble. My brother and cousin taught me everythin' they knew about cars, and whatever they didn't teach me I figured out on my own when I took apart junkers in the back of the shop.

I get under the hood of the SUV and work on the inside screws. The sound of metal clinking on metal echoes through the shop and for a second I feel like we're back in Chicago at Enrique's.

"Nice girls," my brother says sarcastically as we work side by side.

"Yeah, I know. I was thinkin' about askin' both of them to Homecoming." I shove the Phillips in my back pocket. "Oh, and before I forget to tell you, Kiara invited me over for *cookies* yesterday."

"Why didn't you go?"

"Besides the fact that I didn't want to, she uninvited me."

Alex turns his focus from the bumper to me. "Please tell me you weren't a complete *pendejo* to her."

"I just had a little fun, that's all. Next time you want to arrange an escort for me, make sure it's one who doesn't wear oversized shirts with stupid sayings on them. Kiara reminds me of a dude I knew back in Chicago, Alex. I'm not even sure she's female."

"You want me to p-p-prove it?" my ex–peer guide's voice echoes from the doorway.

Oh, hell.

6

Kiara

"Yeah," Carlos says, challenge and amusement written all over his face. "Prove it."

Alex holds up a hand. "No. Don't." He shoves Carlos against the car and mutters something in Spanish. Carlos mutters something back. I have no clue what they're saying, but neither sounds happy.

I'm not too happy either. I can't believe I just stuttered. I'm so pissed at myself for letting Carlos get me so emotional I stumbled over my words. That means he has power over me, and that fact makes me angrier. I can't wait until Friday, when Operation Cookie will finally go into effect. I have to wait until the cookies are good and stale in order for it to work right. At least he won't be expecting it.

A frustrated Alex stomps away from Carlos and pulls a box from behind the cashier's desk. "I tested your radio, and I think a spring is missin'. I don't think it's gonna work, but I'd like to give it a try. Give me your keys and I'll pull your car in." He turns to Carlos. "Don't say a word while I'm gone."

The second after Alex leaves, Carlos says, "So if you still want to prove you're not a dude, I'm game."

"Does being a jerk make you feel better about yourself?" I say.

"No. But pissin' off my brother does. And pissin' you off pisses my brother off. Sorry you're the one caught in the crossfire."

"Keep me out of it."

"Not likely to happen any time soon." Carlos crouches in front of the car they were working on and pulls on the bumper cover.

"You need to unhook the clips first," I tell him, pleased to prove that I know more about cars than he does. "It won't come off until you unhook the clips."

"You talkin' bras or bumpers?" he asks, then flashes me a cocky grin. " 'Cause I'm an expert at unhooking both."

I shouldn't have done it. It was immature. It was that sexy and stupid comment Carlos made. That, combined with him making fun of the way I say "marmalade," was what pushed me to make him eat his words.

It's Friday. Tuck and I came to school early this morning to rig Carlos's locker. Tuesday after school Tuck and I made over a hundred double-chocolate chip cookies. When they cooled off, we glued a small but powerful magnet to the back of each one. Now they're stale cookie magnets. When Carlos opens his locker this morning, the inside is going to be decorated with a hundred little cookie magnets.

When he tries to pull each magnet off, the cookie will break into pieces and crumble in his hand. I got superstrong little magnets the size of a dime. It'll be messy, that's for sure. So he'll have two options: keep the magnet cookies stuck inside his locker, or take them off one by one and be showered with little broken cookie pieces.

"Remind me never to get in a fight with you," Tuck says as he acts as a lookout. School won't start for another forty-five minutes, so there are only a few people passing in the hallway.

I open Carlos's locker using the combination that was written on top of his schedule, which Mr. House gave to me. I feel guilty, but not guilty enough not to do it. I place a few cookies, then look at Tuck. He's on the lookout for Carlos or anyone else who might get suspicious. Each time I place a cookie, the clink of the magnet against metal makes Tuck laugh.

Clink. Clink. Clink. Clink. Clink. Clink.

"He's going to freak," Tuck says. "He'll know it was you, you know. When you punk someone, the goal is to do it anonymously so you don't get caught."

"Too late now." I attach more magnet cookies, but wonder how I'm going to get all one hundred of them inside. I'm placing them on the top, back, inside door, sides . . . I'm running out of space, but I'm almost done. It looks like the inside of his locker has brown measles.

I reach into the bag. "Only one left."

Tuck peeks his head inside. "This could be one of the best pranks ever at Flatiron High, Kiara. You could go down in the history books. I'm proud of you. Put the last one on the outside, right in the middle."

"Good idea." I close his locker before anyone catches us, attach the last cookie, then check my watch. Homeroom starts in twenty minutes. "Now we wait."

Tuck looks down the hallway. "People are coming. Shouldn't we hide?"

"Yeah, but I have to see his reaction," I say. "Let's hide in Mrs. Hadden's room."

Five minutes later, as Tuck and I peek through the square window in the door, Carlos comes walking down the hall.

"There he is," I whisper. My heart is beating furiously in my chest.

His eyebrows furrow when he reaches his locker and sees a big brown cookie on it. He looks left and right, obviously looking for any sign of who did it. When he pulls the cookie off, it crumbles in his hand but leaves the magnet stuck to his locker.

"What's his reaction?" I ask Tuck, who's taller and has a better view.

"He's smiling. And shaking his head. Now he's tossing the crumbled cookie in the garbage."

Carlos won't be smiling when he opens his locker to find ninety-nine more cookie magnets.

"I'm going out there," I tell Tuck. I emerge from the safety of Mrs. Hadden's room and walk to my locker as if nothing is out of the ordinary.

"Hey," I say to Carlos as he eyes his open locker with all the cookies.

"I'll give you an A+ for originality and execution," he says.

"Does it bother you I get good grades in everything, even pranks?"

"Yes." He cocks a brow. "I'm impressed. I'm pissed off, but impressed." He closes his locker, the ninety-nine cookies still attached to the inside. As if the cookies don't exist, we walk side by side to his first-period class.

I can't help but smile while we walk down the hall. He shakes his head a few times, as if he can't believe what I did.

"Truce?" I ask.

"No way. You may have won this battle, but this war, *chica*, is far from over."

7

CARLOS

I can't get rid of the cookie smell. It's on my hands, it's in my books . . . hell, it's even in my backpack. I tried taking a few of them off my locker, but it was such a mess I gave up. I'll keep 'em in until they get really moldy . . . then I'll collect all the crumbs and shove them into Kiara's locker. Or better yet, superglue them to the inside.

I have to get my mind off cookies and Kiara. Nothing beats *mi'amá*'s cookin', but as soon as I get home from school today I take whatever I can find in Alex's apartment and attempt to make us an authentic Mexican meal. It'll get me to stop thinking about those damn double-chocolate chip cookies. That, combined with the fact that I've been here almost a week and have yet to eat authentic, spicy Mexican food, is drivin' me nuts.

Alex leans into the pot of stewed meat and inhales the scent. I can tell just by the expression on his face it reminds him of home.

"It's called *carne guisada*. It's Mexican." I say the words slowly as if he's never heard of it.

"I know what it is, smart-ass." He replaces the lid, then sets the table and goes back to studying.

We sit down to eat an hour later. I watch as my brother inhales his first serving and takes a second.

"Eat much?"

"Nothin' as good as this." Alex licks his fork. "I didn't know you could cook."

"You don't know a lot of things about me."

"I used to."

I push around the food on my plate, suddenly not hungry. "That was a long time ago." I keep my eyes focused on my food. I don't even know my brother anymore. After he got shot, I guess I was afraid to talk to him because talkin' about it made it real. Alex never said what exactly happened when he got jumped out of the Latino Blood, and I never asked. But yesterday mornin' I got a clue. "I saw your scars yesterday when you came out of the shower."

He stops eating and puts down his fork. "I thought you were still sleepin'."

"I wasn't." The image of his badly scarred back, full of what looks like whip marks, is etched into my brain. When I noticed the bulging skin between his shoulder blades with the letters *LB* permanently branded into him like a head of cattle, my skin crawled with hateful anger and thoughts of revenge.

"Just forget it," Alex says.

"Not gonna happen." Alex isn't the only Fuentes brother who feels a fierce protectiveness toward his family. If I go back to Chicago and find the asshole responsible for branding Alex's body, he's a dead man. I might rebel against *mi familia*, but they're still my blood.

Alex isn't the only one with scars. I have more fights to my name than a professional boxer. Along with my scars, if Alex knew the tattoos on my back marked me a *Guerrero*, he'd shit a brick. I might be in Colorado, but I'm still connected.

"Brittany and I are goin' to visit her sister Shelley tonight. Want to come?"

I know Brittany's sister is disabled and staying in some assisted-living place near the university. "I can't. I'm goin' out," I tell Alex.

"With who?"

"Last time I checked, our *papá* was dead. I don't have to answer to you."

Alex and I stare each other down. He used to be able to kick my ass without even tryin', but not anymore. We're about to get into it again, but the door opens and Brittany walks in.

She must realize there's tension in the air, because her smile fades when she reaches the table. She puts her hand on Alex's shoulder. "Everything okay?"

"Everything's *perfecto*. Right, Alex?" I say, then pick up my plate and weave my way around her to get to the kitchen.

"No. I asked him a simple question, and he can't even answer it," Alex says.

I swear that's something that should only come out of a parent's mouth. I let out a frustrated sigh. "I'm just goin' to a party, Alex. It's not like I'm goin' out to murder someone."

"A party?" Brittany asks.

"Yeah. Ever hear of the concept?"

"I've heard of it. I also know what goes on at parties." She sits next to Alex. "We went to parties in high school, though we learned from our mistakes, and he'll learn from his. You can't stop him from going out," she tells my brother.

Alex points to me accusingly. "You should see those girls he was hangin' with the other day, Brittany. They've got that psycho Darlene written all over them. Remember her? That girl would have screwed the entire football team back in high school if it would have upped her popularity status."

Once again my brother isn't helping my cause. Thanks, bro.

"Well, it was nice listenin' to both of you discuss my life in front of me, but I've got to go."

"How are you gettin' there?" Alex asks.

"Walkin'. Unless . . ." I eye Brittany's keys lying on top of her purse.

"He can use my car," she says to my brother. She doesn't say it to me, because God forbid either my brother or she make a decision without the other one's approval. "But no drinking. Or drugs."

"Okay, Mom," I say sarcastically.

Alex shakes his head. "Not a good idea."

She weaves her fingers through his. "It's fine, Alex. Really. We were going to take the bus to visit my sister anyway."

For a nanosecond I like my brother's girlfriend, but then I remember how she controls his life, and that warm and fuzzy feeling disappears as fast as a streak of lightning.

I pick up Brittany's keys and twirl them in my hand. "Come on, Alex. Don't make my shitty life worse than it already is."

"Fine," he says. "But bring that car back in perfect condition. Or else."

I salute him. "Yes, sir."

He pulls his cell phone out of his back pocket and tosses it to me. "And take this."

Before either of them can change their mind, I head out the door. I forgot to ask where her car is parked, but it's not hard to spot. The Beemer shines like an angel in front of the apartment building, calling to me.

I reach into my back pocket and pull out a sheet of paper with Madison's address on it. I wrote it down before I washed off my arm. After I figure out how to use the thing, I enter the address into the GPS, put the top down, and screech out of the parking lot. Finally . . . freedom.

I park on the street and walk up the long driveway to Madison's house. I know I have the right address because music is blarin' out of the second-story window and kids are hangin' out on the front lawn. The house is huge. At first I'm not sure if it's one house or an entire apartment building until I get close and see that it's just one big mansion. I step inside the monstrosity and recognize a bunch of kids from my classes.

"Carlos is here!" a girl screeches. I pretend not to hear the echo of squeals that follow.

Madison, wearing a short clingy black dress and carryin' a can of Bud Light in her hand, weaves through the crowd and gives me a hug. I think she spilled beer on my back. "Omigod, you're here."

"Yeah."

"We need to set you up. Follow me."

I follow her to a kitchen that looks like it came out of a magazine. It has stainless-steel appliances. Big granite slabs line the top of the counters. Next to the sink is a huge bin stuffed to the rim with ice and cans of beer. I reach in and grab one.

"Is Kiara here?" I ask.

Madison snorts. "As if."

I guess that's my answer.

Madison wraps her hand around my elbow and leads me down a hallway and up a flight of stairs. "I have someone you *have* to meet." She stops when we reach a room off to the side, filled with five huge vintage arcade games, a pool table, and an air-hockey table.

It's a teen guy's dream.

It also reeks of pot. I think I'm gettin' high just by inhalin' the air.

"It's the rec room," Madison explains.

I'm sure it takes the definition of "recreation room" to a whole different level.

A white guy is sitting on a brown leather couch, leaning back as if he's content to stay in that position forever. He's wearing a plain white T-shirt and black jeans and boots. I can tell he thinks he's one cool dude. On a small table in front of him is a bong.

"Carlos, this is Nick," Madison says.

Nick nods to me.

I nod back. " 'Sup."

Madison sits next to Nick, picks up the bong and a lighter lying next to it, and takes a really long hit. Damn, that girl can inhale.

"Nick wanted to meet you," she tells me. I notice her eyes are bloodshot. I wonder how many hits she took before I got here.

Lacey peeks her head in. "Madison, I need you!" she screeches. "Come here!"

Madison tells us she'll be right back and stumbles out of the room.

Nick waves me to the couch beside him. "Take a seat."

The guy is too slick, and my radar goes up. I know his game, because I've seen a hundred Nicks in my lifetime. Hell, I was a "Nick" back in Mexico.

"You dealin' the stuff?" I ask.

He chuckles. "If you're buyin' it, I'm dealin' it." He holds out the bong. "Want a hit?"

I hold up the can of beer in my hand. "Later."

He narrows his eyes at me. "You're not a narc, are you?"

"Do I look like a narc?"

He shrugs. "You never know. Narcs come in all different shapes and sizes these days."

I immediately think of Kiara. She's definitely become my daily entertainment. I try and peg her reactions every time I do my best to piss her off. Her rose-colored lips tighten into a thin line every time I make an outrageous comment or flirt with a girl. No matter what I told her, and no matter how many cookie crumbs are scattered on the inside of my locker, I'm gonna miss havin' her as my peer guide.

I haven't decided what I'm gonna do to get back at her for the cookie stunt. Whatever it is, she'll never see it comin'.

"I hear Madison wants to get into your pants," Nick says as he pulls out a bag of pills from his front pocket. He spills them out on the table.

"Yeah?" I ask. "Where'd you hear that?"

"From Madison. And you know what?"

"What?"

He pops a little blue pill into his mouth and throws back his head to swallow it. "Usually what Madison wants, Madison gets."

8

Kiara

"I'm color-blind," Mr. Whittaker complains in a cranky, scratchy voice as he dips a paintbrush into a cup of brown paint and swipes it on the canvas. "Is this green? How am I supposed to paint anything when these colors aren't labeled?"

There's never a dull moment during art class at The Highlands Long-Term Health Care Facility, otherwise known as a nursing home. The regular art teacher quit, but since I was volunteering to help during art hour I just kind of took over the class. The administration supplies the paint, and I come up with subjects for those who want a painting activity after dinner on Friday nights.

As I rush over to Mr. Whittaker, a little old lady with stark white hair named Sylvia comes shuffling over to us. "He's not color-blind," Sylvia croaks out as she finds an empty easel and sits down. "He's just plain ol' blind."

Mr. Whittaker looks up at me with his thin, weathered face as I kneel beside him and label the colors with a thick, black marker. "She's just sore because I wouldn't dance with her at the social last week," he says.

"I'm sore because you forgot to put your teeth in at dinner yesterday." She waves her hand in the air. "He was all gums. Some Casanova you are," she says in a huff.

"Hussy," Mr. Whittaker growls.

"Next time maybe you should dance with her at the social," I say. "Make her feel young again."

He reaches up with calloused, arthritic fingers and pulls me closer. "I've got two left feet. But don't tell Sylvia that, because she'll give me a hard time."

"Don't they have dance lessons here?" I whisper right into his ear, loud enough so he can hear but the rest of the class can't.

"I can hardly walk. A Fred Astaire I'll never be. Now, if you were the dance teacher instead of that old bat Frieda Fitzgibbons, I'd definitely start coming to lessons." He waggles his overgrown white eyebrows at me and pats me on the butt.

I shake my finger at him. "Didn't anyone tell you that's sexual harassment?" I tease.

"I'm a dirty old man, honey. In my day there was no such thing as sexual harassment and women actually let men buy them sodas and open doors for them . . . and pinch their butts."

"I let guys open doors for me, just as long as they don't expect any favors in return. I could do without the butt-patting and pinching, though."

He shoos me away. "Ach, you girls today want it all . . . and then some."

"Don't listen to him, Kiara," Sylvia says, waving me over. "What you want is a nice boy . . . a real gentleman."

"There are no such things," Mildred says next to her.

A nice boy. I thought Michael was nice, and he couldn't even dump me *like a gentleman*. "Maybe I'll just stay single for the rest of my life."

Both Mildred and Sylvia shake their heads vigorously, their wispy white hair flying from side to side. "No!" they both say.

"You don't want that," Sylvia says.

"I don't?"

"Nope." She looks over at Mr. Whittaker. "Because we need them . . . even if they are the devil incarnate." She motions me closer. "I wouldn't mind if he patted *my* butt."

"Amen to that, sister," Mildred says as she swipes her brush on the canvas. She's painting a silhouette that looks suspiciously like a nude man. "Why don't you ask that nice boy Tuck to come and pose for us? You said we can do live subjects."

"I was thinking of a dog," I tell her.

"No. Get us a male model."

"I'm not drawing some guy," Mr. Whittaker yells from across the room. "Kiara will have to model, too."

"I'm not promising anything," I tell the class. Wait until I call Tuck today and ask him to be a male model for my class. I think he might just go along with it.

9

CARLOS

"Heeeey," Madison sings. "I'm back."

And she's brought about ten other people with her. They all gather by the bong and pass it around, each takin' hits. I wonder what Kiara and her friends are doin' tonight. I bet she's studying for her SATs or something like that, so she can get into a good college, while I'm at a bong-and-little-blue-pill party.

Nick lines up the pills on a tray. It reminds me of what Alex called a pu-pu platter.

When Madison passes the bong to me with a big smile, I want to forget about Kiara and SATs and college and bein' good. I'm a thug, so I better start actin' like one.

I take a hit, inhaling the sweet smoke into my lungs. The stuff is definitely potent, because I feel the effects before I even hand the bong to the person next to me. When it comes back around, this time I take a long, slow hit. By the fourth time, I'm stoned enough not to care about Kiara and her cookies or Alex gettin' on my case all the time, or the fact that I lied to Brittany when I promised I wouldn't drink or do drugs tonight.

Right now I only want to think about life's burning questions, like . . . "Why doesn't Heavy Shevy shave her mustache?"

"Maybe she's a man in disguise," Nick says.

"But why would he choose an ugly woman as a disguise?" I ask. Seriously.

"Maybe he's an ugly man and has no other choice."

"Makes sense." I watch Madison take another hit. She sees me watching her, then smiles at me as she wiggles her way onto my lap and licks her lips. By the length and pointy tip of her tongue I think she might have iguana genes in her family tree. She leans forward, her *chichis* inches from my face.

"Nick has the best shit," she coos, leanin' back and stretching on me like a cat on a rug. Needless to say, I'm the rug. She twists herself around, straddles me, and wraps both arms around my neck. Her eyes are at half-mast. "You're sexy."

"So are you."

"We're a perfect match." She traces my chin with her finger and leans forward. That iguana tongue of hers sneaks out and her body starts writhing against mine. She licks my chin, which I have to admit no girl has ever done to me before. I'm not too keen on having this girl do it a second time, either.

We start makin' out in front of everyone. I think Madison likes the spotlight, 'cause when one of the girls makes a comment to one of the guys to stop watching, Madison leans back and starts pullin' up her shirt like she's a stripper at a club givin' me a lap dance. It's obvious Madison wants to be watched and admired by all the guys, and envied by all the girls.

This girl is definitely an exhibitionist, but when I look to my left and find Nick making out with a shirtless Lacey I start to wonder if everyone is expected to show off their sexual talents in public here.

That's not me. "Let's go somewhere private," I tell Madison as she reaches down to feel me over my jeans.

She pouts for a minute, then wiggles her way off my lap and holds out her hand. "Come on."

The night is moving way too fast. I'd rather chill, and in the back of my mind I remember Ram warned me about Madison, but she grabs my hand and pulls me up.

"Have fun, you two," Nick calls out.

Two minutes later we enter a huge room with a king-size bed against the wall.

"Your room?" I ask.

Madison shakes her head. "It's my parents', but they're hardly home. Right now they're in Phoenix." I sense traces of bitterness in her voice, and I'm sure foolin' around on their bed is her revenge.

Should I tell her I'd rather do this on the floor instead of her parents' bed?

"Let's go to your room," I say.

She shakes her head, then pulls me closer to the bed.

"What did Ram say about me?" she asks.

"It's kind of hard to think about that right now," I tell her. "I'm as baked as you are."

"Just *try* and remember. Did he mention why we broke up? Because if he did, it wasn't all my fault. I mean, it's not like I knew what he knew and that I didn't know what I was doing. And if I did know, it wasn't because I knew that he knew. It's not like his mother would have found out and have us all arrested."

My head aches from listenin' to her. "Okay," I say. I have no clue what she just said, but I figure a response of "okay" might cover the bases. One can only hope.

"Really?" she says, smiling.

Huh? I have no fuckin' clue what I'm talkin' about. Or what she's talkin' about.

She hugs me tight, her *chichis* pressed hard against my chest. I hope they don't burst from the pressure of being squished against me.

Thoughts of bursting *chichis* are creepin' me out. And my mind wanders to thoughts of Kiara and what she looks like under those huge shirts. For a second I think the unknown of Kiara's body is sexier than what Madison flaunts every day.

I squeeze my eyes shut. What am I thinkin'? Kiara isn't sexy. She's frustrating and challenges me more than my own family.

"Did I tell you what Kiara did to my locker?" I ask.

She urges me onto the bed. "I don't really care about Kiara. Stop talking about another girl when you're here with me." She's right. I need to stop talking about Kiara. I like things that come easily to me, and Kiara isn't one of them. Madison is.

Before I know it, we're gettin' hot and heavy on her parents' bed. She's sitting on me, her hair in my face. I think some of her hair is in our mouths as we're kissing, but she doesn't seem to notice. I do.

She leans back. "Wanna do *it*?" she slurs.

Sure I want to do it. But when I look to the side and see a picture of her parents smiling at us from one of the nightstands, it hits me. She doesn't want me because I'm me—she wants me because I'm a drugged-out thug, the exact opposite of who her parents want her to be with.

But tellin' myself I'm a thug is one thing. Actin' like one is another. "I gotta go," I tell her.

"Wait. Oh, no. I'm not feeling well. I think I'm gonna be sick."

She pushes herself up and runs to the bathroom, locking herself in. The sounds of gagging and puking echo through the room a second later.

I knock on the door. "Need help?"

"No."

"Open the door, Madison."

"No. Get Lacey."

When I do, Lacey and a bunch of other girls rush in the room to help. I'm standing in the doorway, watching them treat Madison like she's really sick instead of puking from getting drunk and stoned.

After twenty minutes of standing around being ignored, and confident that Madison is having her every need taken care of, I figure I've had enough of this party.

Outside, I pull out Brittany's pink heart keychain. I rev the engine and put the car in drive, but when I look up and the lines on the road are blurry I know I can't do it. I'm too stoned, too drunk, or a mixture of both.

Shit. I have two options. Go back in Madison's house and find a place to crash, or sleep in the car.

It's not even a contest.

I push the button to recline the seat and close my eyes, hopin' tomorrow I can figure out what actually happened tonight.

Bright. It's too bright. I open my eyes to the morning sun hittin' me right in the face. I'm still in Brittany's car. With the top down. When I get back to Alex's place, I find him sitting at the table with a mug of coffee in his hands.

He stands when I toss Brittany's keys on the table.

"You told me you'd be home in a couple of hours. Are you aware it's nine? *De la mañana*."

I rub my palms over my eyes. "Please, Alex," I moan. "Can you wait until at least noon to yell at me?"

"I'm not gonna yell at you. I'm just not gonna let you drive Brittany's car again."

"Fine." I notice the air mattress is still set up. I fall onto it and close my eyes.

Alex pulls the pillow out from under my head. "Are you *high*?"

"Not anymore, unfortunately." I grab the pillow back.

I hear my brother sit on his bed and let out a heavy sigh. Poor guy probably needs to smoke some weed to relax. I swear I can feel his eyes boring into my skull like two little lasers.

"What do you want?" I mumble into my pillow.

"Do you not fuckin' care about anyone but yourself?"

"Pretty much."

"Didn't you realize I would worry about you?"

"Nope. That thought didn't cross my mind even once."

Someone knocking on the door thankfully stops him from askin' me more questions.

I hear my brother say, "Hey, *chica*."

Let me guess—it's Brittany.

"Carlos forgot to put my top up," she tells Alex. "And it's starting to rain. He left your phone in the passenger seat. I hope it still works."

If they ever get married, I feel sorry for their kids. I hope those *niños* never fuck up . . . because Brittany and Alex are both lookin' at me as if they want to ground me for life.

Too bad for them, they're not my parents.

10

Kiara

On Monday, rumors are flying about Madison Stone's party. Most of them revolve around Madison and Carlos getting it on in her parents' bed.

On Tuesday and Wednesday, I notice Madison sitting with Carlos at his lunch table.

On Thursday, Carlos isn't even at lunch. Neither is Madison. The happy couple must be off by themselves somewhere.

On Friday morning, Carlos is at his locker, the cookies still stuck on the inside. "Hey," he says.

"Hey," I say back.

I enter my combination, but the locker won't open.

I try again. I know I have the numbers right, but when I pull the handle, it doesn't budge.

I try again.

Carlos is looking over my shoulder. "Havin' trouble?"

"No."

I try again. This time, I pull the handle harder and jiggle it. Again, nothing happens.

He taps his fingers on the metal. "Maybe you forgot the combination."

"I know my combination," I say. "I'm not stupid."

"You sure? 'Cause that's a turn-on."

My thoughts turn to the rumors about him and Madison. I don't even know why, but the idea of them hooking up fuels my anger. "Just go away."

He shrugs. "If you say so." The first bell rings. "Well, good luck. If you ask me, it looks like someone rigged it." He grabs his books out of his locker and struts down the hallway.

I run after him and grab his arm. "What did you do to my locker?"

He stops. "I might have changed the combination."

"How?"

He chuckles. "If I tell you, then I'd have to kill you."

"Very funny. Tell me what you changed it to."

"I will totally give you that information . . ." He taps the tip of his forefinger on my nose. "When every last cookie is out of my locker. Includin' all the crumbs. See ya," he says, ducking into the classroom and leaving me alone in the hallway to figure out how I'm going to do it . . . and then plot my next move.

In English class, Mr. Furie hands back our essays. He calls out our names and one by one we have to go up to his desk.

"Kiara," he calls out.

I walk up to get my paper. When Mr. Furie hands it to me, he's not smiling. "You can do a lot better than this, Kiara. I know you can. Dig deeper next time, and don't try to give me the answer you think I want."

I pass Madison on the way back to my desk. "How's Carlos?" she asks.

"Fine."

"You know he only pays attention to you because he feels sorry for you. It's kind of sad, if you think about it."

I ignore her and sit at my desk. A big, red C is written on the front of the paper Mr. Furie just gave back to me. Not good, especially if I'm going to apply for an academic scholarship.

"For the next fifteen minutes, you're going to write a persuasion paper," Mr. Furie says.

"About what?" Nick Glass asks.

"The topic is . . ." Mr. Furie pauses, obviously to heighten the anticipation and get the attention of all the students. He sits on the edge of his desk and says, "Should people on reality shows be considered celebrities?"

The class starts buzzing about the topic.

"Keep the noise level to a minimum, people."

"How can we write a persuasion paper when we don't have time to do research?" someone in the back of the class asks.

"I'm looking for your thoughts, not research. When you're talking with a friend and you need to persuade him to do something, or to change his opinion, you can't say, 'Hold on, I need to do research or write down statistics.' You just come up with arguments off the top of your head. That's what I'm asking you to do."

Mr. Furie wanders around the room as we write. "If you want extra credit, you can read the paper aloud to the class."

That's good. I need extra credit, and I know I can say my speech without stuttering. I just know I can.

"Pens down," Mr. Furie orders fifteen minutes later. He clasps his hands together. "Okay, any volunteers to read first?"

I raise my hand high.

"Ms. Westford, come on up and share your thoughts."

"*Oh, no. Not her,*" I hear Madison groan beside me. Lacey laughs, along with a bunch of their friends.

"Do you have a problem, Madison?"

"No, Mr. Furie. I almost broke a nail!" She wiggles her manicured fingers at him.

"Please save your nail issues for after class. Kiara, come on up."

I pick up my paper and walk to the front of the class. I tell myself to take deep breaths and think about the words before they come out of my mouth. When I'm standing in front, I look over at my teacher. He's smiling warmly at me. "Go ahead."

I clear my throat. And swallow, but feel my tongue getting thicker before I even start talking, because of Madison. She's thrown me off, but I can overcome it. I don't have to give her power over my stuttering. *Relax. Think about the words. Don't forget to breathe.*

"I th-th-think . . ." I stare down at my paper. I can feel all eyes on me. Some are probably giving me the pity stare. Others, like Madison and Lacey, probably look amused. "I th-th-think that p-p-people on r-r-reality shows . . ."

A burst of laughter erupts from one girl. I know who it is before I look up.

"Madison, I don't find this funny. Be respectful to your classmate," Mr. Furie says, then adds, "That's not a request. That's an order."

Madison puts her hand over her mouth. "I'm good," she says through her fingers.

"You'd better be," Mr. Furie says in his stern voice. "Go ahead, Kiara. Continue."

Okay. I can do this. If I can talk to Tuck and not stutter, maybe I should just pretend I'm talking to Tuck. I look up at my best friend.

He gives me a small wave of encouragement from his seat in the back of the room.

". . . people on reality shows are celebrities . . ." I pause and take a deep breath, then continue. *I can do this. I can do this.* ". . . because we let the m-m-media—"

Another burst of laughter echoes in the room, this time from both Lacey and Madison.

"Miss Stone and Miss Goebbert!" Mr. Furie points toward the door. "Out of my class."

"You're not serious," Madison argues.

"I've never been more serious. And I'm also giving you and Miss Goebbert three days of after-school detention starting today."

"Don't do that," I whisper to Mr. Furie, hoping no one else can hear me. "Please don't do that."

Madison gets a shocked look on her face. "You're giving us detentions *for laughing*? Come on, Mr. Furie. That's not fair."

"Tell it to Principal House if you have a problem with my punishment." Mr. Furie opens the top drawer of his desk and pulls out two blue detention slips. He fills out both and motions for Madison and Lacey to come get them. Both girls shoot me a furious look. Oh, no, this is not good. Now I'm on Madison's radar, and I don't know if there's any way I can get off it.

When he hands them the blue slips, Madison shoves hers in her purse. "I can't have detention after school. I have to work at my mom's boutique."

"You should have thought about that before you disrupted my class. Now, both of you, apologize to Kiara," our teacher orders.

"That's okay," I mumble. "You d-d-don't have to."

"Oh, I insist. We're s-s-s-s-sorry," Madison says, and suddenly

Madison and Lacey start giggling again. Even after they hurry out the door, I can hear their laughter echoing as they walk down the hall.

"I apologize on their behalf for their inappropriate behavior, Kiara," Mr. Furie says. "Would you still like to share your paper?"

I shake my head and he sighs, but he doesn't argue when I return to my desk. I wish the bell would ring so I could go to the girls' bathroom and hide. I'm so mad at myself for letting them affect me.

For the next twenty-five minutes, Mr. Furie calls on other students to read their persuasion papers. I keep looking up at the clock, praying for the minutes to go by faster. It's hard holding back tears that are threatening to pour out any minute.

As soon as the bell rings, I grab my books and practically sprint out of class. Mr. Furie calls my name, but I pretend not to hear him.

"Kiara!" Tuck says, grabbing my elbow and spinning me around.

A stupid tear falls down my face. "I want to be alone," I choke out, then run down the hall.

At the end of the corridor, there are stairs that lead to a vacant locker room rival teams use during tournaments. Nobody uses it during the day, and just the thought of being alone where I don't have to put on a fake smile sounds like heaven right now. I'm aware I'll be late for study hall, but Mrs. Hadden doesn't usually take attendance and even if she does, I don't care. I don't want everyone to see me an emotional mess.

I push open the locker room door and sink onto one of the benches. All the energy I used during the last half of English class to stop myself from losing it rushes out of me. I wish I could be stronger and not care what people think, but I do. I'm not strong like Tuck. I'm not strong like Madison.

I wish I was content just being *me*, Kiara Westford, speech issues and all.

Fifteen minutes pass before I walk to the sink and look at my reflection in the mirror. I look like I've been crying. That, or I have a very bad cold. I wet paper towels and dab them on my eyes, attempting to erase the puffiness. After a few minutes, I think I look halfway decent. Nobody will know I've just been crying. I hope.

The door to the locker room opens, startling me.

"Anybody here?" one of the janitors yells out.

"Yeah."

"You'd better get to class because the police are here. They're doing a drug search."

11

CARLOS

In bio, Shevelenko finishes a lecture on dominant and recessive genes. She has us draw square boxes and tells us to write different scenarios about eye-color traits in the offspring of humans.

"I'm havin' a couple guys over tonight," Ram says as we work. "You wanna come?"

Even though Ram is a rich kid, he's pretty cool. The past week he's given me notes from the first two weeks of school, and his stories about going skiing last winter are hilarious.

"¿A qué hora?" I ask him.

"Around six or so." He rips out a piece of paper from his notebook and starts writing on it. "Here's my address."

"I don't have a car. Is it far?"

He turns the paper over and hands me his pen. "No problem, I'll just pick you up. Where do you live?"

As I write down Alex's address, Shevelenko walks over to our table. "Carlos, did you get all the notes from Ramiro?"

"Yeah."

"Good, because there's a test next week." She's handing out worksheets when five beeps echo over the loudspeaker.

The entire room seems to gasp at once.

"What's that?" I question.

Ram looks shocked. "Holy shit, man. We're in lockdown."

"What's 'lockdown'?"

"If it's some psycho with a gun, I'm jumping out the window," another student named John says. "You guys with me?"

Ram rolls his eyes. "It's not someone with a gun, dude. That would be three long beeps instead of five short ones. This is a drug lockdown. It must not be routine, 'cause I haven't heard anything about it."

John seems amused. "Call your mom, Ram. Ask if she knows what's up."

Drug lockdown? I sure hope Nick Glass doesn't bring his pu-pu platter of drugs to school with him. I look over at Madison, who came late to class. She pulls her phone from her purse and starts texting someone underneath the lab table.

"Everyone calm down," Shevelenko says. "Most of you have been through this before. In case you haven't guessed it, we're in lockdown. No student can leave the building."

Madison raises her hand. "Can I go to the bathroom?"

"Sorry, Madison."

"But I *really* have to go! I promise I'll be quick."

"Lockdown rules state no wandering in the halls." Shevelenko glances at her computer. "Take this time to study for the test next wednesday."

Fifteen minutes later a cop knocks on Shevelenko's door.

"Who do you think got busted?" a guy named Frank whispers as our teacher meets the officer outside the room.

Ram holds his hands up. "Don't look at me, man. I'm not risking getting kicked off the soccer team. Besides, my mom would have me arrested herself if she found out I was doing illegal shit."

Shevelenko walks back in the room. "Carlos Fuentes," she says loud and clear.

¡Carajo! She called my name. "Yeah?"

"Come here."

"Dude, you are so busted," Frank says.

I walk up to Shevelenko, and all I can focus on is her mustache hairs moving up and down as she says, "There are some people who want to talk to you. Follow me."

I know everyone in my bio class knows why I've been called out. Thing is, I don't have any drugs in my pockets or in my locker. Maybe they found out I came from Mexico and want to deport me, although I was born in Illinois and am an American citizen.

In the hallway two cops step toward me. "Are you Carlos Fuentes?" one of them asks.

"Yeah."

"Can you show us where your locker is?"

My locker? I shrug. "Sure."

I walk to my locker, the *policía* following so close I can feel their breath on the back of my neck. I turn the corner down J Hall and see a K9 police dog barking at my locker. What the hell?

The dog is ordered to sit by its handler.

Mr. House is standing next to my locker.

"Carlos, is this your assigned locker?" he asks me.

"Yeah."

He makes a dramatic pause before saying, "I'll only ask this once. Do you have drugs in your locker?"

"No."

"Then you wouldn't mind opening it, would you?"

"Nope." I enter the combination and open the door.

"What are those things?" one of the cops asks as he points to Kiara's cookie magnets. He steps forward to take a closer look and the K9 dog goes nuts. He pokes one. "They're cookies," he says dumbly.

"I think your dog is hungry," I tell him.

The second cop gives me a level stare. "You, be quiet. They're probably laced with drugs and you're selling them."

Laced cookies? Is he kiddin' me? They're *fucking stale cookie magnets*. I start to laugh.

"You think this is funny, punk?"

I clear my throat and try to keep a straight face. "No, sir."

"Did you make those cookies?"

"Yes, sir," I lie, because it's none of their business who made them. "But you should probably not pull 'em off."

"Why not? Scared we'll find out what's in them?"

I shake my head. "No. Trust me, they're not laced."

"Nice try," the cop says.

Ignoring me, the principal tries to pick off one of the cookie magnets. The cookie breaks in his hand. I cough again, trying to cover up another laugh, as he holds the crumbled brown pieces in his hand and sniffs them. I wonder what Kiara would think if she knew her cookies were under investigation.

One of the cops crumbles another cookie off and takes a small bite to see if he can taste traces of illegal substances. He shrugs. "I don't taste anything." He holds the rest of the cookie under the K9's nose. The dog goes still. "The cookies are clean," he says. "But there's something else in the locker. Take everything out," he orders, then crosses his arms on his chest.

From the top shelf, I take out a couple of books and place them on the floor. I take more books out from the bottom. When I pull down my backpack, the dog starts freakin' out again.

That dog is certifiably nuts. If we watch it long enough, I'm sure its head will turn around and its eyes will roll to the back of its head.

"Take everything out of your backpack and place the items on the floor in front of you," House says.

"Look," I tell House. "I have no clue why that dog is about to attack my backpack. I don't have drugs in there. Maybe the dog's got a disorder."

"The dog isn't the problem, son," the K9 officer barks out.

My pulse races when the guy calls me "son." I want to lash out at him, but he's got a psycho dog he can sic on me. While I think I'm a hard-ass, I definitely know a trained psycho K9 can kick my ass.

One by one I pull out each thing from my backpack. I lay them out in a straight line.

One pencil.

Two pens.

One notebook.

One Spanish book.

One can of Coke.

The dog starts barking again. Wait, I didn't put a can of Coke in there. The principal picks up the can, starts unscrewing the top and . . . oh, shit. It's not a can of Coke. It's a fake one with . . .

One bag of weed. A big bag. And . . .

One bag with a bunch of white and blue pills inside.

"That's not mine," I tell them.

"Whose is it, then?" the principal asks. "Give us names."

I'm pretty sure it's Nick's, but I'm not about to rat on him. If there's one thing I've learned in Mexico, it's that you don't open your mouth. Ever. Even if I don't give a shit about Nick, I'm about to take the fall whether I like it or not. "I don't have any names. I've only lived here a week, give me a break."

"We don't give breaks. Not on school property, which makes this a felony," one of the officers says, eyeing my tattoos. He takes the bags from the principal, then opens the one with the pills. "This is Oxy-Contin. And this," he says, opening the bag with the weed, "is enough marijuana for us to know you're not just smoking it, you're selling it."

"Do you understand what this means, Carlos?" the principal asks.

Yeah, I know what it means. It means Alex is gonna kill me.

12

Kiara

When I found out Carlos got arrested, I immediately had the instinct to call my dad. He said he'd call Alex and find out what was happening and where Carlos was taken.

At home, my mom greets me at the door. "Your father said he'll be home soon with some news about Carlos."

"So you know what happened?"

She nods. "Alex told your dad that Carlos keeps insisting the drugs aren't his."

"Does Alex believe him?"

My mom sighs, and I know she wants to give me better news. "He's skeptical."

My dad comes home with hair that looks like he ran his hand through it too many times today. "Family-meeting time," he says.

When the entire family is in the living room, my dad clears his throat. "How would you all feel about having Carlos stay here for the rest of the school year?"

"Who's Carlos?" Brandon asks, clueless.

"The brother of one of my former students. And one of Kiara's friends." My dad looks from me to my mom. "Turns out the place where he's living is subsidized student apartments. Since Carlos isn't a student at the university, the judge said it's against policy for him to stay there."

"I get a brother? Cool!" Brandon yells. "Can he sleep in my room? You can buy us bunk beds and everything."

"Don't get too excited, Bran. He'll stay in the yellow room," my dad tells my brother.

"How's Carlos holding up?" my mom asks.

"I don't know. I think underneath it all he's a good kid who'll thrive in a positive and stable drug-free home environment. I'd like to help out if we're all in agreement. It's either our house, or he goes back to Mexico. Alex said he'd do just about anything to keep him here."

"I'm okay with him staying here," I say, realizing after I say it that I actually mean it. Everyone deserves a second chance.

My dad looks at my mom, who reaches out and brings his head closer to hers. "My husband is going to save the world one kid at a time, huh?"

He smiles at her. "If that's what it takes."

She kisses him. "I'll make sure there are clean sheets on the bed in the guest room."

"I married the best woman," he tells her. "I'll call Alex and tell him it's a go," he adds excitedly. "Monday we'll meet with the judge again. We're going to lobby to get him into the REACH program at Flatiron instead of being expelled."

I watch as my dad leaves the living room and heads for his office.

"He's on a mission," my mom says. "He's has that spark in his eye when he's got a challenge in front of him."

I just hope he keeps that spark alive, because I have a feeling my dad's patience—which is probably at the sainthood level—is about to be tested big-time.

13

CARLOS

"Just send me back to Chicago and be done with me already," I tell Alex on Sunday morning after I hang up with *mi'amá*. Alex forced me to tell her what's going on.

When the police escorted me out in handcuffs, I was fine with it. Seeing my brother come to the station with frustration and disappointment etched on his face didn't faze me. But talking to my mom just now and hearing her cry and ask me what happened to her *niñito* was my undoing.

She also told me I shouldn't come back to Mexico. "It's not safe here for you," she told me. "*Auséntese*, Carlos, stay away." I wasn't surprised. My entire life has been full of people leavin' me or tellin' me to stay away from them—*mi papá*, Alex, Destiny, and now *mi'amá*."

Alex is lying in his bed, his forearm covering his eyes. "You're not goin' back to Chicago, either. Professor Westford and his wife are lettin' you live at their house. It's a done deal."

Livin' with the Professor means I'll also be livin' in the same house as Kiara. That's a bad move on so many levels. "Don't I have any say in this?"

"No."

"*¡Vete a la mierda!*"

"Yeah, well, you created the bullshit you're livin' in," my brother tells me.

"I told you those drugs weren't mine."

He sits up. "Carlos, since you came here all you've done is talk about drugs. They found *chora* in your locker, along with an insane amount of OC. Even if they weren't yours, you've made yourself the scapegoat."

"This is such bullshit."

A half hour later, after I get out of the shower, Brittany is back. She's sitting at the table, wearing a hot pink velour sweatsuit that hugs her curves. I swear that *chica* should just live here . . . she's around all the time.

I walk over to my bed, suddenly wishin' this wasn't a studio apartment. I'm a pissed-off guy thirsty for revenge. I won't rest until I know who stuck those drugs in my locker. Whoever it was is gonna pay.

"I hope you don't get expelled," Brittany says in a sad tone. "But I know Alex and Professor Westford will do all they can to help."

"Don't sound so depressed," I tell her. "Now that I gotta move out, you can be here whenever the hell you want. Lucky you."

"Carlos, *retroceda*," Alex says roughly.

Why should I back off? It's the truth.

"Believe it or not, Carlos, I want you to be happy here." Brittany pushes a brand-new cell phone toward me. "I got you this."

"For what? So you and Alex can check up on me?"

She shakes her head. "No. I just thought you'd want one so you can call us if you need us."

I pick up the phone. "Who's payin' for it?"

"Does it matter?" she asks.

My family obviously can't afford it. I turn my back on Brittany and the phone. "I don't need it," I tell her. "Save your money."

The three of us pile into Brittany's Beemer a few hours later. I should have known Brittany would come on this little adventure to drop me off at the Professor's house, probably to make sure I'm really out of her and my brother's hair.

Alex pulls onto one of the winding roads leading up into the mountains. When I look out at the big houses on either side of the road, it's obvious we've entered the rich side of town. Poor people don't post signs like NO TRESPASSING, PRIVATE DRIVE, PRIVATE PROPERTY, MONITORED BY CAMERA SURVEILLANCE. I should know because I've been poor my entire life, and the only person I know who ever posted a sign like these is my friend Pedro, and he actually stole the sign off a rich guy's yard.

We pull up a brick driveway leading to a two-story house built right into the mountain. I sit up and take in my surroundings. I've never lived in a place where you couldn't easily throw a stone at your next-door neighbor's window.

You'd think I'd be thrilled at the chance to live in this fancy house, but it just reminds me I'm an outsider. I'm not an idiot; I know as soon as I leave here I'll be as poor as I always was—or in jail. This place is just a tease, and I can't wait to get the hell out of here.

As soon as we park, Westford comes out of the house. He's a tall guy with gray hair and a lot of wrinkles around his eyes as if he's smiled too much over the years and his skin is rebelling.

Before I even step out of the car, three more people pile out. It's like a fuckin' parade of white folks, one whiter than the next.

When Kiara walks out, her familiar face is as much a relief as it is an annoyance. In one morning I went from rigging her locker to being handcuffed and thrown in jail. My life went from amusement to completely fucked-up in a matter of hours.

Kiara has her light brown hair pulled back, and is wearing jean shorts and a baggy, puke green–colored T-shirt. She definitely didn't dress up for my arrival, that's for sure. She's even got smudges of brown dirt or grease on her cheek and hands.

Next to Kiara is her brother. He must've been a mistake or an afterthought, 'cause he looks like he could be in kindergarten. The little kid is a mess. He's got leftover chocolate smeared all over his chin.

"This is my wife, Colleen," he says, gesturing to the thin woman next to him. "And my son, Brandon. Of course you already know my daughter, Kiara."

The Professor and his wife are wearing matching white golf shirts. I can totally see them playin' golf at a fancy country club on the weekends. Brandon could be in movies or commercials—he's so annoyingly energetic it almost makes you want to give him Z-Tabs to make him zone out.

While Brittany and Alex do the handshake thing with the Professor's wife and kids, Kiara steps closer to me.

"You okay?" she asks so softly I can hardly hear her.

"I'm fine," I mumble. I don't want to talk about bein' arrested and taken away in the back of the squad car to juvie.

Damn, this is awkward. The little kid, Brandon, pulls at my pant leg. His fingers have melted chocolate all over them. "Do you play soccer?"

"No." I look over at Alex, who doesn't seem to notice or doesn't care the runt is messin' up my jeans.

Mrs. Westford smiles as she guides Brandon away from me. "Carlos, why don't you take a few minutes to get settled, then come to the backyard for some lunch. Dick, take Carlos upstairs and show him around."

Dick? I shake my head. The Professor doesn't have a problem being called *Dick?* If my name was Richard, I'd go by Richard or Rich . . . not *Dick*. Hell, I'd even settle for being called Chard.

I grab my duffel.

"Carlos, follow me," Westford says, "I'll show you around. Kiara, why don't you show Alex and Brittany your car."

The rest of the crew follows Kiara while I follow Professor Dick.

"This is our home," Westford says. Just as I suspected, the inside is as massive as the outside. It's not as big as Madison's place, but it's still bigger than any place I've ever lived. Big paintings line the hallway. They've got a nice flat-screen TV hanging on the wall over the fireplace. "Just make yourself at home."

Yeah, right. This is as much my home as the White House.

"Here's the kitchen," he says, leading me into a huge room with an oversized stainless-steel fridge and appliances to match. Their counters are black with little pieces of what looks like diamonds in them. "If you want something from the fridge or pantry, feel free. Don't feel like you have to ask."

Next, I follow him up a flight of carpeted stairs. "Any questions so far?" he asks.

"Got a map of this place?" I ask.

He chuckles. "You'll get used to the layout in a couple of days."

Wanna bet?

I feel a big, pounding headache coming on and I long to be somewhere where I don't have to pretend to be a reformed kid living in a minimansion with a girl who put cookie magnets in my locker and a little runt who thinks all Mexicans play soccer.

Upstairs, at the end of long hallway, is the parents' bedroom. We turn the corner and Westford points to one of the rooms. "That's Kiara's room. The door across the hall, next to Brandon's room, is the bathroom you'll share with the kids." I peek inside the bathroom, which has two side-by-side sinks.

He opens the door next to Kiara's room and gestures me inside. "This is your room."

I scan what will be my bedroom. The walls are painted yellow, with polka-dotted drapes hanging from the windows. It looks like a damn girl's room. I wonder if I stay here long enough I'll be forced to hand in my Man Card. There's a desk on one side with a closet next to it, a dresser on the other side of the room, and a bed with a yellow blanket next to the window.

"I know it's not the most masculine room. My wife decorated it a while back," Westford says, looking apologetic. "It was supposed to be her porcelain-doll room."

Is he kiddin' me? Porcelain-doll room? What the hell are porcelain dolls, and why would an adult want a room full of 'em? Maybe it's a rich-white-people thing, 'cause I don't know any Mexican families who have a bedroom just for their damn dolls.

"I figure we can get some paint and make this room a little more guy friendly," he says.

My eyes focus on the polka-dotted curtains. "It'll take a lot more than paint," I mumble. "But it don't matter, 'cause I'm not plannin' on hangin' around here much."

"Well, I guess now is a good time to go over house rules." My temporary guardian settles into the chair by the desk.

"Rules?" A feeling of dread washes over me.

"Don't worry, I only have a few. But I do expect them to be followed.

First off, no drugs or alcohol. As you already know, marijuana isn't hard to find in this city, but you have to stay clean per court order. Second, no profanity. I have a six-year-old who is very impressionable, and I don't need him hearing cuss words. Third, curfew on weekdays is midnight, on weekends it's two. Fourth, you're expected to clean up after yourself and help around the house when asked, just like our own children. Fifth, there's no TV unless you're done with homework. Sixth, if you bring a girl up to your room you must keep the door open . . . for obvious reasons." He rubs his chin, seemingly searching for more rules to spout. "I think that's it. Any questions?"

"Yeah, one." I shove my hands in my pockets, wondering how long it'll take for Professor Dick to realize I'm antirules. Of any kind. "What happens when I break one of your fuckin' rules?"

14

Kiara

I don't know if anyone else in my family noticed, but Carlos looked at us like we were a bunch of aliens sent down to earth to destroy him. He definitely isn't happy about having to live with us.

I wonder what he's going to say when they tell him he'll either be expelled or have to go to the REACH program after school. REACH is for at-risk teens who get in trouble. They can attend school on a probationary basis. My dad told me Carlos doesn't know that REACH is his only choice. I do not want to be in the house when Alex and my dad give him the news.

Alex is checking out the new rearview mirror I just installed. Not being able to resist, Alex lifts up the hood and inspects the engine.

"It's a standard V8," I tell Brittany, who's standing beside him.

Alex laughs. "That won't mean anythin' to my girlfriend. Brittany doesn't even like to pump gas."

Brittany punches him lightly on the arm. "Are you kidding me? Every time I even try to fix something with my car, Alex totally takes over. Admit it, Alex."

"*Mamacita*, no offense, but you wouldn't know a gasket from an alternator."

"And you wouldn't know acrylic from gel," Brittany says smugly, her hands on her hips.

"Are we still talkin' cars?" he asks.

Brittany shakes her head. "I was talking fingernails."

"I thought so. You stick to nails, I'll stick to cars."

The corner of Alex's mouth quirks up as he pulls his girlfriend close.

"I think we're ready for lunch," my dad yells from the front door.

My mom waves to my brother. "Brandon, sweetie, show Brittany and Alex where the patio is."

While Brandon races to the backyard, I help my mom in the kitchen.

"You've got grease on your chin," my mom tells me. I rub my chin, then realize it's not grease. It's black epoxy.

"Now you're smearing it. Here—" She tosses me a kitchen towel.

"Thanks." After I wipe my chin clean, I wash my hands and then toss my special walnut salad.

On the patio, my mom has set up pink flowery place mats and her favorite ceramic dishes painted with images of colorful butterflies that match the teacups. She opened up an organic tea store called Hospitali-Tea a few years ago. If you live in Boulder, bets are you like the outdoors and live an active lifestyle. And bets are you drink tea instead of coffee.

Mom's store is very popular with the locals. I work there on weekends bagging loose teas, logging in new teas, and pricing ceramic teapots. I even help with her accounting, especially when her calculations are off and she needs someone to find where she made a mistake.

I'm the mistake-finder in the family, at least when it comes to doing the books.

I help bring out the salad. I actually made up the recipe and have kept the dressing a secret so even my parents don't know how to replicate it. It's made with spinach leaves, walnuts, blue cheese, and dried cranberries . . . and "Kiara's special, secret sauce," as my mom likes to call it. When I get outside, I hold out the bowl to Carlos.

He peers inside the bowl. "What is it?"

"Salad."

He peers inside again. "That's not lettuce."

"It's s-spinach." I stop talking as I feel my tongue getting thicker.

"Just try it," Alex tells him.

"I don't need to be told what to do," Carlos fires back.

"Carlos, I have some lettuce in the fridge," my mom chimes in. "I can throw a lettuce salad together quickly if you want."

"No, thanks," Carlos mutters.

"I'd like some salad," Brittany says, motioning for me to hand her the bowl. I don't know if she really wants the spinach salad or not, but she's trying hard to divert attention away from Alex and Carlos.

I look over at my dad. He's got his eyes on Carlos. He's probably wondering how long it'll take before he can get Carlos to loosen up and trust us. Problem is, I don't know if Carlos will ever let his guard down now that he got arrested.

"I know you're here due to extenuating circumstances," my mom says to Carlos as she passes around the plate of salmon burgers. "But we're happy to offer our home and friendship."

My dad stabs a burger with his fork. "Kiara can show you around

Boulder this weekend. And introduce you to her friends. Right, sweetheart?"

"Sure," I say, although "my friends" consist of Tuck. I'm not one to hang out with a crowd. Tuck is a guy, but he's my best friend and has been since freshman year when Heather Harte and Madison Stone laughed at me during English class when I was called on to read *A Tale of Two Cities* in front of the entire class. Not only did I embarrass myself with my stuttering, I think Dickens must have rolled over in his grave when I horrifically butchered his words. I stopped immediately after hearing them laugh, ran home, and didn't come out of my room until Tuck came over and convinced me to face the world. Friday in Mr. Furie's class brought me back to that day.

"I think I got an undercooked burger. It's really pink," Carlos says as he stares at the inside of one of my mother's salmon patties.

"It's fish," I tell him. "Salmon."

"There bones in it?"

I shake my head.

He picks out a bun from the breadbasket, examines it, then shrugs. I guess he's not used to whole grains sticking out of his burger buns.

"I have to go to work, but Kiara can take you grocery shopping tomorrow if you want," my mom volunteers. "That way you can pick whatever you like."

"Do you like sports, Carlos?" Brandon asks him.

"Depends."

"On what?"

"Who's playin'. I don't watch tennis or golf, if that's what you mean."

"I'm not talking about *watching* sports, silly," Brandon says, laughing at him. "I'm talking about *playing* them. My best friend, Max, plays tackle football, and he's my age."

"Good for him," Carlos says as he takes a bite of the salmon burger.

"Do you play football?" Brandon asks.

"No."

"Baseball?"

"Nope."

Brandon is on a roll and won't stop until he's found the answer he's looking for. "Tennis?"

"That would be a *nada*."

"Then what sport do you play?"

Carlos puts down his food. Oh, no. He's got a rebellious gleam in his eye as he says, "The horizontal tango."

My mom and Brittany start choking on their food. My dad says, "Carlos . . ." in a warning tone he reserves for extreme instances.

"Dancing really isn't a sport," Brandon tells Carlos, oblivious to the shock at the rest of the table.

"It is when *I* do it," Carlos says.

Alex stands and says through clenched teeth, "Carlos, let's talk. In private. *Ahora*."

Alex walks into the house. I'm not sure Carlos is going to follow. He hesitates, then his chair scrapes the patio tiles and he heads inside. Oh, this is definitely not going to be pretty.

Brittany puts her head in her hands. "Please tell me when they stop arguing."

Brandon turns to my dad with big, innocent eyes. "Daddy, do *you* know how to do the horizontal tango?"

15

CARLOS

"Do you get off on being a *pendejo*?" my brother asks me when we're in the kitchen, out of hearing range of the *gringos*.

"Uh . . . yeah. I had the best teacher. Right, Alex?"

Since our father was murdered when I was four, Alex was the oldest male in our house from the time he was six. He might be older than me, but there was nobody else to look up to but him.

My brother leans against the kitchen counter and crosses his arms over his chest. "Here's the deal: you got busted with drugs. I don't give a shit if they were yours or not, you're the one who got busted. So suck it up and live here without causin' problems, or you get shipped to a youth home for delinquents with guards watchin' your every move. Which is it?"

"Why can't I go back to Chicago? We've got family there. My old friends are there."

"Not an option." Before I can respond, Alex says, "I don't want you to get messed up with the Latino Blood. Besides, Destiny isn't waiting for you, if that's what you're thinkin'."

Destiny and I broke up the day my family packed and moved to

Mexico. She said it was no use havin' a long-distance relationship when we might never see each other again. Truth is, if it wasn't for Alex we'd never have left Chicago. And if we never left Chicago, Destiny and I would have stayed together and I wouldn't be stuck livin' in a room with damn yellow polka-dotted curtains.

I expect everyone in my life to leave me at some point. Since Destiny, I haven't allowed myself to get emotionally involved with anyone. If I let myself care about someone, they'll leave me, push me away, or die. That's the way it's been, and will always be.

"I'll stay here for now, but one day soon I'm gonna get back to Chicago, with or without your help. Just go back to your apartment and stay out of my life." I push past my brother and storm up to my room, slamming the door behind me. But the yellow comforter is a reminder this is not *my* room. *¡Mierda!*

I'm glad Alex didn't follow me. I need to be alone and sort out what happened on Friday. Who put the drugs in my locker? Was it Nick? Madison, who came to bio late? Or was it a sign from the *Guerreros* that no matter where I go they're never far behind?

Eyeing my duffel on the ground, I open it and put my clothes away. Actually I toss them in the drawers, not bothering to hang 'em up. I don't wear clothes that have to be hung up, anyway. I take out my toothbrush and shaver and head to the bathroom across the hall. Assuming the sink with the step stool is Brandon's, I decide to share with him. The last thing I need is to be opening a drawer only to find tampons, makeup, or other female crap.

I stick my shaver and toothbrush in an empty drawer, the one without the cartoon-character bubble bath in it. In between the sinks, taped to the big mirror in front of them, is a small piece of paper.

WEEKDAY MORNING SHOWER TIMES

Monday, Wednesday, Friday: Kiara 6:25–6:35

Monday, Wednesday, Friday: Carlos 6:40–6:50

Tuesday, Thursday: Kiara 6:40–6:50

Tuesday, Thursday: Carlos 6:25–6:35

When should I break the news to Kiara that nobody is going to tell me how long my showers are? I've been known to take hour-long showers when I'm hot, sweaty, and pissed off. Like right about now.

As if it wasn't bad enough I got busted for somethin' I didn't do, now I have to share a house with a bunch of strangers who make salad out of spinach.

I head back to my room, but when I see Kiara's door cracked open I get curious. Knowing she's still eating lunch, I wander inside. Her desk is piled with books and loose papers. There's a corkboard above her desk with different sayings that belong in a self-help manual:

Don't be afraid to be unique

Love yourself before you love another

Give me a fucking break. Does she read that crap before she gets off?

A few pictures of Kiara and that guy she sits with in the lunch-room every day are pinned to the board. One shows the two of them hiking or something on a mountain, and the other is of the two of them on snowboards. In the pictures, Kiara is laughing.

I pick up one of the notebooks on her desk and flip through the pages. I stop when I see RULES OF ATTRACTION written on top of one of the pages. My eyes immediately focus on the words "perky privates" listed under Kiara's traits. I laugh, then scan the next column . . . she's lookin' for a dude who is confident, nice, can fix cars, and likes sports. Who the hell actually writes this stuff down? I'm surprised she didn't write *I'm looking for a guy to rub my feet and kiss my ass.* On the next pages are pencil drawings of her car. I hear the bedroom door squeak. Oh, crap. I'm not alone.

Kiara is standing in the doorway in shock. Behind her is the guy from the pictures. Kiara looks stunned to find me in her room, my paws on her notebook.

"I needed paper," I say, keeping a casual tone as I drop the note-book on her desk.

The guy steps forward. "Yo, yo, wassup homie!" he says.

I wonder what Professor Dick would say if I kicked Kiara's boyfriend's ass on my first day here. He never said one of the rules was not getting into fights.

I narrow my eyes at the guy and step forward.

Kiara quickly rummages through her desk and pulls out another notebook. She pushes it into my hand. "Here," she says, alarm laced in her voice.

I look down at the notebook I didn't need, annoyed that I'm feel-ing like a jalapeño stuck in a bowl of mixed nuts . . . somewhere I don't belong and definitely not a good mix.

I murmur a "Catch you later . . . *homie*," and head back to the canary yellow room I am officially dubbing *infierno*, hell.

Looking out the window, I gauge how far it is to the ground so I can escape every once in a while and get a small taste of freedom. One day I might just escape and never look back.

"Carlos, can I come in?" I hear Brittany's voice say through the bedroom door.

When I open the door, I find my brother's girlfriend alone. "If you're gonna lecture me, save your breath," I tell her.

"I'm not here to lecture you," she says, her bright blue eyes shining with compassion. She weasels her way past me and enters the room. "And although I'm sure your friends back home might appreciate details of your sexual prowess, bragging about it in front of a six-year-old and his parents probably isn't the best idea."

I hold my hand up, stopping her from continuing. "Before you go on, I gotta be honest and say that sounds suspiciously like a lecture to me."

She laughs. "You're right. Sorry about that. Truth is, I came up here to give you the cell phone. I know you and Alex are like oil and water sometimes, so I'm here if you want to talk to someone a little less hardheaded. I programmed both our numbers into the contacts list." She places the phone on the desk.

Oh, no. I feel her trying to get close to me like the sister I never had, but it ain't happenin'. I don't get close, so I decide to go for the asshole route. It actually comes naturally to me; it's not even an act anymore. "You flirtin' with me? I thought you were datin' my brother. Honestly, Brittany, I don't date white *chicas*. Especially ones with blond hair and skin the color of Elmer's Glue. Did'ja ever hear of a tannin' salon?"

Okay, the Elmer's Glue comment was a little over-the-top. Brittany has a golden glow to her skin, but insulting her will push her away. I've done it with *mi'amá*. And Luis. And Alex. It never fails.

I make a big show of opening the desk drawer and dumping the phone inside.

"You're going to want that one day," she says. "I have no doubt you'll call me."

I give a short laugh. "You have no clue who I am or what I'll do."

"Wanna bet?"

I step forward, invading her personal space so she'll back up and know I mean business. "Don't piss me off, bitch. In Mexico I was hangin' with gangbangers."

She doesn't back down. Instead, she says, "My boyfriend was in a gang, Carlos. And neither of you scare me."

"Did anyone tell you you'd be a perfect *mamacita* to prove the dumb-blond theory?"

Instead of cowering in fear or getting furious, she steps forward and kisses my cheek. "I forgive you," she says, then backs out of the room and leaves me alone.

"I didn't ask for your forgiveness. Or want it," I say back, but she's already gone.

16

Kiara

"I don't think he wanted paper," Tuck says as he straddles my desk chair. "He was snooping. Believe me, I know snooping when I see it."

I sigh and sit on my bed. "Did you have to bait Carlos with all that 'yo, yo, homie' talk?" Sometimes Tuck just talks to amuse himself. I don't think Carlos appreciated Tuck's humor.

"Sorry, I couldn't help it. He thinks he's so tough I wanted to bring him down a peg." Tuck's face perks up. "I've got a great idea. Let's snoop back."

I shake my head. "No way. Besides, he's probably in his room."

"Maybe he's back downstairs with the rest of your family. We won't know unless we check."

"That's a bad idea."

"Oh, come on," he moans like my brother does when he doesn't get his way. "Let's have some fun. I'm bored and I have to leave soon."

Before I have time to digest what Tuck is about to do, he disappears into the hall. I hear his footsteps creak as he steps toward Carlos's room. Oh, no. This is definitely not good. Not good at all. I grab

Tuck's arm and try to pull him back, but he doesn't budge. I should know better. When Tuck is on a mission, nothing can stop him. He's kind of like my dad that way.

Carlos's door is open a crack. Tuck peers inside. "I don't see him," Tuck says.

"That's 'cause I was takin' a piss," Carlos says from behind me.

Oh. No. We're. Busted.

I suck in a breath at being caught, and pinch Tuck. This stunt really wasn't one of his brightest ideas. I wonder if Carlos will retaliate with a cookie stunt of his own.

"We were just, uh, wondering how Kiara's notebook was working out for you," Tuck says, not the least bit embarrassed at getting caught and just making up stuff off the top of his head. "Or do you need loose-leaf? 'Cause we could scrounge up some of that if you need it."

"Uh-huh," Carlos says.

Tuck holds out his hand. "By the way, I don't think we've been formally introduced. I'm Tuck. You know, rhymes with luck."

"And *fuck*," Carlos adds.

"Yep, that, too," Tuck says, unfazed. He points to Carlos with a big, cocky smile. "You are quick with the comebacks, *amigo*."

Carlos flicks Tuck's finger away. "I'm not your *amigo*, asshole."

Tuck's cell phone rings. He slides it out of his pants and says, "I'll be right there," then shrugs and says to me, "Well, I'm outta here. My stepdad, Rick, is making me and Mom go to some stupid rope-knotting class. Kiara, I'll see you in school tomorrow." He turns to Carlos. "See you 'round, *amigo*."

Tuck is out of sight in an instant, leaving me standing with Carlos in the hallway. He steps in front of me. When Carlos has his attention fixed on me, it's very intimidating, whether he intends it or not. He's like a panther ready to pounce, or a vampire ready to suck the blood out of anyone who stands in his way.

"By the way, I didn't need paper. Your boy Tuck was right on. I was snoopin'." He walks back to his room, but turns to me before he closes the door. "These walls are paper thin. You might want to remember that the next time you and your boyfriend talk about me," he says, then slams his door shut.

17

CARLOS

In the evening, I'm summoned to the Professor's home office. I expect his wrath. Honestly, I want his wrath. If he or that judge at the juvie courthouse thought bringin' me here would reform me or change me, guess again. It's pure instinct that makes me rebel every time someone tries to control my life and hand out more rules.

Professor Westford tents his fingers and leans forward in his chair, which is facing the small couch I'm sitting on. "What do you want, Carlos?" he asks.

Huh? I'm caught off guard here. I didn't expect him to say that. I want to go back to Mexico and continue living my life on my terms. Or go back to Chicago, where my friends and cousins I grew up with are . . . I sure as hell can't tell him I'd like to bring *mi papá* back from the dead.

Westford sighs when I don't answer. "I know you're a tough kid," he says. "Alex told me you got into some heavy stuff in Mexico."

"So?"

"So I just want you to know that you can create a new life here, Carlos. You started off on the wrong foot, but you can wipe the slate clean and start new. Alex and your mother want the best for you."

"Listen, *Dick*. Alex doesn't know me."

"Your brother knows you better than you think he does. And you're more alike than you want to believe."

"You just met me. You don't know me, either. And to be honest, I don't have much respect for you. You opened your home to a guy who got arrested for drugs. How come you're not afraid of havin' me here?"

"You're not the first kid I've helped, and you won't be the last," he assures me. "And I should probably let you know that before I got my doctorate in psychology I was in the military. I saw more death and guns and bad guys than you'll ever see in your life. I might have gray hair on my head, but I'm just as tough as you are when I have to be. I think we can work together. Now, let's get back to why I called you down here. What is it that you want?"

I better say somethin' to get him off my back. "To go back to Chicago."

Westford leans back. "Okay."

"What'dya mean 'okay'?"

He puts his hands up. "I mean 'okay.' You follow my house rules until winter break, and I'll get you to Chicago for a visit. I promise."

"I don't believe in promises."

"Well, I do. And I don't break them. Ever. Now, enough serious talk for tonight. Relax and make yourself at home. Watch some TV if you want."

Instead, I head straight for polka-dot hell. When I pass Brandon's room the kid is sitting on the floor, wearing pajamas with little baseballs, mitts, and bats splattered all over them. The little kid is playing with plastic soldiers. He looks all innocent and happy. It's easy for him—he hasn't been exposed to the real world.

The real world sucks.

As soon as he sees me, he smiles wide. "Hey, Carlos, wanna play soldiers?"

"Not tonight."

"Tomorrow night?" he asks, hope filling his voice.

"I don't know."

"What does that mean?"

"It means ask me tomorrow and I might have a different answer." On second thought, "Get your sister to play with you."

"She just did. Now it's your turn."

My turn? This kid has serious delusions if he thinks that I actually want a turn. "Tell you what. After school tomorrow I'll play soccer with you. If you can get one goal off me, I'll play soldiers with you."

The kid looks confused. "I thought you didn't play soccer."

"I lied."

"You're not s'posed to do that."

"Yeah, well, when you're a teenager you'll be doin' it all the time."

He shakes his head. "I don't think so."

I chuckle. "Call me when you're sixteen. I guarantee you'll have a different opinion," I say, then head for my room. Kiara is in the hallway. Her ponytail is loose, and most of her hair has managed to escape. I've never met any girl who cares less about her appearance.

"Where you goin' all dressed up?" I joke.

She clears her throat, like she's stalling. "Jogging," she says.

"For what?"

"Exercise. You . . . can come."

"Nah." I've always had the theory that people who exercise are white-collar stiffs, 'cause most of their day is spent sitting on their asses. She starts to walk away, but I call her back. "Kiara, wait." She turns around. "Tell Tuck to stay out of my way. And about your shower-time schedule . . ."

I'm gonna let her know how it is, let her know who's boss here. Her father might try and dictate rules I have no intention of keepin', but nobody, especially not a *gringa*, dictates when I can take a shower. I cross my arms over my chest and tell her straight up, "I don't do schedules."

"Well, I d-do, so get used t-to it," she says, then turns away from me and heads straight for the stairs.

I stay in my room until morning, when the Professor's voice bellows through the door. "Carlos, if you're not up, you'd better get a move on. We're leaving in a half hour."

When I hear his footsteps retreat, I crawl out of bed and head to the bathroom. I open the door and find Brandon brushing his teeth. He's getting toothpaste all over *our* sink and his mouth, and he looks like he's got rabies.

"Hurry up, *cachorro*. I gotta take a leak."

"I don't know what *cha-cha-cho-ro-ro* means."

The kid isn't fluent in Spanish, that's for sure. "Good," I say. "You're not supposed to."

Brandon finishes up while I lean against the doorway. I hear Kiara's door open. She walks out of her room, all dressed. Well, you can't exactly call it dressed. She's got her hair up in her signature ponytail, a yellow T-shirt with the word ADVENTURELAND on it, baggy brown shorts, and hiking boots.

One look at me and her eyes go all wide and her face gets all red. She looks away.

"Ha, ha, ha!" Brandon laughs, pointing to my boxer briefs. I look down to make sure I don't have my own perky private showing. "Kiara saw your underpants! Kiara saw your underpants!" he sings.

She walks downstairs and is out of sight within seconds.

I narrow my eyes at Brandon. "Did anyone ever tell you that you're an annoyin' little shit sometimes?"

Brandon's hand flies to his mouth and he sucks in a breath. "You said a *bad* word."

I'm internally rolling my eyes. I'm definitely gonna have to start speakin' Spanish around this kid so he has no clue what I'm saying. Or beat this kid at his own game. "I did not. I said you were an annoyin' little *spit*."

"No, you didn't. You said *shit*."

My hand flies to my mouth and I gasp. I point at him and wiggle my finger just like a two-year-old and say, "You just said a bad word."

"You said it first, Carlos," he argues. "I was just saying what you said."

"I said *spit*. You said somethin' that rhymed with it. I'm tellin'." I open my mouth to tattle. I'm not really gonna do it, but the little *diablo* doesn't know that.

"Don't tell. *Please*."

"Fine. I'll give you a free pass. *This* time. See, now we're partners in crime."

He furrows his little eyebrows. "I don't know what that means."

"It means we don't tattle on each other."

"But what if you do something bad?"

"Then you keep your mouth shut."

"And if I do something bad?"

"Then I don't tell."

He seems to consider this for a minute. "So if you see me eat all of the cookies in the pantry?"

"I won't say a word."

"And if I don't feel like brushing my teeth?"

I shrug. "You can go to school with rotten breath and cavities for all I care."

Brandon smiles wide and holds out his hand. "You've got yourself a deal, my man."

My man? As I watch Brandon trot back to his room, I wonder if I just outwitted the kid or if he just outwitted me.

18

Kiara

So it's no secret what Carlos wears to bed. His boxers. That's it. I had to look away when I was upstairs in the hallway, because I was staring. He's got more tattoos than the ones on his bicep and forearm. He's got a small one on his chest in the shape of a snake, and when my gaze dropped I caught a glimpse of letters in red and black peeking out of his briefs. While I'm fascinated to know what they all mean and why he got them, there's no way I'm going to ask.

My mom left over an hour ago to open her store. It's my turn to make breakfast for everyone. My dad is wolfing down the eggs and toast I just set on his plate. I know he's expecting Alex in a few minutes and is probably going through the speech he and Alex are going to give Carlos this morning.

I definitely don't want to be here for that talk, and am kind of feeling guilty for challenging Carlos last night. The last thing he needs right now is another person he thinks is against him.

"Dad," I say as I sit down next to him at the breakfast counter. "What are you going to tell him?"

"The truth. That after the judge confirms temporary custody, I hope they'll let him register for the REACH program instead of serving time."

"He's not going to like it."

"He doesn't have a choice." My dad pats me on the hand. "Don't worry, it'll all work out."

"How do you know?" I ask.

"Because deep down I suspect he wants to clean up his life, and the judge wants to keep kids in school. To be honest, I'm not sure Carlos even knows how much he wants to succeed yet."

"He's kind of a jerk."

"It's a cover-up for something deeper. I know he's definitely going to be a challenge." He cocks his head to the side and gives me a thoughtful look. "You sure you're okay with him staying here?"

I think of myself in his situation and wonder if anyone would try to help me. Isn't that why we're put on this earth to begin with, to make it a better place? It's not a religious quest; it's a humanitarian one.

If Carlos can't stay here, who knows where he'll end up. "I'm totally fine with him here," I say. "Really." My dad, with his psychology background and infinite patience, will be able to help Carlos. And my mom . . . well, if you can see past her quirks, she's great.

"Brandon, where's Carlos?" my dad asks when my brother comes bouncing down the stairs.

"I don't know. I think he was in the shower."

"All right. Well, get some breakfast in you. Your bus'll be here in ten minutes."

When we hear the upstairs water turn off, indicating Carlos is out of the shower, it's my dad's cue. "Bran, get your backpack. The bus will be here any second."

As my dad urges Brandon out of the house to catch the bus, I scramble a couple of eggs for Carlos.

I hear him coming down the stairs before I see him. He's wearing dark blue jeans ripped in the knees, and a black T-shirt that looks overworn and overwashed . . . but I can just imagine is totally soft and comfortable.

"Here," I mumble, placing the eggs and toast neatly on the table with a glass of fresh-squeezed juice.

"*Gracias.*" He sits down slowly, obviously surprised I made him breakfast.

As he eats, I load the dishwasher and busy myself with taking out the lunches my mom packed for us. When my dad comes back a few minutes later, he's accompanied by Alex.

"Mornin', brother," Alex says as he sits beside Carlos. "Ready for court?"

"No."

I grab my car keys and backpack, so they can be alone. As I drive to school, I wonder if maybe I should have stayed as a buffer. Because three guys together, especially if two are very strong-willed Fuentes brothers, might be a dangerous mix. Especially when one of them is about to be forced to enroll in an after-school program for delinquents. I guarantee when they tell him, Carlos will go ballistic.

My poor father doesn't stand a chance.

19

CARLOS

"So what're you doin' here?" I ask my brother again.

I look at Westford, a cup of coffee in his hand. Something is definitely up.

"Alex wanted to be here when we discuss what will happen today. We're going to ask the judge to release you into my custody in exchange for your cooperation and participation in a special after-school program."

I look at my food, half uneaten, and toss my fork down. "I thought we were just goin' to court and I was goin' to be released into your custody. Now I feel like I'm at a firin' range about to be blindfolded and given my last cigarette."

"It's not really a big deal," Alex says. "It's called REACH."

Westford sits across from me. "It's a special program for at-risk teens."

I look to Alex to give it to me in plain English.

Alex clears his throat. "It's for kids who've been in trouble with the law, Carlos. You'll go there right after school. Every day," he adds.

Are they kiddin' me? "I told you the drugs weren't mine."

Westford puts his mug down on the table. "Then tell me who the drugs belong to."

"I don't have a name."

"Not good enough," Westford says.

"It's a code of silence," Alex says.

Westford doesn't understand. "A code of silence?"

Alex looks up. "I know a member of the *Guerreros del barrio*," he says. "A code of silence protects all members. He won't talk, even if he knows who was responsible."

Westford sighs. "A code of silence doesn't help your brother any, but I get it. I don't want to get it, but I do. And that leaves us no choice but to ask the judge to let Carlos enter the REACH program. It's a good program, Carlos, and it beats getting kicked out of school or stuck in juvenile detention. You'll get your high school diploma and be able to apply to colleges."

"I'm not goin' to college."

"Then what are you going to do after high school?" Westford asks. "And don't tell me deal drugs, 'cause that's a cop out."

"What do you know, *Dick*? It's easy for you to sit here in your big-ass house and eat your organic shitty food. When you've walked a day in my shoes, you can lecture me. Until then, I don't want to hear it."

"*Mi'amá* wants us to have a better life than she did," Alex says. "Do it for her."

"Whatever," I say as I put my dishes in the sink. I've definitely lost my appetite. "All right, let's get this shit over with."

Westford picks up his briefcase and breathes a sigh of relief. "You ready, boys?"

I close my eyes and rub my palms over them. I guess it's wishful thinking that I'd open them and magically be in Chicago. "You don't really want me to answer that, do you?"

A half smile crosses his face. "Not really. And you're right, I haven't walked in your shoes. But you haven't walked in mine, either."

"Come on, Professor. I'd bet my left nut the biggest problem you've faced is decidin' on what country club to belong to."

"I wouldn't make that bet if I were you," he says as we walk out of the house. "We don't even belong to a country club."

When we reach his car, or what I think is his car, I step back. "What is this?"

"A Smart Car."

It looks like an SUV took a dump and out came the Smart Car. I wouldn't be surprised if Westford had said it was one of those toy cars that kids drive around.

"It's fuel-efficient. My wife drives the SUV, and since I'm just driving to work and back, this was a perfect choice. If you want to drive it, you can."

"Or you could come in my car," Alex says.

"No thanks," I say as I open the door to the Smart Car and climb into the little passenger seat. It doesn't seem as tiny on the inside, but I still feel like I'm in a miniature spaceship.

It takes less than an hour for the judge to grant the Professor temporary guardianship and approve my participation in REACH instead of my being sentenced to either juvie or community service. Alex leaves because he's got a test, so it's up to my new guardian to register me at REACH and then drive me to school.

REACH is held in a brown brick building a few blocks from the high school. After waiting in the lobby, we're brought into the director's office.

A big, tall white guy who probably weighs close to three hundred pounds greets us. "I'm Ted Morrisey, the director here at REACH. And you must be Carlos." He flips through a file and says, "Tell me why you're here."

"Judge's orders," I tell him.

"It says here in my file you got arrested last Friday for school drug possession." He looks up. "That's a serious offense."

Only 'cause I got caught. The problem is, I'm Mexican with gang affiliations. There's no way this guy is gonna believe I was framed. I'm sure he's heard "I didn't do it" from most of the kids here. I'll find out who framed me . . . and in the end I'll get revenge.

For the next half hour, Morrisey recites The Lecture. To sum it up, it's about me having control of my destiny and future. This is my last chance. If I want to succeed, the REACH program will help give me the tools to "REACH my potential," yadda yadda. When I graduate the program, the career counselors are dedicated to helping every REACH graduate secure either a job or entrance to a school of higher education. I have to stop myself from pretending to snore a couple of times, and I wonder how Westford can sit here and listen to Morrisey's bullshit with a straight face.

"And just so you're aware," Morrisey says as he pulls out a student handbook and goes through each page, "we'll be doing random drug tests on all REACH students throughout the year. If we find an illegal substance in your system or on your person at any time, your guardian will be notified and you'll be kicked out of REACH and expelled from school. Permanently. Most teens end up locked up for any violations."

Morrisey hands both Westford and me a copy of the REACH rules. Then he folds his hands on his big belly and smiles, but that smile doesn't fool me. He's a hard-ass who takes no prisoners. "Any questions?" he asks, his voice even . . . but I have no doubt that voice can bellow commands louder than any drill sergeant.

The Professor looks to me, then says, "I think we're good."

"Great. Then we have one more piece of business before you can go back to school." He slides a piece of paper toward us. "This is a responsibility contract stating that I've gone through the REACH rules, that you understand them, and you agree to abide by them."

Leaning forward, I notice three signature lines. One for me, one for a parent or guardian, and one for a REACH staff member. The paper reads:

> I, _____, certify that by signing below I agree to abide by the rules outlined in the REACH Handbook. I understand the rules, which have been properly explained to me by a REACH staff member. I further acknowledge that if I disregard the rules for any reason I will be subject to disciplinary action which may include in-house detention, additional counseling, and/or expulsion from the REACH program.

What it *really* means:

> I, _____, sign my freedom over to REACH staff. By signing this piece of paper, I certify that my life will be dictated by other people and I'll live a miserable existence while I'm in Colorado.

I don't think too hard about it as I scribble my name on the sheet and slide it over so Westford can sign it, too. I just want to be done with it already, so I can move on. There's no use trying to argue. After the paper is signed and tucked in my file, we're ushered out and I'm ordered to report to REACH no later than three p.m. Monday through Friday, or I'll be in violation.

I figure I have so many rules stacked up, it's only a matter of time until I violate one.

20

Kiara

I haven't seen Carlos since school started. Everyone at school is buzzing about Friday's drug bust, and wondering what happened to Flatiron High's newest senior. I heard one person in the hallway say that Carlos spent the weekend in jail and didn't make bond; another said he was deported for being an illegal alien. I keep quiet about Carlos coming to live with us, even though I'd like to tell everyone to shut up and stop spreading false rumors.

At lunch, Tuck and I are sitting at our usual table.

"I can't be your male model on Friday," he tells me.

"Why not?"

"My mom wants me to help with an adventure group she's leading this weekend. They don't have enough instructors."

"The ladies at The Highlands are going to be crushed," I tell him. When I told them they'd have two live models for our painting class, they got really excited. Even after I told them the models would be me and my friend Tuck, and no, we weren't going to be in the nude but in costumes.

"Get someone else to do it with you."

"Like who?"

"I got it!" he says. "Ask Carlos to be your partner."

I shake my head. "No way. He's seriously pissed about getting busted on Friday. I don't think he's in the mood to do favors for other people. Every time he challenges me I feel like I'm going to stutter."

Tuck chuckles. "If no words come, you can always give him the finger. Guys like Carlos respond well to hand gestures."

Just as he says it, Carlos walks in the cafeteria. Every single eye in the room turns to him.

If I were Carlos, I'd avoid the lunchroom for at least a month. But I'm not Carlos. You'd think he didn't notice everyone staring at him and whispering about the latest Carlos gossip. He walks straight over to the table he usually sits at, without an apology to anyone. I admire his confidence.

None of the other guys acknowledges Carlos, until Ram slides over and invites Carlos to sit next to him. After that, the freak show seems to be over. Ram is a popular guy, and if Ram gives Carlos his approval, then suddenly getting busted doesn't mean Carlos is an outcast after all.

After lunch when Carlos is at his locker, I tap him on the shoulder. "Thanks for changing my combination back."

"I didn't do it to be nice," he says. "I did it so I wouldn't get busted and kicked out of school."

When Carlos started here a week ago, he didn't care whether he attended classes or got kicked out. Now that getting expelled is a real possibility, he's fighting to stay here. I wonder if the threat of getting kicked out makes him want to stay more.

21

CARLOS

Mr. Kinney, my assigned social worker, greets me in the REACH lobby after I sign in. In his office, he places a yellow piece of paper in front of me. My name is on the top, and four blank lines are below it.

"What's this?" I ask. I've already signed my life away; what more could they want?

"A goal sheet."

"A *what*?"

"Goal sheet." Kinney hands me a pencil. "I want you to write down four goals you have. You don't have to do it now. Think about it tonight, and hand it in tomorrow."

I hand the sheet back to the guy. "I don't got any goals."

"Everyone has goals," he tells me. "And if you don't, you should. Goals help give your life direction and purpose."

"Well, if I have any I'm not about to share 'em with you."

"That attitude won't get you anywhere," Kinney says.

"That's good, because I don't plan on goin' anywhere."

"Why not?"

"I'm just livin' in the moment, man."

"Does living in the moment include going to jail on a drug charge?"

I shake my head. "No."

"Listen, Carlos. Every student in the REACH program is at-risk," Kinney says. I follow him down a stark white hallway.

"For what?"

"Self-destructive behavior."

"What makes you think you can fix me?"

Kinney gives me a serious look. "Our goal is not to *fix* you, Carlos. We'll supply you with the tools to reach your full potential, but the rest is up to you. Ninety percent of the students in our program end up graduating without a single violation. We're very proud of that."

"They only graduate because you force them to be here."

"No. Believe it or not, it's human nature to want to succeed. Some of the teens here are like you. They've gotten mixed up in gangs and drugs and need a safe after-school environment. And sometimes, just sometimes, it's because teens don't have the tools to deal with the stress of being a teenager. We give them a place where they can succeed and go on to reach their full potential."

No wonder Alex was so excited for me to come here. He wants me to conform . . . graduate from high school, go to college, get a respectable job, then get married and have kids. But I'm not him. I wish everyone would stop treatin' me as if my goal should be to live my life according to Alex.

Kinney leads me to a room with six misfits sitting in a cozy little circle. A woman with a long, flowy skirt who reminds me of Mrs. Westford is sitting with them, a notebook resting on her lap.

"This some kind of group therapy?" I quietly ask Kinney.

"Mrs. Berger, this is Carlos," Kinney says. "He just enrolled this morning."

Berger smiles that same smile Morrisey flashed me in his office this morning. "Take a seat, Carlos," she says. "During group therapy you can talk about anything that's on your mind. Please, sit down."

Oh, goodie! Group therapy! I can't wait!

I am seriously gonna puke.

When Kinney leaves, Berger asks everyone to introduce themselves to me, as if I care what their names are.

"I'm Justin," the kid to my right says.

Justin has his long hair dyed green in front. The front is so long, it's like he's got a curtain in front of his eyes.

"Hey, man," I say. "What're you in for? Drugs? Petty theft? Grand larceny? Murder?" I say as if crimes are things you can order at a restaurant.

Berger puts her hand up. "Carlos, it's REACH policy not to ask those questions."

Oops, I must have been daydreaming during that portion of The Lecture. "Why not?" I ask. "I say lay it all on the table."

"Auto theft," Justin blurts out to our surprise. I think even Justin is surprised he shared his little secret.

After everyone introduces themselves, I come to the conclusion that I've just been assigned the *Group from Hell*. To my left is a white chick named Zana who could easily be cast if they ever decide to make a reality show called *Colorado Sluts*. Next is Quinn—I can't tell if Quinn is a he or a she. There are two other Latinos—a guy named Keno and a hot Mexican *chica* named Carmela with chocolate brown eyes and honey brown skin. She reminds me of my ex, Destiny, except Carmela's got a troublemaking glint in her eye that Destiny never had.

Berger puts down her pen and says to me, "Before you joined us, Justin was sharing the fact that he punches his fist into walls sometimes when he's frustrated, so he can feel pain. We were talking about other outlets for frustration that are less destructive."

It's a little ironic that Justin will hit a wall because he's desperate to feel something, anything, even pain . . . I'm just the opposite. I do anything and everything in my power *not* to feel anything. My goal most times is to be numb.

Hmm, maybe I should write that one down on my goal sheet. *Carlos Fuentes's goal #1: To be numb and stay numb*. I don't think that'll go over too well, but it's the truth.

"So how was your first day?"

After Alex picked me up from REACH at five thirty, he took me to what I assume is downtown Boulder—a place called Pearl Street Mall. To the delight of Mrs. Westford, we stopped at her Hospitali-Tea store/café for a drink and sit at one of the tables on the outdoor patio. Tea is not the kind of drink I had in mind, but as usual I don't have much choice.

Mrs. Westford puts down two specialty teas she made "on the house, just for us" and heads back inside to take orders from other customers.

I look at my brother as he sits across from me, totally relaxed.

"They're a bunch of fuckin' misfits at that REACH thing, Alex," I tell him quietly so Mrs. W. doesn't hear. "One is worse than the next."

"Come on, it can't be that bad."

"Don't say that until you see 'em. And they made me sign this stupid-ass agreement that I'll abide by their rules. Remember back in Fairfield when we had no rules, Alex? After school it was just you, me, and Luis."

"We had rules," Alex says, then picks up his drink. "We just didn't follow 'em. *Mi'amá* was workin' so much, she wasn't around to keep an eye on us."

We didn't live like kings back in Illinois, but we sure did have family and friends . . . and a life. "I want to go back."

He shakes his head. "There's nothin' left there for us."

"Elena and Jorge are there with little JJ. You've never even seen the kid, Alex. My friends are there. I've got less than nothin' here."

"I'm not sayin' I don't want to go back," my brother says. "We just can't go back now. It's not safe."

"Since when did you become afraid? Man, you've changed. I remember when you'd tell the entire world to fuck off and do whatever you wanted without thinking."

"I'm not scared. I care about bein' here for Brittany. There's a point when you have to stop fightin' the whole world. I reached that point two years ago. Look around, Carlos. There are other girls besides Destiny."

"I don't want Destiny. Not anymore. If you're talkin' about Kiara, forget it. I'm not datin' a chick who wants to control my life and cares whether I'm dealin' drugs or in a gang. Look at us, Alex. We're sittin' at a fuckin' teahouse next to rich white people who don't have a clue what it's like outside this fake reality they call life. You've become a *chido*."

Alex leans forward. "Let me tell you somethin', little brother. I like not havin' to watch my back every time I walk down the street. I like that I have a *novia* who thinks I'm the shit. And I sure as hell don't regret givin' up the drugs and the Latino Blood for a chance at a future worth livin'."

"You gonna bleach your skin so you can look like a *gringo*, too?" I ask. "Man, I hope your kids are as pale as Brittany so you don't have to sell 'em on the black market."

My brother is gettin' pissed off, I can tell by the way the muscle in his jaw is twitching. "Being Mexican doesn't mean being poor," he says. "Goin' to college doesn't mean I'm turnin' my back on my people. Maybe you're turnin' your back on our people by perpetuatin' the Mexican stereotype."

I moan and throw my head back. "Perpetuatin'? *Perpetuatin'*? Hell, Alex, our people don't even know the meanin' of that word."

"Fuck you," Alex growls. He shoves back his chair and walks away.

"That's the old Alex I used to know! I understand that language loud and clear," I call after him.

He tosses his cup in a garbage bin and keeps walking. I admit he doesn't walk like a *gringo* yet and still looks like he could kick anyone's ass who gets in his way. But just give it time. He'll look like he's got a pole up his ass any day now.

Mrs. Westford is soon back at the table, gazing into my untouched cup. "You didn't like your tea?"

"It's fine," I tell her.

She notices the now-empty seat. "What happened to Alex?"

"He left."

"Oh," she says, then pulls up his empty chair and sits next to me. "You want to talk about it?"

"Nope."

"Want my advice?"

"Nope." What am I going to do, tell her that tomorrow I'm going to sneak into Nick's locker to see if I can find evidence that he set me up? While I'm at it, I might as well rummage through Madison's locker too. Since she was so intent on having me and Nick meet, maybe she knows something. I'm not sharing my suspicions with anyone.

"Okay, but if you do, just let me know. Wait here." She takes my untouched cup and disappears inside. That was a shocker. *Mi'amá* is the opposite of Mrs. Westford. If my ma wants to give me advice, you can be damn well sure she's gonna dish it out whether I want to listen or not.

Mrs. Westford comes back a minute later and sets down another cup full of tea.

"Just try it," she says. "It's got calming herbs like chamomile, rose hips, elderberries, lemon balm, and Siberian ginseng."

"I'd rather smoke weed," I joke.

She doesn't laugh. "I know smoking pot isn't a big deal to some people, but at this point it's illegal." She slides the cup further toward me. "I guarantee this will calm you," she says. As she walks back inside to wait on other customers she adds, "And it won't get you in a heap of trouble."

I look down into the cup filled with light green liquid. It doesn't look like herbs, it just looks like tea from a cheap ol' teabag. I look left and right, makin' sure nobody is watching, as I bring the cup to my face and breathe in the steam.

Okay, this is no ordinary tea from a cheap teabag. It smells like fruit and flowers and somethin' else I can't place all rolled into one. And while the smell is unfamiliar, it makes my mouth water.

I look up and see Tuck walking toward me. Kiara is beside him, but her attention is on a guy in the middle of the outdoor mall playing the accordion. She pulls a dollar from her purse and kneels down to put it in his case.

While she stops to watch the guy play, Tuck pulls over a chair from another table and sits across from me. "I wouldn't have pegged you as a tea guy," Tuck says. "You look like more of a tequila and rum guy."

"Don't you have other people to annoy?" I ask.

"No." The dude, who I don't think has cut his hair in at least nine months, reaches out and pokes at the tattoo on my forearm. "What does *that* mean?"

I flick his hand away. "It means if you touch me again I'm gonna kick your ass."

Kiara is now standing behind Tuck's chair. She doesn't look happy.

"Speaking of kicking ass, how was your first day at REACH?" Tuck asks, with a grin that makes me want to tip over his chair.

Kiara grabs his sleeve and yanks him away from the table. He falls off the chair. "Kiara has to ask you something, Carlos."

"No. No, I don't," Kiara chokes out, then grabs him again and starts pulling him into the store.

"Yes, you do. Ask him," he says before they both stumble into the store and out of my view.

22

Kiara

I push Tuck inside. "Stop it," I whisper.

We're at the back of the store now, where nobody else can hear us.

"Why?" Tuck asks. "You need a guy to stand in front of old people with you, and he needs something to do besides sit around and count his tattoos all day. It's a perfect idea."

"No, it's not."

My mom shimmies her way next to us and hugs Tuck. "What's up?"

"I can't help Kiara with her painting class on Friday, so she wants to ask Carlos to take my place," Tuck says.

A big smile crosses my mom's lips. "Oh, honey, that's so nice of you to include him in your activities. You're *so* special." She squeezes me in a huge bear hug. "Isn't my daughter *the best*?"

"Definitely, Mrs. Westford. *The best*."

Tuck is such a suck-up when it comes to my parents.

"Kiara, when you and Tuck are done here, take Carlos home. He was with Alex, but I think they had a disagreement or something. I'll be leaving in about an hour, but I need to pick up Brandon from his friend's house and your father is making dinner. Oh, and once you get home, you might want to supervise so there's something edible for us."

After my mom makes us tea, I find Carlos outside drinking what I suspect is one of my mother's special blends. He seems to like it, although I can't be sure because his face is an emotionless mask.

"I'll see you tomorrow," Tuck says, saluting me with his paper cup.

"What did you want to ask me?" Carlos asks. He sounds annoyed.

Will you dress up as a cowboy on Friday night and model in front of old people? "Nothing." I just can't get the words out.

My mom comes out to chat with customers. I watch as she makes conversation with each and every person as if she's their personal friend. When she reaches our table, she leans down to make sure we're drinking our tea.

"I see you liked it," she says to Carlos. My mom takes such pride in her tea blends that if she finds the right custom blend for a hard-to-please customer, it makes her feel like she's won the lottery. "I understand Kiara wants to ask you to be a model for her on Friday at The Highlands. It should be fun."

Carlos gives me a *what the hell is she talkin' about?* look.

"Want more tea?" my mom asks him.

"No, thanks."

"Kiara can drive you home. Right, sweetie?"

"Yeah. Let's go," I say before my mother says anything more.

When we reach my car, Carlos tries to pull on the passenger-door handle.

"You have to climb through the window," I tell him.

"You're kiddin' me, right?"

I shake my head. "I'm not kidding." That's my next project, after I fix the clock and radio."

Carlos climbs in the car with ease, his feet entering first before his whole body slides into the vinyl bucket seat. I wish the radio or old tape player worked, because I think Carlos is getting anxious after five minutes of me driving in silence.

He shifts in the seat. "What's this modelin' thing about?"

"It's modeling for a nursing-home painting class on Friday night. You don't have to do it. I wasn't even going to ask you."

"Why not?"

We're at a stop sign, so I turn to him and say the truth. "Because you'd be posing with me, and I knew you wouldn't agree to do it."

23

CARLOS

I get it. She wouldn't want to pose with a guy who'd get busted for drugs. "I can bring Madison," I tell her in the cocky tone I know grates on her nerves. "She'd pose with me. On second thought, she invited me to her house Friday night, so I can't make your little paintin' party."

"I don't know what you see in her."

"A lot more than I see in you," I lie to push her away. Truth is, I don't see anything in Madison. I've been trying to avoid the girl since she puked at her party, but since she's on my list of people who might have framed me, I've got to get closer to her. Kiara doesn't need to know that. Hell, Kiara shouldn't know I've been thinkin' about her and her cookies way more than I ever should.

When we arrive at the house, Kiara storms out of the car.

I get a snack in the kitchen a little while later and see Kiara cutting vegetables. I wonder if she'd like to see my head on that board along with the carrots.

"Hey, Carlos," the Professor says when he walks in. "How was REACH?"

"It sucked."

"Can you be more specific?" my guardian asks.

"It *really* sucked," I elaborate, sarcasm dripping from every word.

"Your vocabulary astounds me," he says. "Hey, I need both your help today after dinner."

"With what?" I ask.

"Pulling weeds."

"Don't you rich people have gardeners to do that?" I ask.

The answer is no, because after dinner Westford escorts us to the backyard with big paper bags.

He tosses canvas gloves to me and Kiara. "I'll take the side yard. Kiara, you and Carlos tackle the back."

"Daddy!" Brandon yells out from the patio door. "Carlos said he'd play soccer with me today."

"Sorry, Bran. Carlos has to help pull weeds in the yard," Westford says to the little kid.

"You can help," Kiara says to him. Brandon looks all too happy to help her.

I remember when I was younger and Alex invited me to help him do yard work. He always made me feel useful. "Yo, Brandon, I could use your help, too," I say. "After you help me, I'll play with you."

"Really?" the little kid says.

"Yeah. Just make sure the bag is wide open so when I toss in the weeds they fall in the bag."

He rushes over to the bag and holds it open. "Like this?"

"Yeah."

Kiara is on her hands and knees, pulling weeds and tossing them in her own bag. I can't imagine Madison ever kneeling in dirt and subjecting herself to manual labor. I also can't imagine her having a vintage car that doesn't even have a usable passenger door.

"You're going too slow," Brandon observes. "I bet Kiara has more weeds in her bag than you have in yours." The kid runs over to inspect the inside of Kiara's bag. "She's winning."

"Not for long." I grab a bunch of weeds and rip them out of the ground. A few have prickly stems pokin' me through the gloves, but I don't care.

I look over at Kiara, workin' faster than before. She's definitely showing her competitive side.

"Done!" she yells out, standing up at the left side of the yard and pulling the gardening gloves off with attitude. She picks Brandon up and twirls him around until they both fall on the grass laughing.

"You better be careful, Kiara," I call out to her. "Your personality is startin' to show."

While Brandon's back is turned, Kiara flashes me the one-finger salute as she walks to her car.

I have definitely gotten on her bad side.

"Now we can play soccer! Go by the goal," Brandon says, pointing to the little net in the yard. "Remember, if I get it past you, you said you'd play G.I. Joe with me."

I stand by the goal while Brandon tries kicking the ball past me. I have to give the little dude credit. He tries until he's sweating and panting, never giving up even though it's a lost cause.

"This time I'm gonna do it," he says for the fiftieth time. He points to something behind me. "Look! Over there!"

"That's the oldest trick in the book, little man." I appreciate his attempt at cheating, but he picked the wrong guy.

"No, really. Look!" Brandon cries out.

He sounds convincing, but I'm still not taking my eye off of his soccer ball. I'd rather block shots all day than play with dolls.

He kicks the ball, but I block it once again. "Sorry, man."

"Brandon, time for your bath," Mrs. Westford yells from the patio.

"Just a few more kicks, Mom. Please."

She looks at her watch. "Two more, then bath time. I'm sure Carlos has homework to do."

After two more unsuccessful attempts, I tell Brandon to give up. He skips into the house. He's pretty coordinated, but I wonder at what age boys realize they're just not supposed to skip. On my way upstairs, I pass the dining room. Kiara is sitting at the big table, her head in a bunch of thick textbooks.

Strands of hair have escaped her ponytail, falling in her face. It makes me wonder what she'd look like with it all down.

She glances up, then snaps her head back down.

"You should wear your hair down," I tell her. "You might look more like Madison that way."

She answers by flipping me off again.

I laugh. "Be careful," I warn. "I hear in some countries every time you do that, they chop off a finger."

I wait two days to break into Nick's and Madison's lockers, thanks to one of Kiara's cookie magnets (minus the cookie) and a small screwdriver I took from Kiara's car. In the middle of third period, I ask to go to the bathroom but end up searching Madison's locker. In her book bag are books, makeup, and a bunch of notes from Lacey and other girls. In a stroke of luck, she left her cell in the side pocket of her bag. I grab her phone and take it with me to the bathroom, where I scroll through her call log texts, calendar, and contacts. Nothing out of the ordinary here, except that Friday after school she called Nick more times than I can count on two hands.

I put her phone back before I head to class.

That leaves Nick. I see him briefly in the halls at school and have been staking out his locker, but I don't have classes with the guy. During lunch hour the halls are too busy, but right after lunch I sneak into the halls and put the magnet and screwdriver to use again.

Nick's locker is a damn mess. In his backpack are a bunch of names scribbled on pieces of paper with codes on them. They're probably his customers or suppliers, but they're all written in that stupid code.

I've been here too long already. But I feel close, as if Paco or *Papá* is driving me to look further. I dig through his backpack, hoping to find his phone or some other evidence that he was connected to my getting busted. But all I find are a bunch of papers.

Someone is coming up the stairs. I can hear footsteps coming closer. If it's the principal, I'm busted. If it's Nick, I'd better be ready for a fight. I quickly thumb through the mess of papers, until . . . yeah, I got it.

It's the one scrap of paper that's not in code. It's someone's name that I'm all too familiar with . . . Wes Devlin, a drug lord with deep connections to the *Guerreros del barrio*, and a phone number written right below it.

I shove the number in my pocket, then close the locker right before someone comes up the stairs.

Nick better watch out, 'cause very soon I'm gonna pay him a visit . . . one that he won't forget anytime soon.

24

Kiara

After school on Wednesday, I'm washing my car in my driveway when Alex drops off Carlos after REACH. Alex comes over to me and picks up an extra sponge.

"Your dad said you're havin' problems with the radio even after I put the spring in."

"Yeah." I love my car, but . . . "It's imperfectly perfect."

"I guess that's one way to describe it. Sounds like some people I know." Alex peers inside the car. "Brittany's car is fast, but this thing has some juice left." He sits in one of the bucket seats. "I could get used to this. One of our customers has a '73 Monte Carlo for sale. I'm thinkin' about buyin' it. Did Carlos tell you he worked at my cousin's auto body back in Chicago?"

"No."

"I'm surprised. Carlos always hung out with Enrique at the shop. He loves workin' on cars probably more than me."

"Don't you have somewhere else to be?" Carlos asks. He's been leaning against our garage this entire time. I know this because, well, when Carlos is anywhere near me I can sense it.

I've purposely been avoiding him since Monday, which has been working out fine for both of us.

When Alex leaves a little later, Carlos steps forward. "Need help?"

I shake my head.

"Are you ever gonna talk to me again? Dammit, Kiara, enough with the silent treatment. I'd rather have you say your little two-word sentences than stop talkin' altogether. Hell, just flip me off again."

I toss my backpack in the backseat and start the engine.

"Where are you goin'?" Carlos asks, stepping in front of my car.

I beep.

"I'm not movin'," he says.

My response is another beep. It's not an intimidating, deep beep like most cars, but it's the best my car can give.

He places both hands on the hood.

"Move," I say.

He moves all right. With pantherlike quickness, Carlos jumps through the open passenger window, feet first. "You should get the door fixed," he says.

Guess he's coming along for the ride. I pull out of the driveway and head into Boulder Canyon. The wind is blowing through the open windows, the fresh air hitting me in the face and whipping my ponytail against the back of my neck.

"I could fix the door," Carlos tells me. He puts his hand out the window, letting the wind rush through his fingers.

I drive up Boulder Canyon Road in silence, taking in the scenery. You'd think I'd be immune to the beauty of it after living here so long, but I'm not. I've always felt a strange fascination and peace with the mountains.

I park by The Dome; I occasionally mountain climb with Tuck here. I reach in the backseat to get my backpack and step out of the car.

Carlos sticks his head out the window. "I'm assumin' this isn't your destination."

I admit I get a little satisfaction when I say, "Guess again." Slinging on my backpack, I start walking toward the bridge suspended over Boulder Creek.

"Yo, *chica*," he calls after me.

I keep walking, heading for my sanctuary in the mountains.

"*¡Carajo!*" I don't turn around, but by the sounds he's making and the Spanish swear words flying out of his mouth I can tell he's trying to open the passenger door to get out. He's hopelessly unsuccessful. When he climbs out the window and falls on the makeshift gravel parking lot, I hear him curse again.

"Kiara, dammit, wait up!"

I'm at the base of the mountain now, at the beginning of my usual route.

"Where the hell are we?" he asks.

I point to the sign, then start toward the big boulders.

I can hear him slipping on pebbles as he tries to keep up. We're on the trail now, but soon I'm going to veer off and follow my private path. He's definitely not wearing appropriate hiking shoes. "You've got some *serious* problems, *chica*," he growls.

I keep walking. When I'm halfway to my destination, I stop and pull out a water bottle from my backpack. It's not too hot, and I'm used to the altitude, but I've seen people get dehydrated here and it's not pretty.

"Here," I say, holding the bottle out to him.

"Are you kiddin' me? You probably poisoned it."

I take a long gulp, then offer it to him again. He makes a big deal of wiping the mouth of the bottle with the bottom of his T-shirt, as if I have cooties; then he takes a long drink.

When he hands it back, I make a bigger deal of wiping off his germs with the bottom of my own T-shirt. I think I hear him chuckle. Either that or he's covering up his heavy breathing from the climb.

When I start walking again, Carlos is huffing and puffing. "Is this fun for you? 'Cause this is definitely not my idea of a good time."

I keep up my pace. Every time Carlos slips, he curses. You'd think he'd concentrate hard on hiking and not slipping on the rocks, but he keeps jabbering on.

"Did I tell you it's annoyin' that you hardly say anythin' to me anymore? You're like a mute who doesn't use any hand gestures. I mean, seriously, it's irritatin' the hell outta me. Don't you think I have enough to deal with, bein' framed, arrested, and havin' to go to that stupid REACH program?"

"Yes." I come to the place where I have to go over a small ledge and grab on to overhanging rocks for support. I'm fully supported and even if I fall it's only a few feet down to a flat area.

"Is this a joke?" he asks, following my lead just because at this point he probably doesn't think he has a choice. "Are we goin' somewhere, or are you just wanderin' around aimlessly until I slip and plunge to my death?"

Climbing over the big rock that shields my spot from hikers, I stop when I reach the open area with a big, lone tree. I stumbled upon this place years ago, when I needed a place to just come and . . . think. Now I come a lot. I do homework here, I draw, I listen to the birds, and I take in the smell of fresh mountain air.

I sit on a flat rock, open my backpack, and place the water bottle next to me. I open my calculus book and start doing my homework.

"Are you actually *studyin'*?"

"Uh-huh."

"And what am I supposed to do?"

I shrug. "Look around."

He quickly looks left and right. "I don't see nothin' but rocks and trees."

"That figures."

"Give me your keys," he demands. "Now."

I ignore him.

I hear him huff and puff. He could easily overpower me, grab my backpack, and fish the keys out himself. But he doesn't.

I keep my head in my book, going through equations and writing notes on scratch paper.

Carlos takes a deep breath. "Okay, I'm sorry. *Perdón.* Madison and I are history, and I'd much rather model with you than hang out with her. Wow, being in nature has restored my faith in humanity and made me a better person. Now are you happy?"

25

CARLOS

I watch as Kiara closes her book, looks up at me, then reaches in her backpack. She tosses me the keys to her car. I catch them with one hand.

"You just gonna stay here?"

"Yeah," she answers.

"I'm leavin'," I warn her.

"So go," she says, waving.

I will. I sure as hell am not waitin' for her to finish studying. I'm hot, sweaty, and totally pissed off. And I'm thinking of ways to get revenge, the first of which is taking her car and makin' sure it comes back without a lick of gas.

Shoving the keys into my back pocket, I start to climb down. I slide a few times and fall on my ass. I'm gonna have more than one bruise in the morning, thanks to Kiara.

I briefly feel sorry for that dude Tuck for having to deal with her, but then I figure they deserve each other. My thoughts turn to Destiny. If *she* was up on this mountain all alone, I wouldn't let her out of my sight. I'd play her knight in shining armor. Hell, I'd even carry her up the mountain on my back if that's what she wanted.

And while Kiara isn't my girlfriend and never will be, I can't just leave her. I know there are bears here. What if she gets attacked by one? Did she seriously expect me to leave, or is this a test to see what a good guy I am?

She's outta luck 'cause I'm not a good guy.

I keep slippin' down the mountain. Just when I think I've found a path, I get to a dead end or a fucking cliff.

I grab a rock and chuck it. Then another one. And another. Hearing the echo of them bouncing off the rocks below eases my frustration just a fraction.

I take off my shirt, wipe my forehead, and tuck the shirt into the back of my jeans.

I'm not in Mexico anymore, that's for sure. Nobody I know would wander in the fucking mountains just to study. Now, if the aim was to do drugs or get drunk, I could understand it.

I storm back up the rocks, cursing the lack of traction in my shoes, and cursing Alex, *mi'amá*, and Kiara, and just about everyone else I've ever met.

"You're *loco, chica*," I yell when I climb back over the rock that shields her private spot. "I mean, seriously, did you expect me to follow you up here just so you could toss me the keys to your car and leave?"

"I didn't ask you to follow me," she says.

"Like I had a choice?"

"We both have f-f-free will."

"Yeah, well, my free will got taken away the minute I got on that plane to Colorado."

I sit on the ground, facing her. Kiara continues taking notes. We came up here together, and we're gonna leave here together. I'm not gonna like it, but at this point I don't see any other option. Every once in a while she looks up and catches me staring at her. Yeah, I'm doing it to make her uncomfortable. Maybe if I annoy her enough she'll want to pack up and leave.

But after five minutes I can tell my strategy isn't workin'.

Time to change tactics. "Want to make out?"

"With who?" she asks, not bothering to look up.

"Me."

She lifts her head from her book just long enough to give me a once-over. "No, thanks," she says, then goes back to her homework.

She's fuckin' with me.

She's *got* to be fuckin' with me, right? "Because of that *pendejo* Tuck?"

"No. Because I don't want Madison's leftovers."

Wait. *Un. Momento.* I've been called a lot of things before, but . . . "You callin' me *leftovers*?"

"Yeah. Besides, Tuck is a great kisser. I wouldn't want you to feel bad when there's no way you can compete."

That guy hardly owns a pair of lips. "Wanna bet?"

I'm anything but leftovers. After we moved to Mexico and Destiny broke up with me, all I did was date one girl after another. Hell, I could write a book on kissing *chicas* if I wanted to.

I lean toward Kiara and get a small dose of satisfaction when I hear her breath hitch and notice her pencil stop moving. She doesn't move an inch as my lips get close to that place right below her right earlobe. I reach up with my left hand and touch the sensitive spot below her left ear with my thumb while my lips hover over her neck. She can definitely feel my hot breath on her bare skin.

She tilts her head the slightest bit, giving me more access. I'm not even sure she realized she's doing it. I stay where I am. She moans almost silently, but I don't give in. She's definitely being turned on. She likes this. And she wants more. But I'm holding back . . . *leftovers, my ass.*

The problem is, I'm not prepared for what Kiara smells like. Usually girls smell too much like flowers or vanilla, but Kiara has a distinctly sweet raspberry scent that's totally turning me on. And while my mind is telling me I'm flirting with her just to prove a point, my body wants to play "you show me your perky privates and I'll show you mine."

"D-d-do you m-m-mind?" she says. She might be trying to mask her reaction to me being so close, but her words betray her. "I'm trying to work and you're blocking my sun," she whispers. I'm guessin' she doesn't stutter when she whispers.

"We're in the shade, under a tree," I say, but pull away anyway because I need to cool down and stay in control.

I lean back against a rock, the rough edges rubbing into my bare back. I bend one knee and get in a relaxed position even though I'm anything but relaxed. While I'm trying to get comfortable, Kiara is still sitting under that damn tree doin' her homework. She's not sweating at all, and she appears totally relaxed. I don't know if I'm hot because of what just happened, or didn't happen, between us. Or if it's because of the weather. You'd think I'd be used to the hot weather from Mexico, but I was born in Chicago and spent most of my life there. The summers in Chi-Town are humid and hot, but it only lasts a few months.

My insides are going nuts. My heart is beating furiously and there's a crackling energy in the air that wasn't there before I leaned close to her.

What's going on? The altitude must be screwing with my head. I need to change the subject fast and direct the conversation away from anything sexual. "So what's the deal with your stutterin'?" I ask.

26

Kiara

My pencil immediately stops moving. I try and concentrate on my calculus equation, but I can't focus on anything on the page. Nobody who wasn't a speech therapist has ever come right out and asked me about my stuttering before. I'm not prepared to answer, especially because I don't know why I stutter. It's just who I am, how I was born, and everything in between.

Before Carlos asked about my stuttering, all I could think about was our almost-kiss. His hot breath seared my skin and made my stomach do flips. But he was just teasing me. I knew it and he knew it. So as much as I wanted desperately to turn my head and find out what his lips felt like on mine, I didn't want to humiliate myself.

I shove everything into my backpack, then sling the bag onto my back and head down the mountain.

I walk fast, hoping he'll fall far enough behind he'll have to concentrate on keeping up and not ask more questions. I made a huge mistake by bringing him here. It was impulsive and stupid. Worst of all, I didn't expect to want to kiss him more than anything in this world right before he confronted me about my stuttering.

I cross the bridge over Boulder Creek and head for my car. I reach in my backpack for my keys, but then realize Carlos still has them. I hold my hand out.

He doesn't give me the keys. Instead he leans against the car. "I'll make you a deal."

"I don't make deals."

"Everyone makes deals, Kiara. Even smart girls who stutter."

I can't believe he brought it up again. I turn and head for home on foot. Carlos better drive my car back, because they'll tow it if it's parked there all night.

I hear Carlos swear again. "Come back here," he says.

I keep walking.

I hear my car tires spin on the gravel behind me. Carlos drives up next to me. He's got his shirt back on, which is good because I get distracted when he's half naked.

"Get in, Kiara."

As I keep walking, he inches the car forward. "You're gonna get in an accident," I say.

"Do I look like I give a shit?"

I glance in his direction. "No. But I do. I love my car."

Someone beeps at him from behind. He doesn't flinch and keeps the car moving slowly beside me. At the first bend in the road, he screeches ahead of me and cuts me off. "Don't test me," he says. "If you don't get in right now, I'm comin' out there to get you." We stare each other down, the muscle in the side of his jaw twitching in determination. "If you get in, I'll wash your car."

"I just washed it."

"I'll do your chores for a week, then," he says.

"I don't . . . I don't mind doing chores," I tell him.

"I'll let your brother get a goal off of me and I'll play with his G.I. Joe dolls."

Every day Brandon has been trying to get a goal off of Carlos, with no luck. My little brother would love to beat Carlos. "Fine," I say. "But I drive."

He slides over the center console and hops in the passenger seat while I get behind the wheel. When I glance at him, I can't help but notice the look of triumph on his face.

"You know what your problem is?" I'm not surprised he doesn't wait for me to respond before he goes into his assessment of me. "You make everythin' a big deal. Take kissin', for example. You probably think if you kiss someone it's supposed to mean somethin' monumental."

"I don't just go around kissing people for fun like you."

"Why not? Kiara, didn't anyone tell you that life is supposed to be fun?"

"I have fun in other ways."

"Oh, please," he says in total disbelief. "You ever smoke weed?"

I shake my head.

"Take Ecstasy?"

My top lip curls in disgust.

"Have wild sex on top of a mountain?" he questions.

"You have a demented view of fun, Carlos."

He shakes his head. "Okay, *chica*. What do you consider fun? Walkin' up mountains? Doin' your homework? Watchin' Madison make fun of you in class? I heard about that, you know."

I pull off the side of the road, my poor tires screeching to a stop. "Being rude . . . doesn't make y-y-you . . ." I'm about to get caught up on my words. I swallow, then take a deep breath. I hope the panic and frustration doesn't show as I stumble over my words. I know when it's coming, but I can't stop it. ". . . tough."

"I'm not aimin' for tough, Kiara. See, you pegged me all wrong. My goal is to be an asshole." He flashes me a big, cocky smile.

I shake my head in frustration and steer the car back on the road. At home, I find Dad playing with Brandon in the backyard.

"Where have you two been?" my dad asks.

"Kiara took me hikin'," Carlos says. "Right, K.?"

"A little practice?" my dad asks me, then explains to Carlos, "We're going on a family camping trip."

"Dick, I don't hike or camp."

"But he does play soccer." I tilt my head and smile. "Didn't you tell me you were dying to play with Brandon?"

"I almost forgot," Carlos says, the cocky grin gone.

"Oh, that's great," my dad says, patting Carlos on the back. "It'll mean so much to him. Bran, you ready to play soccer with Carlos?"

We all look over at my brother, hurrying to set up the goal. "Awesome! Carlos, I'm gonna beat you today."

"Don't count on it, *muchacho*." Carlos kicks the ball and starts bouncing it up and down on his knees like a soccer pro. No matter what he claimed before, he's definitely played a lot.

"I was practicing with my dad," Bran calls out. "I'm ready for you."

Practice or not, my little brother doesn't stand a chance against Carlos unless he purposely lets him win. I can't wait to see the triumph in my brother's face as he sails the ball past Carlos and scores a goal. I sit on the patio and watch as they warm up.

"Don't you have homework to do or somethin'?" Carlos asks.

I shake my head.

He's definitely trying to challenge me in this little game of who's going to get the upper hand. "I think I see some weeds that you missed on your side," he says.

"Kiara, come play with us!" Brandon cries out.

"She's busy," Carlos says.

Brandon looks at me in confusion. "She's just sitting watching us. How can she be busy?"

Carlos has the ball under his arm now.

"I'll just watch," I say.

"Come on," Brandon says, then runs over to me. He takes my hand and pulls me until I get up. "Play with us."

"Maybe she doesn't know how to play," Carlos says to my brother.

"Sure she does. Give her the ball."

Carlos kicks it to me in the air. I dribble it on my knees, then bounce it off my head back to him. The guy looks stunned. And impressed. In a rare diva moment, I brush invisible dust off my shoulders.

"Surprise, surprise, Kiara can dribble," Carlos says as he positions himself in front of the goal. "You've been holdin' out on me. Let's see you try and get it past me."

When I have the ball back, I kick it to Brandon. He kicks it back, then I whack it toward the goal.

Okay, so I'm not really surprised Carlos intercepted it with hardly any effort. But now he's brushing invisible dust off his shoulders like I did and I'm sorry I didn't get it to sail past him. "Want a second chance?" he asks.

"Maybe another day," I tell him. I'm not sure if I'm talking about that almost-kiss or about soccer.

Carlos's eyebrows go up, and I think he realizes my words have double meaning. "I'll look forward to the challenge."

"My turn!" Brandon screams.

Carlos sets himself in front of the goal and leans over, deep in concentration. "You get three chances, but face the fact, Brandon. You're just not good enough."

Immediately, my brother's tongue shoots out the side of his mouth. He's deep in competitive/concentration mode. I'm sure when he gets older he'll give Carlos a run for his money.

My brother sets the ball down and takes five steps back, counting each one. He kneels down as if he's a golfer lining up his shot. Is Carlos going to let him win? I've had no signal or sign from him that our little agreement is still on, and he looks determined to stop my brother's ball.

"Give up now, *cachorro*. You'll never get it past me, and then afterward you're going to call me the All-Powerful-Master-Goalie, the one, the only . . . Carlos Fuentes!"

His taunting makes my brother even more determined; his lips are pressed tight and his hands are balled at his sides. He kicks the ball as hard as a six-year-old can, even grunting as his foot connects with the ball. It flies in the air.

Carlos flies in the air to catch it . . .

And misses by an inch. Even better, Carlos falls and rolls to his back as he comes crashing to the ground.

I've never seen a more triumphant expression on my brother's face. "I did it!" he screams. "I did it! On the first try, even!" He runs over to me and gives me a huge high five, then jumps on Carlos's back. "I did it! I did it!"

Carlos groans. "You ever hear of a sore winner?"

"No." Brandon leans down to Carlos's ear. "This means you get to play G.I. Joe with me tonight!"

"Can we do a rematch?" Carlos asks. "Like two out of three. Or three out of five?"

"No way, José."

"My name's Carlos, not José," Carlos says, but Brandon isn't listening. He's running inside the house to tell my parents that he beat Carlos.

Carlos is still on the ground when I kneel beside him. "What do you want?" he asks.

"To say thanks."

"For what?"

"Holding up your end of the bargain by letting Brandon beat you. You pretty much succeed in being a jerk most of the time, but you've got potential."

"To be what?"

I shrug. "A decent human being."

27

CARLOS

After dinner, I dig up the cell phone and call Luis and *mi'amá*.

"*¿Te estás ocupando de Mamá?*" I ask my little brother.

"*Sí.* I'm takin' care of her."

Loud pounding on my door reminds me that I lost the competition this afternoon. "It's G.I. Joe time, Carlos!" Brandon's voice bellows through the door.

"*¿Quién es ése?*"

"The little kid who lives here. He reminds me of you sometimes."

"He's that good, huh?" Luis says, then laughs. "How's Alex?"

"*Alex es buena gente.* He's the same."

"Ma said you got in trouble."

"*Sí*, but everything will be fine."

"I hope so. 'Cause she's savin' up to come there for the winter. If I'm good, she said I can come, too. *Podemos volver a ser familia, Carlos.* Won't that be great?"

Yeah, it would be great if we could be a family again. A complete family to Luis is the four of us—me, *Mamá*, Alex, and Luis. Our *papá* was dead before Luis could talk. I never want kids, because I'd never want to leave behind a wife struggling to put food in my kids' mouths or have my kids think a family is complete without me in the picture.

Knock, knock, knock. Knock, knock, knock. "You in there?" Brandon yells again, this time his voice coming through the bottom of my bedroom door. I can see his lips through the tiny space between the door and carpet. I should open the door with no warning and see the little *diablo* scramble to his feet.

"It'll be great if you and *Mamá* can come here. *Déjame hablar con Mamá.*"

"She's not home. *Está trabajando*—she's at work."

My heart wrenches. I don't want her working, slaving away for almost no pay. I provided for the family when I was in Mexico. Now I'm going to school while she's working like a dog. It doesn't feel right.

"Tell her I called. *¡Que no se te olvide!*" I say, knowing my little brother is so busy havin' fun with his friends he's likely to forget I even called.

"I won't forget. I promise."

We hang up as Brandon pounds on the door again. "Stop poundin', you're givin' me a headache," I say as I open the door.

Brandon scrambles to his feet quicker than I've ever seen anyone move before in my life. If his swaying is any indication, I think he just got a head rush. Good.

"Brandon," Westford calls out as he walks by. "I told you not to bother Carlos. Why aren't you in your room reading?"

"I wasn't bothering Carlos," he says innocently. "He said he'd play G.I. Joe with me. Right, Carlos?" He looks up at me, his light green eyes practically begging.

"Right," I say to Westford. "Five minutes of G.I. Joe, then I'm done playing big brother."

"Ten minutes," Brandon shoots back.

"Three," I shoot right back. Two can play this game, kid.

"No, no, no. Five's fine."

In his room, he pushes a doll in my hands. "Here!"

"Kid, I hate to break the news to you, but I don't usually play with dolls."

He looks offended as he huffs loudly. "G.I. Joe isn't a *doll*. He's a marine, like my daddy was." Brandon pulls out miniature plastic soldiers from a bucket and places them around the room. You'd think the kid was making a random mess, but I've got a feeling there's a method to his madness. "Didn't you have a G.I. Joe when you were a kid?"

I shake my head. I don't remember having many toys . . . we pretty much played with sticks, rocks, and soccer balls. And the odd times Alex would sneak into my mother's dresser, we'd make up the craziest games with rocks inside her panty hose. A few times we cut the legs off and made slingshots. Other times we filled them with water balloons and whacked each other. Alex and I did get our butts bruised by *mi'amá* a bunch of times for those incidents, but it didn't matter. The punishments were worth it.

"Well," the kid says, getting serious. "The Cobras are the bad guys who want to take over the world. The G.I. Joes need to capture them. Got it?"

"Yeah. Let's get on with it already."

Brandon holds his hands up. "Wait, wait, wait. You *can't* be a G.I. Joe unless you have a code name. What'd you want your code name to be? Mine is Racer."

"I'll be *Guerrero*."

He tilts his head to the side. "What does it mean?"

"Warrior."

He nods his approval. "Okay, *Guerrero*, our mission is to get Dr. Winky." Brandon faces me with big, round eyes. "Dr. Winky is the biggest, baddest, toughest bad guy on earth. Badder than Cobra Commander."

"Can't we change the name to something scarier? Sorry, but Dr. Winky doesn't sound tough at all."

"Oh, no, you can't change the name. No way."

"Why not?"

"I like the name. Dr. Winky winks all the time."

I can't help but be amused by this kid. "Fine. So what did Dr. W. do that's so bad?"

"Dr. *Winky*," Brandon corrects me. "Not. Dr. W."

"Whatever." I hold up G.I. Joe and say to the plastic dude, "Joe, you ready to kick Dr. W.'s butt?" I turn to Brandon. "Joe says he's ready."

Brandon perks up as if he's on a secret mission. "Follow me," he says, crawling across the room. "Come on!" he whispers loudly when he notices I haven't followed.

I crawl behind him, pretending I'm a six-year-old kid who has the patience to play this game.

Brandon cups his hand over my ear and whispers, "I think Dr. Winky is hiding in the closet. Call in the troops."

I look at the plastic miniature soldiers scattered all over the room, then say, "Troops, surround the closet."

"You can't be a G.I. Joe in your own voice. You have to sound like a marine," Brandon says, obviously not impressed with my action hero role-playing skills.

"Don't push it, or I'm outta here," I say.

"Okay, okay. Don't leave. You can be G.I. Joe in your own voice."

Brandon and I set the miniature soldiers around the closet door. As long as I let myself get sucked into playing, I figure I might as well spice it up a bit. "Joe here told me he got some info on Dr. Winky."

"What is it?" Brandon asks, totally getting into it.

But now I've got to think of something fast. "Dr. Winky's got a new weapon. If he winks at you, you're dead. So make sure not to look directly at his eyes."

"Okay!" Brandon says excitedly, reminding me of my little brother, Luis, who gets excited about the smallest things.

Thinking of Luis makes me think of *Mamá* and how I rarely saw her smile these past few years. As much as I rebel, I'd do anything to make her smile again.

28

Kiara

I watch from the doorway as Carlos and my brother play with the toy soldiers. Carlos set up an elaborate scene with Brandon's T-shirts as tunnels held up with string. One side is tied on his window latch and spans the entire length of Brandon's room. The opposite end is attached to his closet handle.

From his relaxed expression, I'd bet Carlos was having almost as much fun as my brother.

My mom rubs my shoulder. "You okay?" she mouths.

I nod.

"I worry about you."

"I'm fine." I think back to this afternoon, playing in the yard with Brandon and Carlos. I admit I had fun, too. I give her a huge hug. "More than fine."

"They seem to be having fun," she says, nodding to the war scene going on in Brandon's room. "You think Carlos is warming up to the idea of living here?"

"Maybe."

"Five minutes was up a long time ago," I hear Carlos say.

My mom rushes into the room and picks up Brandon, heading off what's sure to be an attempt at a typical Brandon negotiation tactic. "Time for bed, Bran. You've got school tomorrow." After she tucks him in, she asks, "You did brush your teeth, didn't you?"

"Yep," my brother says, nodding. I notice he's got his mouth totally closed when he nods. I'm guessing my brother isn't telling the exact truth.

" 'Night, Racer," Carlos says as he follows my mom out of the room.

" 'Night, *Guerrero*. Kiara, since Carlos won't tell me a story, can you sing me a song? Or play the letter game? *Please*," Brandon begs me.

"Which one?" I ask.

"The letter game." My brother sits with his back to me and lifts up the back of his shirt.

I've been playing this game with him since he was three. With my finger, I trace a letter on his back. He has to guess which letter I'm tracing.

"*A*," he says proudly.

I trace another one.

"*H!*"

And another.

"*D* . . . no, *B!* Am I right?"

"Yep," I tell him, then say, "Okay, one more. Then bedtime." I trace another letter.

"*Z!*"

"Yep." I kiss him on the forehead and tuck him in one last time. "Love you," I say.

"Love you, too. Kiara?"

"Yeah?"

"Tell Carlos I love him, too. I forgot to say it."

"I will. Now go to sleep."

In the hallway, Carlos is leaning against the wall. My mom has disappeared, probably to watch television in the family room with my dad.

"I heard what he said, so you don't need to tell me," Carlos says. His usual cockiness is gone. He looks vulnerable, as if hearing Brandon say *I love you* broke down some emotional barrier he's been holding up. He's showing a glimpse of the real Carlos.

"Okay." I look at my shoes because, honestly, I can't look into his eyes. They're mesmerizing and too intense right now. "Thanks again for, you know, playing with my brother. He really likes you."

"That's 'cause he doesn't really know me."

29

CARLOS

Before school starts, I go behind the football bleachers to find Nick. Sure enough, he's smokin' a joint.

A look of panic crosses his face, until a second later he masks it with a smile. "Hey, man, wassup? I heard you got busted last week. That sucks." He holds out his joint. "Want a hit?"

I grab him by the collar and push him into a metal bar. "Why did you set me up?"

"You're crazy! I don't know what you're talkin' about," he says. "Why would I set you up?"

I punch him in the face and he goes down. "Remember now?"

"Oh, shit," Nick cries out as I stand over him. I'll kick the crap out of him until he gives me info. If he's involved in any way with the *Guerreros del barrio* and Wes Devlin, that means Kiara and the Westfords could be in danger because I'm living with them. I can't let that happen.

I grab the front of his shirt and hold him up. "Tell me why you put the drugs in my locker. And you better do it quick, because I haven't been in a good mood since those cops put me in handcuffs."

He holds his hands up in surrender. "I'm a pawn, Carlos, just like you. My supplier, this guy Devlin, told me to plant the drugs. I don't know why. He had a gun. And gave me the can and said to put it in your backpack or else. I don't know why. I swear it wasn't my idea."

That leaves me to find out whose idea it was. The problem is, now I have to contact Devlin and watch my back every second of the day.

"Carlos, it's your turn to share."

All eyes are on me after school at REACH. Berger expects me to spill my guts in front of everybody. Isn't it bad enough I have to hear about their stupid problems, like how Justin's dad tells him he's an idiot all the time and how Keno is a hero because his friends all drank beer over the weekend and he didn't give in to the peer pressure?

What. A. Bunch. Of. Crap!

Mrs. Berger looks at me over the top of her glasses. "Carlos?"

"Yeah?"

"Would you like to share something you did over the past week that had an impact on you?"

"Not really."

Zana sneers, curling her lip-glossed lips. "Carlos thinks he's too cool to share with us."

"Yeah," Carmela chimes in. "Why do you think you're better than us, huh?"

Keno gives me a hard stare, obviously tryin' to intimidate me. I wonder if he knows anything about Devlin.

It's clear I shouldn't expect Mexican Power on my side right now, so I look to Justin.

"You can do what you want," Justin, the green-haired kid says. "Just as long as it doesn't involve me."

What the hell is that supposed to mean?

Quinn is looking at the floor.

Berger leans forward. "Carlos, you've been here a week already and haven't opened up. Each of the other group members has shared a part of themselves with you. Why not share just a tiny bit of what's been happening so your peers can feel connected to you in some way."

She's actually assumin' I want to be connected to these people. Is she nuts?

"Just say something already," Zana urges.

"Yeah," Keno agrees.

Berger gives me that we're-here-for-you pity gaze. "Our group is held together when everyone contributes a part of themselves. Think of your sharing as the glue that makes us a unit where everyone helps each other and nobody is left out."

She wants glue, I'll give her glue. I'm not tellin' them crap about Nick or Devlin, but something else is on my mind. I hold my hands up in surrender. "Fine. I almost kissed this girl, Kiara, on Wednesday. It was on top of this stupid mountain she made me climb." I shake my head in frustration just thinkin' about it. The problem is, for the past two days I haven't been able to stop thinkin' about what that kiss would have been like.

Keno leans forward in his chair. "You like her?"

"No."

"Then why did you almost kiss her?" Zana asks.

I shrug. "To prove a point." They're all quiet and totally focused on me.

"What point would that be?" Berger asks.

"I kiss better than her boyfriend."

Justin's hand flies to his shocked, open mouth. If that's scandalous to him, I bet I can count how many girls he's kissed on *less* than one hand.

"Did she kiss you back?" Carmela asks.

Keno raises his eyebrows. "Is she *Mexicano*?"

"We didn't kiss. We *almost* kissed, and it wasn't a big deal."

"You like her," Zana says. When I sneer she says, "Oh, please. People say 'it was no big deal' when it *is* a big deal."

"What does it matter, Zana?" Justin chimes in. "He didn't actually kiss her, and she has a boyfriend. Whether he likes her or not, she's taken."

"You have to work on yourself, Carlos, before you can have a healthy relationship," Zana says like she's some sort of expert.

Yeah, whatever. I don't like Kiara. The last thing I want is a *healthy* relationship . . . and I'm not even convinced that a healthy relationship even exists.

I lean back and cross my arms. "Just so you know, Mrs. B., I'm done talkin'."

Berger gives me a nod of approval. "Thanks for sharing, Carlos. We all appreciate your willingness to give us a glimpse into your personal life. Believe it or not, our group is more cohesive now because of you."

I'd give a hand gesture to show what I think of her theory, but it's probably a violation of the damn rules.

I suffer through the rest of our group therapy session with the misfits, although I swear they're all actin' as if we're friends now. When I walk out of the building at the end of the day, Alex is in the parking lot waiting for me with Brittany's car.

When we're at a stoplight, I see a couple walking hand in hand in front of us. I never see Tuck and Kiara holdin' hands, so maybe one of them is a germ freak. "Kiara's got this boyfriend who's a total *pendejo*," I blurt out. "The two of them are ridiculous together."

Alex starts shaking his head.

"What?" I ask.

"Don't get messed up with her."

"I won't."

He laughs. "That's what I said to Paco when he warned me about Brittany."

"Let's get this straight once and for all. I'm not you. I'll never be you. And if I tell you there's nothin' between Kiara and me, I mean it."

"Fine."

"She annoys the shit out of me most of the time, anyway."

My brother's response is another laugh.

When we get to the Westfords' house, nobody is home. Kiara's car is in the driveway with the passenger window open as usual.

"She needs it fixed," I tell Alex as we head toward it. I don't think either one of us can resist imagining what the car would be like if it were fixed up. "The passenger door doesn't open."

Alex pulls the handle, testing it. "You should take it apart and see if you can fix it."

I shrug. "I might."

"Fixed up or not, it's a sweet ride."

"I know. I drove it." I poke my head inside the window and slide in.

"What if I told you I bought one just like it?" Alex asks.

"Really? You finally have your own car?"

"Yeah. It needs work, so I'm keepin' it in the shop until I can rebuild the engine."

"Speakin' of engines, I think this one is draggin'," I tell him, then pop the hood on Kiara's car.

"You sure it's okay we're doin' this?" he asks me.

"She won't care," I tell him, then hope it's true.

As we're inspecting the engine and talking cars, it's as good a time as any to tell my brother what I found out. "I think Devlin was behind me bein' set up."

Alex picks up his head so fast he bangs it on the hood. "Devlin? *Wes* Devlin?" he asks.

I nod.

"Why Devlin?" He wipes his hand over his eyes, as if he can't imagine how I got myself into this mess. "He recruits gang members from all over, turnin' them into hybrids no matter what their affiliation is. How the hell did you let this happen?"

"I didn't actually let it happen. It just happened."

My brother looks me straight in the eye. "Have you been lyin' to me, Carlos? Have you been contactin' the *Guerreros* back in Mexico and had this drug thing planned all along? Because Devlin doesn't fuck around. Hell, he even had connections with the Latino Blood back in Chicago."

"Don't you think I know that?" I pull out Devlin's number that I found in Nick's locker and hand it to Alex. "I'm gonna call him."

He takes one look at the number and shakes his head. "Don't."

"I have to. I've got to find out what he wants."

Alex gives a short laugh. "He wants to own you, Carlos. The *Guerreros* obviously told him about you."

I look my brother straight in the eye. "I'm not afraid of him."

My brother jumped out of the Latino Blood and almost got killed.

He knows what it means to challenge the top when it comes to gangs. "Don't you dare do anythin' without me. We're brothers, Carlos. I'll always fight with you side by side, no questions asked."

That's what I'm afraid of.

30

Kiara

After school Tuck and I decided to take a jog before Tuck's Ultimate Frisbee practice. We talked the first half mile, but have been running in silence ever since. Our feet slapping on the pavement is the only sound. The heat of the day is gone, but today a chill lingers in the air.

I like jogging with Tuck. It's a lonely sport, but having someone to do it with makes it way more fun.

"How's The Mexican?" Tuck asks, his voice echoing off the mountain slope.

"Don't call him that," I say. "It's racist."

"Kiara, how is calling him *Mexican* racist? He is Mexican."

"It's the *way* you said it, not *what* you said."

"Now you sound like your dad, all sensitive and PC."

"What's wrong with being sensitive?" I ask him. "What if Carlos called you *The Gay Guy*?"

"I wouldn't accuse him of being racist, that's for sure," Tuck says.

"Answer the question."

Tuck chuckles. "So did he really call me The Gay Guy?"

"No. He thinks we're a couple."

"I bet he doesn't even know any homos. That guy's got a testosterone shield a mile high."

When we reach the entrance of the jogging path through Canyon Park, I stop. "You never answered the question," I say, out of breath. I'm used to the run, but today my heart is racing faster than usual and I'm suddenly anxious for no reason.

Tuck holds his hands up. "I wouldn't care if he called me gay, because I *am* gay. He's Mexican, so what's the big deal if I call him Mexican?"

"Nothing. It's calling him *The Mexican* that's annoying."

Tuck narrows his eyes at me. His face gets scrunched up, as if he's trying to figure out what my motivations are. "Oh my God."

"What?"

"You *like* The Mexican. I should have seen it all along. That's why you started stuttering again . . . it's all because of him!"

I roll my eyes and sneer. "I do not like him." I start running down the path, ignoring Tuck's theory.

"I can't believe you like him," Tuck croons, poking me in the side with his index finger.

I jog faster.

"Slow down." I hear Tuck panting behind me. "Okay, okay. I won't call him The Mexican. Or say that you like him."

I slow down and wait for him to catch up. "He thinks you and I are dating, and that's just fine with me. Don't let him know anything different, okay?"

"If that's what you want."

"I do."

At the top of the mountain, we stop and admire the city of Boulder below, then jog back home.

Alex and Carlos are standing next to my car in my driveway.

Carlos takes one look at us and throws his head back. "You guys are wearin' matchin' outfits. I'm gonna be sick." He points to us. "You see, Alex. Along with everything else, I have to deal with this: matchin' white people."

"We're not matching," Tuck says defensively. He shrugs when he checks out my T-shirt and realizes the truth. "Okay, we are."

I hadn't noticed. Obviously, Tuck hadn't noticed, either. We're both wearing black T-shirts with big white letters that read DON'T BE A WIENER, CLIMB A 14'ER! We each bought one after we hiked to the peak of Mount Princeton last year. Before Princeton, we'd never climbed one of the "fourteeners," the nickname for the Colorado mountains that top fourteen thousand feet.

Carlos is looking at me.

"What are you doing with my car?" I ask him, changing the subject.

He looks to Alex.

"We were just checkin' it out," Alex says. "Right, Carlos?"

Carlos backs away from my Monte Carlo. "Yeah. Right." He almost looks embarrassed as he clears his throat and shoves his hands in his pockets.

"My mom said to take you grocery shopping. Let me just go get my purse and keys and then if you want we could go."

As I head to my room I wonder if I shouldn't have left Carlos and Tuck together. The two of them don't mix well at all. I grab my purse off my bed and am ready to run back outside, but Carlos is standing in my doorway.

He rubs a hand over his head and sighs.

"Everything okay?" I ask, taking a step closer to him.

"Yeah, but can we just go alone? You and me, without Tuck." He shifts from one foot to the other as if he's anxious.

"That's fine."

He doesn't move. He looks as if he wants to say something more, so I stay where I am. The more we stand here staring at each other, the more nervous I get. It's not that Carlos intimidates me; when he's around, the air just seems more electrified. Seeing him vulnerable like this is another glimpse into the real Carlos, the one without the protective wall.

I held back so much when he threatened to kiss me at The Dome on Wednesday, and now even though Tuck and Alex are outside, I'm feeling an intense attraction to Carlos I've never experienced before.

"You gonna change?" he asks, looking at my DON'T BE A WIENER, CLIMB A 14'ER! shirt with sweat spots on it from my jog. "That shirt has got to go."

"You're too focused on looks."

"Better than not bein' focused on it at all."

I slide my purse on my shoulder, then motion for him to move out of the way.

He moves aside. "Speakin' of looks, you ever takin' that rubber-band thing out of your hair?"

"No."

"'Cause it looks like a dog's tail."

"Good." As I pass him, I whip my head and try to hit him with my ponytail. He catches it just as it's about to lash across his face. Instead of pulling it, he lets my hair slide through his fingers. I look back at him and find him smiling. "What?"

"Your hair is soft. I wasn't expectin' that."

The fact that he actually paid attention to what my hair felt like as it fell from his fingers makes me catch my breath. I swallow hard as he reaches out and runs my hair through his fingers again. It feels intimate.

He shakes his head. "One of these days, Kiara, we're gonna get in trouble. You know that, don't you?"

I want to ask him to elaborate on what he means by trouble, but I don't. Instead, I say, "I don't do trouble," and walk away from him.

Outside, Tuck and Alex are waiting for us.

"What were you guys doing in there for so long?" Tuck asks.

"Wouldn't you like to know," Carlos fires back, then looks at me. "Tell him he's not comin' with us."

Tuck drapes his arm around my shoulders. "What is he talking about, babycakes? I thought we were going to hang out at my house and, well, you know." He wiggles his eyebrows up and down, then pats me on the butt.

My best friend does such an over-the-top impression of a boyfriend I don't think he's convincing at all, but Carlos seems to be buying it, if the look of disgust on his face is any indication.

I lean close to Tuck's ear. "Tone it down, *babycakes.*"

He leans close to my ear. "Okay, snookie-wookie."

I push him away before I laugh.

"I'm out of here," Tuck says, then jogs off.

Alex leaves right after him, so it's just me and Carlos standing on the driveway.

"I can't believe it took me so long to figure it out," Carlos says. "You and Tuck are just friends. I don't even think you're friends with benefits."

"That's ridiculous." I get in my car and avoid eye contact with him.

Carlos slides through the window. "If he's the champion kisser you claim he is, how come I've never seen you guys lock lips?"

"We kiss all the time." I clear my throat, then add, "We just . . . do it in private."

A smug expression crosses his face. "I don't buy it for a second, 'cause if you were my girlfriend and a stud like me was livin' in your house, I'd kiss you in front of the guy every chance I got as a reminder."

"A reminder of w-w-what?"

"That you were mine."

31

CARLOS

I push a cart through the grocery store, thankful for a chance to shop for food I can actually identify. As I weave around the other customers in the vegetable aisle, I pick up an avocado and toss it to Kiara. "I bet you've never had real Mexican food before."

"Sure I have," she says as she catches it and places it in the cart. "My mom makes tacos all the time."

"What kind of meat is inside?" I ask, testing her. I bet Mrs. W. doesn't know the first thing about authentic tacos.

Kiara mumbles something I can't make out.

"What? Can't hear ya."

"Tofu. I admit tofu tacos probably isn't the most authentic Mexican dish, but—"

"Tofu tacos are *not* Mexican. I think putting tofu on anything and calling it Mexican is an insult to my people."

"I doubt that's true."

She walks down the aisle, watching as I pick up tomatoes, onions, cilantro, lime, poblano, and jalapeños. The fresh smell of each item reminds me of *mi'ama's* kitchen. I grab something we always had in our kitchen back home. "This is a tomatillo."

"What do you do with it?"

"I can make a mean *salsa verde* with it."

"I like red salsa."

"That's only because you haven't tasted mine."

"We'll see," she says, unconvinced. I might have to make a special extra-spicy batch for her so she'll remember not to challenge me.

Kiara follows me around the grocery store. I buy all the necessities—beans, rice, and masa flour, and different kinds of meat (which Kiara insisted on being organic even though it cost almost double what the non-organic meat was). Then we head back.

In the Westfords' kitchen, I pull out the groceries and volunteer to make dinner. Mrs. W. is grateful because Brandon has a project for school. Supposedly he tried to make a map on his body with permanent markers, and it's not coming off.

"I'll help," Kiara says as I set out bowls on the counter and place pans on the stove.

For once I think it's a good thing Kiara is wearing a T-shirt so I don't have to make her pull up any sleeves.

"It's gonna get messy," I tell her after we wash our hands.

She shrugs. "That's okay."

I place the masa flour in a bowl, then add water.

"Ready?" I ask her.

She nods.

I dig in with my hands and knead the masa into the water. "Come on, help me."

Kiara stands next to me and dives in, squishing the now wet and sticky dough between her fingers. Our hands touch a few times, and I think one time I accidentally mistook her finger for dough.

I add more water and stand back, watching her.

"What consistency do you want?" she asks as her hands are busy working in the dough.

"I'll tell you when to stop." I don't know why I'm standing like an idiot leaning against the counter watching her. Maybe it's because this girl doesn't complain about doing anything. She's not afraid to climb mountains, fix cars, challenge jerks like me, or get her hands dirty in the kitchen. Is there anything this girl can't—or won't—do?

I look into the bowl. The masa mixture definitely looks like a solid mass of dough. "I think that's good. Now roll it into balls and I'll mash them with this pan. Since I'm sure you don't own a tortilla maker, we'll figure somethin' out. Be careful, you wouldn't want to mess up that ridiculous shirt you're wearin'."

While I'm searching the cabinets to find plastic wrap to put in between the pan and ball before I smash it into a tortilla shape, I feel something hit my back. I look on the floor. One of the dough balls is rolling away from me.

I look at Kiara. In her hand is another ball, aimed right at me.

"You didn't just throw that at me, did you?" I ask, amusement laced in my voice.

She takes another dough ball in her other hand. "I did. It's punishment for calling my shirt ridiculous." She smiles in triumph, then whips the ball at me, but this time I catch it. In one movement I pick up the one on the floor so now I'm holding two balls.

"Punishment, huh?" I say as I toss the one I caught up in the air and catch it again. "And it's got your name written all over it. Payback's a bitch, *chica*."

"Really?" she asks.

"Yeah. Really."

"You're gonna have to catch me first." Like a little kid, she sticks her tongue out at me, then makes a dash for the backyard. I let her get a head start while I grab the entire bowl of dough and go after her. My arsenal just multiplied drastically. "Don't ruin my balls!" She laughs as the words leave her mouth. I watch in amusement as she scrambles to take a side table off the patio and use it as a shield.

"Better yours than mine, *chica*." I toss the dough balls at her, one by one, until I've got none left.

Our dough war continues until the entire backyard is scattered with little balls.

Westford comes outside with a confused look on his face. "I thought you two were making dinner."

"We were," Kiara tells him.

"While you two have been playing around, the rest of us are hungry. Where's dinner?"

Kiara and I look at her dad, then each other. Without even saying a word, we pelt him with dough balls until he joins the war. In the end, Mrs. W. and Brandon get in on the dough wars, too.

I'm tempted to call Alex and Brittany over, 'cause I wouldn't mind pelting them with a few. Maybe I should suggest to Mrs. Berger to have dough wars during REACH. It beats group therapy any day of the week.

32

Kiara

"Come over tonight," Madison says to Carlos at his locker Friday morning. "My parents are still gone, so we can play house all weekend."

I'm standing at my locker and hear her. Carlos is supposed to go with me to The Highlands to help with the painting class tonight. Will he blow me off for her?

"I can't," Carlos tells her.

"Why not?"

"I've got plans."

She steps back, shocked. I don't think anyone has ever rejected her before. "With a girl?"

"Yeah."

"Who?" she says, her word as sharp as a knife.

Before I know what's happening, Carlos pulls me to his side. "With Kiara."

While I'm still in shock, Madison sneers at both of us. "That's a joke, right?"

"Actually—," I start, ready to out him, but Carlos squeezes me closer and almost cuts off the circulation in my arm.

"We've been secretly datin' since last week." He gives me a smile and a look that says I'm his one-and-only. That smile might deceive Madison, but I know he's full of it. "Isn't that right, K.?"

He squeezes me tighter. "Uh-huh," I squeak out.

Madison shakes her head fast, as if she can't believe what she's hearing. "Nobody in their right mind chooses Kiara Westford over me."

She's right. We're busted.

"Wanna bet?" My eyes go wide when Carlos bends his head down to me. "Kiss me, *cariño*."

Kiss? In the hallway in front of everyone? I can't even talk in front of Madison, let alone kiss the guy she's interested in, in front of her. "I-I-I d-d-don't . . ."

I try to come up with something, but keep stuttering. As if Carlos doesn't even notice I'm struggling with my speech, his fingers cup my cheek, then trace a gentle path down to my lips. It's something a boyfriend would do to a girlfriend that he's crazy about and . . . and . . . and Carlos is full of complete bullshit. I know it. He knows it. But Madison doesn't know it.

I can feel his hot breath on my face, and hear an almost silent word of thanks before he tilts his head and puts his lips on mine. I close my eyes and try to shut out the rest of the school and just focus on trying to savor the moment. Even if the kiss is fake, it doesn't feel fake. It feels exciting and sweet. I know I should push him away, but I can't.

I reach up and wrap my arms around his neck. At the same time, he pulls me closer and without warning teases my mouth open with little erotic licks of his tongue. I don't know where he learned to kiss like this, but it's hard not to moan into his mouth and feel something deep in my body awaken when our tongues touch.

When Carlos pulls back and unwraps my arms from his neck, he sighs. "She's gone."

"W-w-what was th-th-that all about?" I ask.

He looks around to make sure people aren't eavesdropping. "I need you to be my girlfriend. There, I said it." When I don't respond, he takes my elbow and pulls me down the hall until we get to the computer lab. It's empty, except for the thirty computers in neat little rows.

The guy is confusing me, and it doesn't help that my lips are still tingling from his erotic kiss. I compose myself and think about the words before I say them. I'm not going to stutter. "What about Madison? You had sex with her in her parents' bed."

"I didn't have sex with her, Kiara. That's a rumor she started, not me. I knew her for a whole five days before I went to her stupid party. Give me a little credit."

"Why should I? You're always t-t-talking trash." I turn my back to him and start walking out of the computer lab. I guess I'm getting mad because it looked and felt like a real kiss, when in reality Carlos kissed me as a ploy to dupe Madison.

"Okay, I admit it. I talk trash. But I didn't have sex with her, and the only reason she's after me in the first place is because she wants to make Ram jealous. I need her off my back, so will you pretend we're a couple or what?" He shoves his hands in his pockets. "Name your price."

"Why me?"

"Because you're too smart to fall for my bullshit, and I don't want a real girlfriend. I had one once, and it was a complete disaster. Come on, name your price."

I don't care about dressing up every day, but just once I'd like to go to a school dance with an actual date. It's my last year at Flatiron, and I might not get another chance.

"Go to Homecoming with me."

"I don't do dances." He shakes his head. "Homecomin' is out of the question. And don't even think about makin' me go to prom."

"Then forget it."

I head for the door, but he grabs my elbow and urges me to face him. "I don't know anyone else here who can help me."

"Homecoming or nothing," I tell him, staying firm.

Carlos gnashes his teeth. "Fine. Homecoming. But you have to wear a dress . . . and heels. And I'm not talkin' those thick granny ones."

"I don't own heels."

"Then go buy some." He holds out his hand. "Deal?"

I take a second to think about it, then put my hand in his and give it a hard shake. "Deal."

I try to hide my excitement, but I can't just shake on it. I open my arms wide and hug him tight. I think he's surprised, but I don't care. I'm going to Homecoming! And not just with any boy . . . with Carlos, a boy who might just be the most perfect fake boyfriend. Now if I could only cut out the fake part . . .

I pick up Carlos at the REACH facility at five and drive him over to The Highlands. The entire group is waiting for us at their easels, eager to start drawing.

I take Carlos to Betty Friedman, one of the administrators who schedules the classes. "Betty, this is Carlos," I say, introducing them. "He's helping me today."

Betty looks up from her desk. "Thanks, Carlos. I'm glad you're here. Everyone has been excited to have live models. One of our resident artists is here to supervise and help you out today." We follow her to the front of the recreation area, where a guy wearing a black turtleneck and matching tight black pants is setting out different color paints in jars.

"Here are your models," Betty tells him. "Kiara and Carlos, this is Antoine Soleil."

"I brought costumes," I tell Antoine as I pull out a red checkered shirt and cowboy belt for Carlos and a cowgirl outfit for me. I borrowed them from the theater department at school.

Carlos takes one look at the costume and takes two steps back. "You never said anythin' about costumes."

"I didn't?"

"No."

"Sorry," I tell him. "We're wearing costumes."

Betty points to a room off to the side. "You can dress in the conference room, if you want. Or wait until one of the guest bathrooms becomes available, although I just saw Mrs. Heller walk in and it might be some time until she resurfaces."

Carlos grabs the shirt and belt from me, then walks into the conference room. I follow behind with the cowgirl outfit.

"Remind me why I agreed to do this?"

"Because you wanted to do something nice for me," I tell him as I lock us in the room so nobody accidentally walks in.

"Right." He pulls his shirt over his head, revealing a rock-hard stomach any guy would envy and any girl would drool over. "Next time I want to do somethin' nice, slap me." He looks at me and the side of his mouth quirks up. "I was kiddin'."

"I figured." I pull the denim and lace cowgirl dress over my head, glad to have the table hiding me at least a little. When it's in place, I weave my hands through my own shirt and toss it aside, then shimmy out of my pants. Whoa. This dress is short. Really, really short. I look at my bare legs. I try pulling the dress down, but the lace is so layered and frilly it stands out like petals.

"Please don't tell me I have to actually wear this ridiculous belt," Carlos says from across the room as he secures the oversized silver buckle on the belt.

"Pretend you're a rodeo champion," I tell him.

"More like a champion wrestler by the size of this thing. What are you wearin'? You better look as ridiculous as I do."

I look down at my short, frilly dress with the fake jean vest sewn into the front. "Mine is worse."

"Come out from behind the table and show me."

"No."

"Come on. We're a couple now, aren't we?"

"We're a *fake* couple, Carlos."

He sits on the edge of the conference table. "Well, I was thinkin' . . . I figure as long as we know it's not goin' anywhere, we could, you know, hang out."

"What does 'hang out' mean?" I ask.

"You know, spend more time with each other. You make me laugh, Kiara, and right now I need some fun in my life." He moves around to my side of the table and looks at my outfit, then whistles appreciatively. "Nice legs. You should show 'em more often."

I shrug. "I'll think about it."

"What, showin' your legs more often or hangin' out with me?"

"Both." While the very idea of being with Carlos is exciting, I need to protect my heart from being broken. Hanging out to Carlos means keeping an emotional wall up so we don't get too involved. I don't know if my wall is that strong.

In the rec room, I introduce Carlos to Sylvia, Mildred, Mr. Whittaker, and the others. Sylvia grabs my sleeve. "He's a looker."

"I know. The problem is, he knows it, too."

Mildred waves Carlos over. "Let me look at you." She eyes him up and down. "I saw you when you walked in. What's with all those tattoos? Makes you look like a hooligan."

"I suspect I am a hooligan," he says to her. "Whatever that means."

"It *means* that you're trouble," Mildred says, pointing her paintbrush at him. "Nothing but trouble. My husband was a hooligan. Trouble followed him wherever he went. He used to ride around on his motorcycle like he was James Dean."

"What happened to him?" Carlos asks her.

"The old coot died ten years ago in a car accident." She pats Carlos's cheek. "You look a little like him. Come closer." When he does, she closes her eyes and reaches out to touch his face, almost tracing it with her fingers. Carlos is still, letting her fantasize about going back to a happier time and pretend for the moment that she's touching her husband's face instead of Carlos's. Mildred sighs, then opens her eyes. "Thank you," she whispers, tears welling in her eyes.

Carlos nods in silent understanding at the gift he just gave her. I'm standing here in awe of him. On the outside, Carlos is a tough jerk who doesn't let anyone get close to him. But when I get little glimpses of his hidden warmth and compassion, I feel that inner wall of mine start to crumble.

"All right, let's get this class started," Antoine says.

Antoine has set up a little stage in the front of the room. "You two," he says, pointing to us. "Stand here and pose."

Carlos gets on the stage first, then grabs my hand and helps me up. "Now what?" Carlos asks.

"We're supposed to pose," I whisper.

"How?"

Antoine pounds his hand on the stage, getting our attention. "I'll tell you how. Kiara, grab his shoulders. Carlos, hold her around her waist."

We do as he instructs. "Like this?" I ask, trying to ignore what Carlos's hands feel like holding me.

"You look like you're afraid to get close to each other," Antoine says. "You're too stiff. Kiara, lean toward Carlos with your upper body. Yes, that's it. Now bend one knee . . . Carlos, make sure you support her weight or else she'll fall . . . Kiara, look up at him as if you're in love, waiting for that promise of a kiss . . . and Carlos, you look down at her as if Kiara is the cowgirl you've been waiting for your entire life. Perfect!" he says. "Now don't move for the next half hour." He turns to the residents of The Highlands and talks about silhouettes and the human form . . . but all I can do is get lost in Carlos's eyes.

"You were great with the residents," I tell him. "I appreciate you being here."

"And I appreciate you wearin' that dress."

For the next half hour as we're trying not to move, I'm gazing into Carlos's deep dark eyes and he's looking into mine. Even though my body is starting to feel stiff, I feel safe and happy. There's nothing else I can do except to say, "I've made a decision."

"About what?"

"Us. I'd like us to hang out more."

He cocks a brow. "Really?"

"Yeah."

"Are we gonna shake on it?"

"My hands are kind of busy at the moment," I tell him.

He smiles, that cocky smile that's so a part of him he wouldn't be Carlos without it. "Your hands might be busy, but your lips aren't."

33

CARLOS

Most mornings, I'm awakened by Brandon's voice singing one of his usual songs, which gets stuck in my head—*"Good morning to you, good morning to you. We're all in our places with bright shining faces. And this is the way, we start a new day!"* It could drive anyone insane.

No, today it's not Kiara's little brother who wakes me up. It's Tuck's voice bellowing in the hallway. *"La cucaracha, la cucaracha, ya no puede caminar, porque no tiene, porque le falta, I don't know the rest la la la la!"*

And while Brandon doesn't mean to annoy me, Tuck's reason for living might just be to piss me off.

"Don't you ever shut up?" I yell, hoping he can hear me out in the hallway.

"Hey, *amigo*," Tuck says, opening the door. "Rise and shine!"

I pick up my head. "Didn't I lock the door to keep people like you out?"

He holds up a bent paper clip and wiggles it. "Yep. Lucky for me I know how to use the magic door-opener."

"Get out."

"I need your help, *amigo*."

"No. Get out."

"Do you hate me so much because Kiara likes me better than you?"

"Not for long. Get the *fuck* out. Now," I tell him. The guy doesn't move.

"Okay, seriously, I don't know if this is true or not, but I heard people who use profanity are trying to compensate for their lack of, you know, *size*."

I whip off the covers and jump out of bed and chase him into the hallway, but he's gone.

Kiara's door is suspiciously open. "Where is he?" I ask her.

"Um . . . ," she says.

I scan her room, then open her closet door. Sure enough, Tuck is standing inside. "I was just kidding. Can't you take a joke, man?" he says.

"Not at seven in the mornin'."

He laughs. "Put some clothes on so you don't scare poor Kiara with your morning hard-on."

I look down at my shorts. Sure enough, I've got *la tengo dura* in front of Kiara and Tuck. Shit. I reach out for the first thing I can grab and put it in front of me to shield myself from view. It happens to be one of Kiara's stuffed animals, but I don't have much choice right now.

"That's Kiara's Mojo," Tuck says, laughing. "Get it? Mojo?"

Without a word, I rush back to my room and toss Mojo on the floor. Knowing Kiara, she'll probably make me buy her a new stuffed animal.

I sit on my bed, wondering how I'm going to get closer to Kiara with Tuck in the picture, and wondering why I even want to. I like kissin' her, that's all. A knock at my door interrupts my thoughts.

"What do you want?" I say, the words coming out as a growl.

"It's Kiara."

". . . and Tuck," comes another voice.

I open the door. "He wants to apologize," Kiara says.

"I am very sorry I opened your door without permission," Tuck says as if he's a little kid sent to apologize by his mother. "I promise not to do it ever again. Please forgive me."

"Fine." I start to close the door, but Kiara puts her palm on it.

"Wait. Tuck really does need your help, Carlos."

"With what?"

"My Ultimate team only has six players and we need seven. We have three people out with the flu, and two more got hurt in the quarterfinals and can't play. Kiara thinks you'd be halfway decent."

Halfway decent? "Why don't *you* play?" I ask Kiara. "You're athletic."

"It's not a coed team," she tells me. "It's an all-male team."

Tuck holds his palms together in a praying position, and I can just sense the bullshit about to fly. "Please, *amigo*. We need you, Kimosabe, O Mighty Powerful One. We need you more than the earth rises in the west."

"The sun rises in the east, dickhead."

"Only if you're standing on the earth. If you're on the moon, the earth rises in the west." He takes a deep breath. "All right, I'm done sucking up. You in or out? The game starts in less than a half hour and I need to know if we have to forfeit or not. Unfortunately, you're probably our only hope."

I look at Kiara.

"Tuck really needs your help," she says. "I'll come watch."

"Fine, I'll do it. I'll do it for you," I tell her.

"Wait, what . . . what is he talking about *that he'll do it for you?*" Tuck looks from me to Kiara, but neither of us say a word. "Is anyone going to tell me what's going on here?"

"Nope. Give me five minutes," I tell them.

On the drive to the game, Kiara insists I call my brother and ask him to come to the game. "Just call him," she says. "Or I will."

"Maybe I don't want him there."

She holds out her cell. "Maybe you want him there so bad, but you're too stubborn to admit it. I dare you."

Now why did she have to go and do that?

I grab the phone out of her hand and call my brother. I tell him about the game, and without hesitation he says he'll be there.

After I hang up and toss the cell back to Kiara, Tuck goes over the rules with me. I focus on the important ones: once I catch the Frisbee I have to stop and throw it to another teammate within ten seconds.

"This isn't a contact sport, Carlos," Tuck reminds me for the, like, tenth time. "So if you feel like punching, pushing, or fighting with someone, make sure it's after the game."

On the field, Tuck introduces me to our team. A thought keeps running through my head: *if I help Tuck's team win, will Kiara think I'm a hero?*

I'm practicing with the guys in the minutes before the game. Even though I haven't thrown a disc in a few years, I have no problem makin' it sail through the air to my teammate.

One of the guys on my team runs past me, winks at me, then smacks me on the ass.

What the hell was that, some sort of Ultimate ritual? I don't do rituals that involve other guys' hands on my ass.

I walk over to Tuck, who's stretching out on the sidelines. "Am I delusional, or was that guy hitting on me?"

"His name's Larry. Don't ask me why, but he thinks you're hot. He hasn't stopped drooling since you got here. Just don't lead him on."

"Don't worry."

"Here." Tuck reaches into his duffel and tosses me a shirt. "It's our team uniform."

I hold it out in front of me. "It's pink."

"You got something against pink?"

"Yeah. It's gay."

Tuck smacks his lips together. "Um, yeah. Carlos, now's probably a good time for me to tell you something. You're probably not gonna like it."

As Tuck talks, I take close inventory of my teammates. Dennis, a guy who looks mighty feminine. The guy who hit me on the ass is now biting on his lower lip as if he wants to get with me. And the pink shirts . . . "This is a team of gay dudes, isn't it?"

"What gave it away? The pink shirts, or half our team drooling over you?"

I shove the shirt back in his hands. "I'm not doin' this."

"Calm down, Carlos. Playing on a team with gays doesn't make you gay. Don't be a homophobe. That's so un-PC."

"Ask me if I've ever given a shit about bein' PC?"

"Think of all the fans you'll disappoint. Kiara . . . and your brother."

I don't know if my brother is laughing or cringing: all I know is that he's givin' me a thumbs-up from the bleachers. Brittany has suddenly shown up here, too. Kiara and Brittany have their heads huddled together, deep in conversation.

I know I shouldn't ask this, but I can't help it. "What's the name of our team?"

"Ultimate Queers," Tuck says, then starts laughing.

I, on the other hand, am not laughin'.

"What, you don't like our team name? You're one of us now, Carlos."

I'm still not laughin'.

He catches a practice toss from one of the other guys, then tosses it back. "Oh, and just so you know, before we go out on the field we all get in a huddle and yell 'Go Queers!' really loud."

That's it. "I'm quittin'."

I start walking off the field. If anyone back home saw me, my ass would be kicked from Atencingo to Acapulco and back again.

"I'm just kidding, man," Tuck calls after me.

I stop.

"And our name isn't Ultimate Queers." He holds his hands up in surrender. "Okay, okay, truth is we don't yell 'Go Queers,' although Joe over there with the spiked hair suggested it at the beginning of the season. Our team name is The Ultimates. We couldn't come up with a cool name, so Larry came up with The Ultimates and that's what we've been ever since. Happy now?"

I shake my head and grab the shirt back. "You so owe me for this," I say as I pull my T-shirt over my head and exchange it for the pink one.

"I know. Name your price, *amigo*."

"I will. Later." I gaze over at Kiara in the stands. "Has Kiara ever had a boyfriend?"

He taps his chin with his index finger. "Did she tell you about Michael?"

"Who's Michael?" I ask.

"The guy Kiara dated over the summer."

She's never mentioned the guy. "How serious was it?"

Tuck grins wide. "My, my, aren't we curious."

"Answer the question."

"He told her he loved her, then he text-dumped her."

"What a dick."

"Exactly." Tuck points to the other side of the field where the opposing team is practicing. "He's the tall guy picking up his water bottle right over there, with the last name of Barra on his shirt."

"That guy with the green bandanna?"

"Yep, that's the one," Tuck says. "Michael Barra, the text-dumper."

"Is he bald?"

"No, Barra protects his precious hair so it doesn't get messy when he plays." Tuck puts his hand on my chest to get my attention. "But remember what I told you in the car on the way over here when I explained the rules. This is a *no-contact* sport, Carlos. We get penalized for unnecessary roughness."

"Uh-huh." In the opposite end zone I watch Kiara's ex as he tosses his water bottle toward the sideline after taking a swig and doesn't give a damn that it almost hits one of the spectator's dogs. I hate that guy and I've never even met him.

When the game starts, Dennis throws his arm back and whips the disc across the field to our opponents. The game is going fine until one of the guys on the other team mumbles a fag comment when I intercept his throw. The blood in my veins fires up in the same way it does when I've been called a dirty Mexican.

I'm competitive, tough, and I'm ready to kick some Ultimate ass.

I wonder if now is a good time to let Tuck know he should expect some very necessary roughness coming from one very fired-up *Mexicano*.

34

Kiara

It's weird seeing Michael again. I knew he'd be here, but I didn't know how I'd feel about seeing him again after our breakup. I thought I'd still feel at least a little spark or remember why I started dating him, but I look over at him and feel absolutely nothing. I have definitely moved on. The problem is that the person I'm falling for hard and fast doesn't want more than a fling. I don't want a fling with Carlos. I'll go along with pretending this thing between us is temporary and casual, but every time we're together it feels too right to be temporary or casual.

I find myself daydreaming about him when I wake up in the morning, in school when something reminds me of him, and when I fall asleep at night. Even when Michael and I were dating, just thinking about him didn't brighten my day as much as thoughts of Carlos do.

While he does his best to be a jerk, every day I get glimpses of the true Carlos. When he's playing with my brother, I see a soft side he doesn't show the rest of the world. When he's joking around with me, his playful side comes out. When he kisses me, I sense his desperate need for affection. When he's cooking Mexican dishes or inserting Spanish into his English, his loyalty to his heritage and culture comes shining out of him like a beam of light.

I know the great things about Carlos and why I'm feeling attached to him like I've never felt with anyone else before. But he hasn't given me glimpses into his dark side, the side that makes him angry and jealous and beaten down. And I know it's that part of him that won't let him get emotionally involved.

I watch as the teams line up in each of their end zones and Tuck's team tosses the disc in play. Michael is the first to run out and catch it, then quickly aims for another player on his team. The problem is that Carlos is there to intercept the disc almost the second it leaves Michael's hands.

In the first two minutes of the game, The Ultimates have scored. Tuck gives Carlos a high five. I have to admit it's nice seeing them celebrating instead of arguing.

"Carlos is really good," Brittany says to both Alex and me.

"He's a Fuentes, of course he's good," Alex says proudly.

I also knew Carlos would be good, because Carlos wouldn't agree to play if he didn't think he'd be decent at it.

The next time Carlos has the disc, Michael gets in his face and says something. I have no clue what they're saying, but both look like they're ready to fight. In fact, after Carlos tosses the disc to another guy on his team, he gives Michael a shove, and Michael lands hard on his butt.

"Foul!" someone on Michael's team yells.

"Foul, my ass," Carlos argues. "He was in my face."

"I heard him taunt our player," Tuck calls out, then points to Michael. "That guy should get a taunting violation."

Michael stands and points to Carlos. "You've been in my face since the game started!"

"We're playing one-on-one," Tuck says. "He was defending you."

"He *pushed* me. You saw it. Everyone saw it. He should be kicked out!"

If Carlos is kicked out, the game is over because The Ultimates have to forfeit. Carlos looks at me and my heart turns over. He isn't playing because Tuck asked, he's doing it for me . . . and I have a sneaking suspicion he was getting aggressive with Michael because of me.

Thankfully the confrontation ends before it gets out of hand, and they start the game again. I watch for the next hour as both teams battle it out. In the end, The Ultimates win 13–9.

When I climb down off the bleachers, Michael is walking toward me. He still looks the same, just sweatier than usual. With his bandanna now off, his light brown hair is neatly combed to perfection in a side part. I used to be in awe that he never had a hair out of place, but now it's just irritating me.

Michael wipes the sweat off his face with a towel. "I didn't know if you'd come to the game or not."

"Tuck was playing," I say, as if that explains everything. "And Carlos."

His eyebrows furrow. "Who's Carlos? That gay guy I almost got in a fight with?"

"Yeah. Except he's not gay."

"Don't tell me you're *involved* with him."

"*Involved* isn't exactly what I'd call it. We're—"

Carlos suddenly appears in front of us. He's shirtless as he slides between Michael and me, his sweat making wet streaks across Michael's forearm. Michael looks at his arm in disgust, then swipes Carlos's sweat off with his towel. As if that didn't make enough of a scene, Carlos parks himself beside me and drapes his arm across my shoulder.

"We're . . . hanging out," I tell Michael.

Michael completely ignores the fact that Carlos is standing beside me and asks, "What does that mean?"

"It means she's got her hands full with a hot Latino every night, dude," Carlos interrupts, then pulls me closer and bends his head to kiss me.

Instead of kissing Carlos, I push his arm off me and step away from him. He made it sound like I'm someone he screws around with, like we're friends with benefits . . . maybe even without the "friends" part.

"Stop it," I tell him.

"Stop what?"

"The act. Just be normal," I tell him, trying to save face with Michael while trying to hide my hurt from Carlos.

"Normal? I'm not *normal* enough for you?" Carlos says. "You want this guy instead? Did you notice his hair doesn't move? That's *not* normal. You want to date him again, go ahead. Hell, if you want to marry him and be Kiara Barra the rest of your life, be my guest."

"That's not what I—"

"I don't want to hear it. *Hasta*," Carlos says, ignoring me and walking away.

I feel my face heat up in embarrassment as I look back at Michael. "Sorry. Carlos can be abrasive sometimes."

"Don't apologize. The guy obviously has major issues and, for the record, my hair moves . . . when I want it to. Listen," he says, changing the subject. "My team is going to Old Chicago at Pearl Street Mall for lunch. Come with me, Kiara. We need to talk."

"I can't." I look back at Tuck, Brittany, and Alex. "I came with other people . . ."

Michael waves to one of his teammates. "I've got to go. If you change your mind about lunch, you know where to find me."

I find Brittany and Alex talking to Tuck by my car. Carlos is nowhere in sight.

"You okay?" Brittany asks me.

I nod. "Yep."

"Excuse me for being nosy," Brittany says, "but I saw Carlos with his arm around you. He looked pretty angry when he stalked off, and we haven't seen him since. Are you and Carlos—,"

"No. We're not."

"They're pretending to date, but Kiara's not pretending," Tuck tells them.

"I'll go find him," Alex says, shaking his head in frustration. "I'll set him straight."

"No, don't," I say in a panic. "Please don't."

"Why not? He can't just go around pretending to date girls and treat them like—"

"Alex," Brittany interrupts, "let Kiara and Carlos figure it out themselves."

"But he's being stu—" He stops midsentence as Brittany squeezes his hand.

"They'll figure it out," Brittany assures him, then smiles. "Don't interfere just yet."

"Why are you so logical?" he asks her.

"Because my boyfriend is hardheaded and always ready for a fight," she responds, then turns to me and Tuck. "Those traits run in the Fuentes family tree. It'll be fine in the end, Kiara," she assures me.

I just don't know if my heart will be shattered into pieces before that happens.

35

CARLOS

"Carlos, can you give me a hand with my wife's car?" Westford asks later in the afternoon.

I'm drinking one of Mrs. W.'s special cups of tea on the patio. "Sure," I say. "What's the problem?"

"Can you help me change the oil? I also want to make sure the muffler is attached properly. Colleen said it's been making a rumbling sound."

Soon I'm helping the Professor jack up the car and steady it on bricks he has stashed in the garage. We both shimmy under the body while the oil drains into a small bucket.

"Did you have fun at the game this morning?" the Prof asks.

"Yeah, 'cept I didn't know I was going to be playin' for a gay team."

"Did it matter?"

At first, yeah. But in the end we were all just a bunch of guys on a team. "No. Did you know Tuck was gay?"

"He made it clear when he came to live with us a few years back. His parents were in the middle of a messy divorce and he needed a place to stay." He puts down his flashlight and looks over at me. "Kinda like you needed a place to stay."

"Speakin' of that: you might regret your decision after I tell you that Kiara and I have been hangin' out a lot."

"That's good. Why would that make me regret letting you stay here?"

I wish we weren't under a car right now as I'm sayin' this. "What if I told you I kissed her?"

"Oh," he says. "I see."

I wonder if he has the urge to tie me under the car and drop it on me so my guts splatter all over his driveway. Or make me drink the dirty car oil until I promise to keep my Mexican paws off his daughter.

"You were probably gonna find out sooner or later from someone else," I tell him.

"I appreciate your honesty, Carlos. That shows integrity, and I'm proud of you. It probably wasn't easy for you to tell me."

"So are you kickin' me out of your house, or what?" I need to know if I'll be out on the streets tonight.

Westford shakes his head. "No, I'm not kicking you out. You're both old enough to be responsible. I was a teenager once, too, and I'm not naive enough to think kids today are any different than I was. But you better not hurt one hair on her head or force her to do anything she doesn't want to do, or else I will not only kick you out of the house, I'll dismember you limb by limb. Got it?"

"Got it."

"Good. Now take this flashlight and check the radiator to see if I need to flush it."

I take the flashlight from him, but before I get out from under the car I say, "Thanks."

"For what?"

"Not treatin' me like a gangbanger."

He smiles. "You're welcome."

After I help Westford with the car, I call *Mamá* and Luis. I tell them about the Ultimate game, and Kiara, and the Westfords, and all the other bullshit. It feels good to talk to *mi familia*. When I tell them I haven't ditched school I feel like I have a family cheering section. I haven't felt that way in a long time. Obviously I leave out the part about Devlin, because there's no way I'm putting *mi'amá* through the stress of knowing that detail.

After the call, I walk into the kitchen but there's no sign of any Westford. "We're in the den," Mrs. W. calls out to me. "Come join us."

The entire Westford family is sitting in front of the television in the small room off to the side of the house. The professor and his wife are in separate chairs, and Kiara and Brandon are sharing the couch. Slices of lasagna are set on the coffee table in front of them.

"Take a plate, some lasagna, and a seat," Westford instructs.

"It's Family Fun Night!" Brandon yells as he jumps up and down on the couch.

"Family Fun Night?" I question. "What's that?"

Mrs. W. picks up a plate and hands it to me. "It's where we pick an activity and do it together, as a family. It's a once-a-month thing we do."

"You guys are kiddin' me, right?" I look around at all of them and realize they're not joking. They really do have Family Fun Night, and they really do want to hang out together on a Saturday night.

When I look over at Kiara, I think it wouldn't be so bad to spend the night just chilling in front of the TV. I pile my plate with food and head for the couch.

"Move over, *cachorro*."

Brandon scoots between me and Kiara.

After we finish dinner, I help bring the dirty plates to the kitchen while Kiara makes the popcorn.

"You don't have to do all this family stuff with us if you don't want to," Kiara tells me.

I shrug. "I didn't want to go out anyway." I toss a piece of popcorn into the air and catch it in my mouth.

I walk back in the family room with my mind more on Kiara than anything else. Even when the cartoon movie comes on that Brandon picked, I sneak glances at her.

"Bran, time for bed," Mrs. W. says after the movie is over.

"I want to stay up," he whines, then grabs on to Kiara's arm.

"No way. You've been going to bed too late," Mrs. Westford says. "Now give your sister and Carlos a hug and come with me."

Brandon stands on the couch and whips himself into Kiara's arms. She hugs him tight and kisses him on the cheek. "Love you more than you love me," he tells her.

"Not possible," she says back.

He wiggles out of her arms and hops on the couch over to my side. He opens his arms wide and wraps them around my neck. "Love you, *amigo*."

"You speakin' *Español, cachorro?*"

"Yeah. I learned it in class this week. *Amigo* is friend."

I pat him on the back. "You are my little *Mexicano* wannabe, aren't you?"

"What's a wannabe?"

"He'll explain it in the morning. Time for bed, Bran," Mrs. W. says. "Now. No more wasting time."

"You kids pick the next movie," Westford says, tossing us the remote. "I'm going to make more popcorn. Bran, I'll be up to say good night after you get in pj's and brush your teeth."

Mrs. W. takes Brandon upstairs and the Professor leaves with the empty popcorn bowls. I'm alone with Kiara. At last.

I sit with one arm over the back of the couch and the other resting on my knee. I'm all too aware of this girl beside me. She gets up and walks over to a cabinet lined with rows of movies—obviously the Westfords' personal collection. I've never been in a house with an entire collection of movies before.

"I can't be normal with you," I tell her.

She turns to me, confused. "What are you talking about?"

"This morning in front of Michael you asked me to be normal." I take a deep breath and tell her what I should have said after the game. Instead of lettin' her ignore me when I finally got home, I should have told her the truth. "I can't. When Tuck told me you'd dated Michael, all these visions of you with another guy drove me nuts. I don't want you with another guy."

"I don't want to be with another guy. I want to be with you. Now pick a movie before I say something you don't want to hear." She waves me over. "Pick one."

"Whatever you want to watch is fine," I tell her, pushing aside the comment about her not telling me what I don't want to hear. I've heard enough. She wants to be with me. I want to be with her. Why complicate it by sayin' anything else?

She pulls out *West Side Story* and I laugh. "You like that movie?"

"Yeah. I like the dancing. And the singing."

I wonder if she can move as well as she fixes cars. Or if she thinks an interracial couple is doomed because they're too different. "Do you dance?"

"A little. Do you? I mean besides the, um, horizontal tango."

Kiara surprises me sometimes. I'm always shocked when she shows glimpses of her spicy attitude. "Yeah. Back in Mexico my friends and I went to clubs every weekend. We danced, met girls, drank, got high . . . fun stuff. Now I'm here, having Family Fun Night with the Westfords. Times have definitely changed."

"You shouldn't do drugs."

"Don't you do things you shouldn't do? Come on, Kiara, give it up. There's no way you're as innocent as you let everyone think you are. You're just like the rest of us sinners. So you don't smoke, drink, or do drugs. But you have other vices. Everyone does." When she doesn't answer, I continue. "Tell me somethin' you do that would shock me."

She sits back on the couch. "Shock you?"

"Yeah. Shock me to the core."

She sits up on her knees and leans toward me. "I've thought about you, Carlos," she whispers in my ear. "At night, in bed. I think about kissing you, our tongues sliding against each other's, while your hands are buried in my hair. When I think about feeling those ripples in your naked chest I touch my—"

"Here's more popcorn!" Westford says, barging into the room with two big bowls filled to the rim with freshly popped popcorn. "Kiara, what are you doing?"

The scene must look pretty racy. Kiara is leaning over me on all fours. Her face is just inches from mine.

I swallow. What she was about to say formed an image in my mind that was almost too much to bear. I stare right into Kiara's eyes to see if she's bullshitting me or not, but I can't tell. She's got a fire in her eyes, but I'm not sure if it's from passion or from her excitement at trying to beat me with my own MO.

I stay silent and let Kiara take this one.

She leans back on her heels. "Um . . . I . . . um . . . nothing really."

Westford looks to me for an explanation.

"Trust me, you don't want to know," I tell him.

"Know what?" Mrs. W. asks, walking into the room.

The Professor hands me the bowl of popcorn as Mrs. W. settles back in her chair. I start munchin' so I don't have to talk.

"I can't get a straight answer out of either one of these teenagers," Westford says.

Kiara settles herself on the other side of the couch. "Mom, Dad, what would you do if you came in here and found us kissing?"

36

Kiara

I really meant to ask the question as a hypothetical. I didn't mean for Carlos to start choking on his popcorn, which he is.

"You okay?" I ask him as he coughs repeatedly.

Carlos looks at me like I'm the craziest person on the planet. "What the hell are you askin' them that for?"

"Because I want to know the answer."

I can tell my parents are trying to telepathically communicate to each other to come up with an answer.

"Well . . . ," my mom starts. "Um . . ."

"What your mother is trying to say," my dad chimes in, "is that we were teenagers once upon a time, too, so we understand that experimentation is a normal part of growing up . . ."

"And you know to always respect yourself and your bodies," my mom says. I suspect she's not answering the question on purpose.

"Yes, Mother."

My dad picks up the remote. "Okay, now that that's settled, which movie did you pick?"

I get a little shy when I say, "*West Side Story*."

We watch the movie, but every now and then Carlos snickers as if some of the parts are ridiculous to him. By the end, I'm crying so hard Carlos has to pass me a tissue from the end table nearest him.

"Pass me one of those tissues, too," my mom says as she sniffs away. "I cry every time I see that movie."

"I hate the ending," I declare to everyone in the room as I take the movie out of the player and replace it with another one.

My dad turns around to face Carlos. "What can I say? My women want a happy ending."

My mom, with her hair up in a clip like a teenager herself, looks at my dad. "What's wrong with a happy ending?"

"They're not realistic," Carlos chimes in.

"On that note . . . I'm going to bed. I'm beat," my dad says, then moans and stretches as he stands up from his chair. "These old bones can't stay up past midnight anymore. I'll see you all in the morning."

My mom calls after him, "I'll be up in a bit."

We all agree to start another movie. This time it's an action film that's probably right up Carlos's alley. Ten minutes into it, my mom yawns. "I'm younger than your father, Kiara, but I can't stay up much past midnight anymore, either. I'm going to bed." She gets up to leave, but before she turns the corner, she pauses the movie and wiggles her forefinger at us. "Trust and respect." She says those few choice words, then tosses Carlos the remote before she disappears.

"Your ma sure does know how to kill the mood," Carlos drawls.

As we continue watching the movie, I glance at Carlos a few times. I can tell he's into the movie because his features are relaxed, unlike his usual tense appearance.

One time he catches me watching him. "Want some water?" he asks.

"Sure."

He disappears into the kitchen, then reappears a few minutes later carrying two glasses of ice water.

It's dark except for the glow of the television. His fingers graze mine as I take the glass from him. I don't know if he felt it, but I can't ignore my body's reaction to the soft touch of his hand brushing against mine. It's not like this morning after the game, where he did it for show.

He hesitates, then his eyes meet mine. It's dark, it's just us, and I'd love nothing more than to tell him I want his hands on me, all over, although he'd already said that my mom broke the mood.

Trust and respect. I trust Carlos not to hurt me physically, but not emotionally. I immediately break the connection and quickly raise the glass to my lips to drink the cold water, because if I didn't I might be tempted to ask him to kiss me again and force myself not to think about the consequences.

Without talking, he eases his lean body back on the couch. Our thighs are almost touching, and while the movie is still playing, all I can think about is him.

The hero is stuck in a warehouse with a beautiful blond woman. He suspects she might be one of the bad guys, but he can't resist her and they start making out.

Carlos shifts, clears his throat, then takes another chug of water. Then another. And another.

I wonder if the scene reminds him of my detailed fantasy about us. I take a slow, deep breath and try to keep my mind on the movie and not on the fact that our knees are now touching.

A while later I glance at him. He looks like he might be sleeping, but I'm not sure.

"Carlos?" I say tentatively.

He opens his eyes, those black depths shining from the light of the TV. The passion and desire are evident in his gaze. "Yeah?"

"Were you sleeping?"

He chuckles. "No. Not by a long shot. I was just tryin' to convince myself not to make a move on you."

The movie forgotten, I push my fears aside and decide to test what we have together. I get off the couch to close the door to the den and lock it, giving us privacy.

"You locked the door," he says.

"I know."

I'm not good with words, and if I did try to say anything I'd probably stutter and break the mood. If I can't effectively tell him how I feel, I can definitely show him. I suddenly realize that I trust this boy even if he doesn't trust himself.

Kneeling next to him on the couch, I slowly raise a shaky hand to his face. My fingers trace random designs in the stubble growing on his jaw. His breath hitches in response.

"Kiara—"

I put my fingers on his beautiful full lips and cut him off. "Shh."

"Are . . . we . . . about to get into . . . trouble?" he asks.

I lean forward. His words fade the closer my lips are to his. I move my palms to his chest and brace myself against his hard body as I move closer. And closer. I can feel the warm heat of his breath mingling with mine and I can't hold back any longer. "Loads of trouble," I say. I know I can't hope to be his permanently, but I want to show him what intimacy with real emotion can feel like.

When my lips touch his the slightest bit, a quiet moan escapes from his mouth. His heart beats fast against my palms. The sweet sound of our lips parting and coming together again is melting my insides. He's letting me be in control by keeping his hands at his sides, but each time I lower my lips to his only to separate them a few seconds later, he starts breathing heavier.

"Let me taste you," he whispers.

The next time I dip my head, I kiss him softly a few times, then gather enough courage to open my mouth and deepen the kiss. I get a surge of energy when our tongues meet for the first time, wet and slippery and, oh, I want more.

The sound of the movie is just white noise in the background.

He cradles my face in his hands and forces me to look into his dark, sexy eyes filled with passion and desire. "You're playin' a dangerous game, *chica*."

"I know. But I trust you."

37

CARLOS

Her words echo in my head. *I trust you.* She's the first girl who's ever said that to me. Even Destiny said I had to earn her trust when we first met, because she thought I was a player. And here's Kiara, a girl who knows I'll never be her knight in shining armor, gifting me with her trust without hesitation. She's straddling me, her lips wet from our kisses. She's crazy to think I'll do the right thing.

My hands are still cradling her face. I respect this girl too much to be dishonest. "Don't trust me."

A pink blush creeps up her cheeks as she reaches behind her head and pulls that band out of her hair. "But I do."

She shakes out her hair. It falls in a curtain over her shoulders, the ends landing just above her breasts. I've never seen anythin' sexier in my life, and she's not even naked yet.

Yet? What am I thinkin'? I'm not gettin' her naked. I want to. Hell, I'd love to peel away the layers and study the curves of her body with my eyes and hands. My body says *Go for it! You want it. She wants it. What's the problem?*

The problem is that damn word . . . trust.

She trusts me.

I squeeze my eyes shut. What can I say to prove to her I'm the bad boy she knows I am? She'd be stupid to trust me. I'll take advantage of her every chance I get, but how can I prove that to her?

Knowing how ready I am to take this to the next level might scare her off. I reach around and grab her butt, then grind against her in a way that makes no mistake of my intent.

Problem is, she starts moving with me. Damn. This is not good. She's definitely got power over me. I thrive on control, but right now I've totally lost it.

I pull her toward me and press her body to mine, my hands feelin' up and down her back. Our heavy breathing is filling the room. I'm glad the movie is still on to mask any sounds we're making.

I lean back and look into her trusting face.

"You gotta stop before this gets out of hand, 'cause I won't." I'm ignoring the fact that we've already gotten out of hand and she doesn't look the least bit ready to stop.

She stills and presses her cheek to mine. "I'm a virgin," she whispers in my ear as if it's a secret she's only going to share with me.

Oh, hell.

I lean my head back on the couch and tell her the truth. "You're not actin' like one."

"That's because it's *you*, Carlos. Only you do this to me."

Power shift. She shouldn't have said that. Now I know I have control, if not physically, at least mentally. Givin' me control isn't a wise move on her part.

I'm taking this girl to the danger zone, but that's where I'm used to spendin' most of my life. My hands inch over to her waist.

"Take your shirt off, *chica*."

Her hands go to the bottom of her shirt. The anticipation of seeing what she's hiding underneath makes me hold my breath. I look up into her face, her eyes filled with uncertainty and something else I refuse to acknowledge.

In one swift movement, she lifts her oversized T-shirt over her head and reveals a body to kill for or die for. Or both.

"I don't have a body like Madison's," she says shyly, her hands crossing her midsection in an effort to hide it.

"What?"

"I'm not skinny."

Skinny to me equals fake body or no body. I need a girl who I can hold on to and not be afraid to break.

I gently remove her hands and hold them lightly at her sides. I lean back and stare, completely dumbfounded, at her pink bra modestly covering her breasts. She's got nothin' to be embarrassed about. This girl has got it goin' on and has no clue she's got a better body than Madison, hands down. Kiara's got curves where God intended them to be, and I have the urge to caress those curves and memorize every inch of her. I feel like the luckiest guy on earth. "*Eres hermosa . . .* you're beautiful."

Her eyes are cast downward. "Look at me, *chica*." When she does, I repeat, "*Eres hermosa*."

"What does it mean?"

"You're beautiful."

She leans forward and trails little kisses across my lips. "Your turn," she whispers, then bites her bottom lip as she waits for me to strip off my shirt.

I immediately toss my shirt to the side.

"Can I touch you?" she asks, as if she doesn't have complete owner-ship of my body at this moment.

I take her hand in mine and guide her to my bare skin. When I let go so she can explore on her own, her fingers trail slow paths up and down my chest. Each touch sears my skin from the inside out, and when her fingers linger on the tattoo peeking out of my jeans and dip into the waistband, it's almost my undoing.

"What does that say?" she asks as she lightly traces one of my tattoos.

"Rebel," I tell her. My fingers weave into her hair and I lean her toward me. I need to taste her again. I need to feel her soft lips on mine. We start making out like it's the first time and maybe our last, our breaths and tongues collide almost desperately.

While she continues her exploration, I focus all my attention on her. I slide her bra straps down until they fall loosely on her arms. She leans back and I can't imagine a sexier image or a sexier girl than the one sit-ting atop me. My pulse quickens in hot anticipation as I slide the silky fabric aside.

Her fingers go still as my hands touch the sides of her waist and slide up until my thumbs reach the curve of her breast. Nothing could prepare me for the wave of emotions I'm feeling right now as I look into Kiara's sparkling eyes.

"I think I'm falling in love with you," she says so softly it might be my imagination, then I hear the sound of gunfire.

Pop! Pop! Pop!

In a frenzied panic, I pull Kiara down on the couch and lay atop her to save her from danger.

I look up, confused. Wait, nobody is in the room besides us. What the hell?

I look at the television screen and see the hero of the movie standing over the body of a dead guy with blood streaming out of his chest. The gunshots were coming from the television.

I look back at a stunned, scared, half-naked Kiara.

"Sorry," I say, moving off her and shifting to the other side of the couch. "Sorry. It was only the TV." My heart is beating faster than a drum at a rock concert. When I heard the gunshots I'd have done anything to protect her life. Even if it meant sacrificing my own. The thought of losing her in the same way I lost my father and almost lost Alex is just too much. I'm practically hyperventilating from the thought of it.

Fuck.

I broke my number one rule: never get emotionally involved.

Whatever happened to foolin' around only with girls who want nothin' more than a good time? The word *"amor,"* or the English equivalent, "love," isn't in my vocabulary. I'm not boyfriend material. If you want love and commitment, don't come knockin' at my door. I have to get out before I'm in too deep.

"It's okay." She sits up and leans over me, her body too close. I can't think straight when I can feel the heat of her body penetrate mine. I feel claustrophobic and trapped. I have to get out of here.

I gently move her away so there's distance between us.

"No, it's not okay. *This* isn't okay." My reaction to the gunshots puts everything back into perspective. I can't do this with Kiara. I press my palms against my eyes and breathe out a frustrated sigh. "Cover yourself," I say, then pick up her shirt.

When I toss the oversized T-shirt to her, I tell myself to avoid meeting her gaze. I don't want to see the hurt in her eyes and know I was the one who put it there.

"I w-w-wanted th-th-this," she stutters in a shaky voice. "Y-y-you d-d-did, t-t-too."

Shit. Now she's so emotional she can hardly get a word out without stumbling all over it. It would be better for her to hate me than fall in love with me.

"Yeah, well, I want a girl who'll fuck around with me, not declare her undying love."

"I d-d-didn't—"

I put up a hand, stopping her. I know what she's gonna say, that she never said this would turn into something more. "You said you were fallin' in love with me, and that's the last thing a guy like me needs to hear. Admit it, Kiara. Girls like you want to cut guys' nuts off and hang 'em from your rearview mirror."

I'm rambling like a complete *pendejo*, the words streaming out of my mouth without my even thinking about what I'm saying. I know I'm hurting her with each word. It's practically killin' me to do this to her, but she needs to know I'm not the one who'll be there to catch her when she falls. I've still got Devlin to deal with, and I might not come back alive. The last thing I'd ever want is for Kiara to be mourning someone who didn't deserve her love in the first place.

"We can be friends—," I tell her.

"Friends who fool around, without any emotion?"

"Yeah. What's wrong with that?"

"I want more."

"Not gonna happen. You want more, go find yourself another sucker." I head for the door, needing to get away from her before I kneel down and beg her to take me back into her arms and finish what we started. As I leave her, I try to shove all images of her out of my head. Fat chance of that anytime soon.

Back in my room, I sit on my bed. There's no use tryin' to get any sleep. I know that's not gonna happen tonight. I shake my head, wondering how I got myself into this mess. Leavin' her in that room was the first selfless thing I've done since I came to Colorado.

And I feel like complete crap.

38

Kiara

I sit in the den and go over in my head what happened tonight. As much as I told myself that fooling around with him wouldn't make our relationship serious, I hoped otherwise. I knew exactly what I was doing, and the fact that it backfired just brought home the fact that Carlos is right. He's not boyfriend material. He only wants a girl who'll take her clothes off for him without a commitment or promise.

He wants a girl like Madison.

I made a complete fool out of myself tonight. To think that sharing my body with him would make him change was stupid. Did I really think an amazing physical connection between us could make him want a permanent relationship with me? The fact is, I did.

When we kissed tonight it was perfect. It was everything I wanted and expected and hoped for. As soon as he cupped my face in his hands, I was lost. I knew nothing I had or could have with Michael would ever compete with the intensity of what Carlos and I were sharing.

Now all of that is shattered, because Carlos pushed me away.

After that, my tongue got heavy and every word I uttered came out as a stutter.

Oh, I am beyond embarrassed. How am I going to face him in the morning? Worse, how am I going to face myself?

39

CARLOS

I got about two hours of sleep last night. When the sun wakes me up, I moan and roll over to try and get more sleep. It's hard to do when the entire room is painted the same color as the damn sun. Next time I'm at the hardware store I need to get some black paint to darken this place to match my mood.

I lie on my side and hold a pillow over my eyes. The next time I open them, it's ten.

I call *mi'amá*, just because I need to hear her voice again. She says that she's trying to get tickets to visit, and I detect an excitement I haven't heard from her in years. It reminds me that I told Mrs. W. I'd help out at the store today. I'll send *mi'amá* the extra money I make so she can add it to the trip fund.

After I shower, I knock on Kiara's bedroom door. She's not there, so I head downstairs.

"Where's Kiara?" I ask Brandon, who's playin' some computer game in the Professor's office.

He's either ignoring me or doesn't hear me.

"Yo, Racer!" I yell.

"What?" Brandon says, not turning around.

I stand next to him and check out the game he's addicted to. On the screen are a bunch of cartoon characters walking in a park. In the corner of the screen it says: **Commodities: Cocaine, 3 grams; Marijuana, 7 grams.**

"What kind of game is this?" I ask the kid.

"A trading game."

The kid is a damn cyber drug dealer. "Turn it off," I tell him.

"Why?"

" 'Cause it's stupid."

"How do you know?" Brandon looks up at me with innocent eyes. "You've never played it."

"Yeah, I have." The real-life game. And that's only because I had to do it to survive. But Brandon has choices in life, and doesn't need to deal drugs to survive. No use in havin' him play a game that simulates it when he's in kindergarten. "Turn it off, Brandon, or I will. I'm not kiddin'."

He sticks his chin in the air and continues playing. "No."

"What's the problem?" Westford says, walking into the room.

"Carlos told me I have to turn off my game. Daddy, you told me I can go on your computer and play a trading game. All my friends play it."

I point to Brandon. "Your son and his friends are cyber drug dealers," I tell his father.

Westford's eyes go wide and he rushes to the screen. "Drug dealers? Brandon, what are you playing?"

I walk out of the room when Westford tells Brandon that illegal drugs are not a commodity. Then he mumbles something about parental controls and how they can't replace parents and he should have supervised more closely.

I wander outside and find Kiara working on her car, her legs and feet sticking out of the driver's side door. I watch as she works upside down, her head under the dash, and a screwdriver in her hands.

"Need help?" I ask.

"Nope," she says without looking up.

"Can I take a look at the door? Maybe I can fix it."

"It's fine."

"No, it's not. It's busted. You can't go around with it like that forever."

"Watch me."

I lean against the side of the car. And wait. And wait. If she doesn't shimmy herself out in a few minutes I'm tempted to drag her ass out.

Westford walks out of the house. "Kiara, what time are you and Carlos going to Hospitali-Tea?"

"As soon as I can tape this wire together, Dad. It won't cooperate."

"You probably need to solder it," I tell her, although at this point it's pretty obvious she doesn't want any suggestions from me.

"Let me know when you're ready to go. In the meantime, I need a word with Carlos." Westford crooks his finger at me. "Meet me in my office."

He doesn't look or sound too happy with me. Truth is, he shouldn't be. Last night I had my hands full with his daughter.

I pass Brandon watching some cartoon in the den on my way to the Professor's office.

"What's goin' on?" I ask as I take a seat.

"Obviously not this." He tosses me my shirt from last night. "I found it on the floor of the den. It's obvious there was some hanky-panky going on."

Okay, so he knows we fooled around. But at least he didn't find Kiara's bra on top of my shirt.

"Yeah . . . things kinda got a little heated after you and Mrs. W. left the den last night," I tell him.

"I was afraid of that. Colleen and I believe in open communication with our kids. And while you're not one of my own, I'm responsible for you at this point." The Professor rubs his hand across his face and sucks in a breath. "You'd think I'd be prepared for this talk. Once upon a time I was a teenager and did the same thing in my parents' house." He looks up. "Of course, I was a little more diligent about hiding the evidence."

"It won't happen again, sir."

"What, leaving the evidence or you fooling around in my house with my daughter? And please cut the 'sir' bullshit. This isn't the military."

"I was the one who forced myself on him, Dad," Kiara says, appearing in the doorway. "It was not his fault."

The Professor winces as he says, "It takes two to tango. I'm not placing blame or fault. I'm just discussing. I wish your mother was here to have this talk. Did you, uh, protect yourselves at least?"

Kiara moans, totally embarrassed. "Dad, we didn't have sex."

"Oh," he says. "You didn't?"

I shake my head.

I can't believe I'm in the middle of this conversation. Mexican dads don't have these kinds of talks, especially with the boys their daughters are foolin' around with. They'd kick the boy's ass first, then ask questions. After that, they'd forbid their daughter to go outside without a chaperone. There's none of this "open communication" bullshit.

I feel like I'm on a white people self-help show, and I'm not sure what I'm supposed to say. I'm also not used to a father who wants to actually talk about shit like this. Is this normal, or does it only happen with dads who happen to be psychologists who're trying to shrink our brains?

"I'm not stupid enough to think that I can prevent you from doing . . . whatever it is you two were doing," Westford continues. "But I'm instituting a new rule: no more monkey business between you two under my roof. If I make it harder for you, maybe you'll make better choices. And I should also tell you, as your father, Kiara, and your guardian, Carlos, to stay a virgin until you get married." He sits back in his chair and smiles at us, mighty pleased with himself for that last sentence. Too bad this discussion is a few years too late, at least for me.

"Were you a virgin when you got married?" I ask, challenging him. Immediately his grin fades.

"Yes, um, well, um . . . when I was a teen it was a very different day and age. Teens today are smarter and more educated. There are *incurable* diseases . . . and dangers for both partners if you're not in a *serious, monogamous, committed relationship*." He wiggles a finger at both of us. "And don't forget the big p-word."

I can't help but chuckle. *¿Perdón?* "The p-word?"

"Pregnancy!" The Professor narrows his eyes at me. "I'm not ready to be a grandpa for a long, long, long, *long* time."

I think about my mom, who got pregnant with Alex when she was seventeen. *Mi'amá* made me promise to always wear a condom if I was ever physical with a girl—she never wanted one of her sons to end up like her and *mi papá*. Hell, she even hid some condoms in a pair of my underwear as a reminder.

Last night scared the shit out of me. 'Cause while I've always had my head on straight when it comes to protectin' myself and the girl I'm with, I can't say I would've been able to stop us last night even though I didn't have a condom within reach. And I wasn't even wasted. If I hadn't been scared half to death from those gunshots comin' from the TV, Kiara and I might be having a very different talk with the Professor right now.

"Dad, we know about all that," Kiara chimes in.

"It doesn't hurt to have a refresher talk, in light of the fact that Carlos's shirt was lying on the floor in the den this morning."

When I hold up the shirt so she knows what he's talking about, Kiara chokes out a surprised, "Oh."

Westford checks the clock on his desk. "I've got to get Brandon outside before he develops ADD from watching too much television." He holds his hands out as if he's about to hand me an offering. "Carlos, are we in complete understanding with each other?"

"Yeah," I say. "As long as it's not in your house and you don't know about it, you're okay with us messin' around."

"I know you're joking with me. You *are* joking with me, aren't you?"

"Maybe."

Kiara steps in the room. "Dad, he was kidding."

The Professor counts off each word on his fingers and gives me a level stare. "Don't forget . . . (1) serious, (2) monogamous, (3) committed relationship, (4) not under my roof, and (5) trust."

"And don't forget (6) the p-word," I remind him.

He nods. "Yes. The p-word. One day in the military, Carlos, and they'd kick that cockiness of yours right out the window."

"Too bad I'm not plannin' on signin' up."

"That *is* too bad. If you ever did sign up and put as much energy into being a good soldier as you do trying to have a major attitude, you'd go far. I'm tempted to put something red inside the laundry so your underwear turns pink. It would be a little reminder of our talk today."

I shrug. "That's okay. I don't wear underwear," I lie.

"Out, wise guy," he orders, shooing us out the door. I think I catch the side of his mouth quirk up, amused at my comeback, but it quickly disappears. "Both of you, out of my office. And let's keep this talk between just us. Now get your butts over to Hospitali-Tea. My wife is expecting to put you both to work today. Don't stop on the way," he calls out when we're in the hallway. "I'm calling there in fifteen minutes to make sure you've arrived."

40

Kiara

"Listen, *chica*—," Carlos says when we're driving to my mom's store a few minutes later.

My hands tighten on the steering wheel. "Don't call me that anymore," I tell him.

"What do you want me to call you, then?"

I shrug. "Whatever. Just not *chica*." I reach down to turn on my stereo but realize it still doesn't work. I grip the steering wheel tighter and concentrate on the road ahead, even when we're at a stoplight.

Carlos holds his hands up. "What do you want from me? You want me to tell you lies, is that what you want? Okay, I'll give you lies. Kiara, without you I'm nothin'. Kiara, you own my heart and soul. Kiara, when I'm not with you I feel like life has no meaning. Kiara, I love you. Is that what you want to hear?"

"Yes."

"No guy who actually says those things really means them."

"I bet your brother says them to Brittany and means them."

"That's because he's lost all common sense. I thought you were the one girl who didn't fall for my bullshit."

"I don't. Consider my wanting you as my real boyfriend as a lapse in judgment," I tell him. "But I'm over it. I expect less than nothing from you from now on, and I've realized you're not my type at all. In fact," I say, glancing at him, "I might call Michael. He wants to go out again."

Carlos reaches down to my purse and pulls my phone from the side pocket. I try to snatch it out of his hand, but he's too quick. "What are you doing?"

"Concentrate on the road, Kiara. You wouldn't want to get into an accident 'cause you weren't payin' attention, would you?"

"Put it back," I order.

"I will. I need to check somethin' first."

At the next stoplight, I reach over and take the phone out of his hand. I read the text message Carlos just sent Michael. *4Q.* "You didn't."

"Yeah, I did." He sits back, looking pretty pleased with himself. "You can thank me later."

Thank him? *Thank him!* I pull off the road, pick up my purse, and swing it like a war club aiming right at Carlos's head.

He grabs the purse before it hits him. "Don't tell me you really wanted to go out with that tool again."

"I don't know what I want anymore."

I get back on the road, heading for my mom's shop. I stop the car and get out, without waiting for Carlos.

"Kiara, wait." Carlos growls as he climbs out of the window. I hear him jog to catch up with me. "I'm gonna fix that damn car door if it's the last thing I ever do." He rubs his hand through his hair. "Listen, if things were different . . ."

"What things?"

"It's complicated."

I turn my back on him. If he won't tell me, there's no use in arguing.

"Hi, guys!" My mom greets us at the front of the store, so our conversation is cut short. "Kiara, I pulled out the receipts from last month and the past week. Feel free to reconcile those. Carlos, come with me."

While I sit in the office and tally receipts and reconcile the books, I hear my mom explain to Carlos how to separate the boxes of loose teas that were just delivered.

At around one, my mom peeks her head in the door and tells me to meet her in the break room for lunch. My mom is oblivious to the tension in the air as we all sit in the break room. She expects everyone to be happy and energetic all the time, so I wonder when she'll notice the happiness quotient in the room is way off.

"I got this from Teddy, the vendor outside the store," she says as she pulls food out from a bag.

"What is it?" Carlos asks as she hands him one.

"Organic vegan dogs."

"What's a vegan dog?"

"A vegetarian hot dog," she says. "With no animal products."

Carlos unwraps his hot dog uncertainly.

"It won't kill you to eat healthy, Carlos," my mom says. "But if you don't like it, I can go out and get you processed food if you want."

I start eating my vegan dog. I don't mind eating all the healthy stuff my mom makes, but I definitely like processed food every now and then.

Carlos bites into his. "It's pretty good. Got any fries to go with it?"

I almost laugh when my mom dumps out a bunch of orange fries on top of a napkin. "They're baked sweet potato fries. With the skin on, to give you more fiber. If I'm not mistaken, I think they've also got omega-3 fatty acids."

"I like to eat without thinkin' about what's inside," Carlos says as he munches away.

My mom pours us glasses of iced tea from a big pitcher she made for us. "You should care about what goes in your body. For example, this tea blend has açaí, orange-peel extract, and mint."

"Mom, eat," I tell her. Before I know it, she'll go through an entire explanation of antioxidants and free radicals.

"Okay, okay." She takes out her hot dog and starts eating. "So how was the movie last night?"

"It was good," I say, hoping she doesn't ask details because I have no clue what the movie was about.

She picks up a fry and bites off the tip. "It seemed a little violent. I'm not into violent movies."

"Me, either," I say. Carlos stays silent. I feel his gaze on me, but I don't look up. I focus my attention on everything else besides him.

Iris, one of my mom's weekend employees, opens the break-room door. "Colleen, you've got a customer specifically requesting you. She seems as if she's in a hurry."

My mom takes the last bite of her dog. "Duty calls."

I get up to leave too, but Carlos reaches out and takes hold of my wrist. God, how I want him to pull me toward him and tell me that last night wasn't a mistake. This thing between us doesn't have to be complicated.

"It's not you, you know. I haven't wanted to be with a girl so bad since . . ." His voice trails off and he lets go of my wrist.

"Since who?" I ask.

"It doesn't matter."

"It does to me."

He hesitates, as if he doesn't want to say her name. When he finally says "Destiny," he can't hide that he still has feelings for her. Her name rolls off his tongue as if he savors each syllable.

I'm definitely jealous. There's no way I can compete with Destiny. Carlos obviously still loves her. "I get it."

"No, you don't. Last night freaked the hell out of me, Kiara. Because I felt somethin' I haven't felt—"

"Since Destiny," I say.

"I won't let myself fall that hard for a girl ever again."

"So am I still supposed to pretend I'm dating you at school?"

"Just for a couple more weeks, until Madison decides she's movin' on." He looks up at me. "Then we can create a fake reason to break up. We made a deal, right?"

"Right."

Back in my mom's office, I look down at the tallies in front of me. The numbers are a blur. Tossing my pencil aside, I put my head in my hands and sigh.

I was so stupid last night to tell Carlos I was falling in love with him. I definitely scared him away. All my life, until now, I've held back. And then I met Carlos, a guy who makes me want to forge ahead and never regret a single moment.

When he played soccer with my brother, and I saw a glimpse of generosity that he only gifts to the few he thinks are worthy, I knew that what you see isn't necessarily what you get when it comes to Carlos.

At the end of the day I find him in the back room, carefully measuring the various ingredients for my mom's homemade blends.

"I came up with a fake reason why we'd break up," I tell him.

"Hit me with it."

"Because you're still in love with Destiny."

His fingers go completely still. "Pick somethin' else."

"Like what?"

"I don't know. Just somethin' else." He puts the ingredients back on the shelves. "I'm gonna walk to the auto-body shop to talk to Alex. Tell your parents I'll be home later."

"I can drive you," I tell him. "I'm leaving now, too."

He shakes his head. "I want to walk." I watch as he heads out the back door a few minutes later, leaving me wondering if he just wants to get away from me as fast as he can.

41

CARLOS

When I'm far enough away from the tea store, I pull out the cell phone Brittany gave me. I punch in Devlin's number and wait.

As soon as I hear him pick up, I say, "It's Carlos Fuentes. You wanted my attention, you've got it."

"Ah, *Señor* Fuentes. I was waiting for you to contact me," a smooth voice says from the other end of the line. It's got to be Devlin.

"What do you want from me?" I ask, letting him know right away I'm not fuckin' around.

"I just want to talk."

I keep walking as I talk because I've got a crazy feeling the guy has people tailing me. "Couldn't you have done that without havin' Nick Glass set me up?"

"I needed to get your attention, Fuentes. But now that I have it, it's time for us to meet."

My entire body tenses. Whether I want to meet Devlin or not, it's gonna happen. "When?"

"How about now?"

"You have guys tailin' me?" I ask, even though I know the answer before I even ask the question.

"Of course, Fuentes. I'm a businessman, and you're my newest apprentice. I've got to keep my eye out for you."

"I haven't agreed to do shit for you," I tell him.

"No, but you will. I've been told you've got what it takes."

"From who?"

"Let's just say a little *Guerrero* told me. Enough talk. When you see one of my guys drive up, get in."

"How will I know it's one of your guys?" I ask him.

Devlin laughs. "You'll know."

The phone goes dead. A few minutes later a black SUV with tinted windows stops right in front of me. I take a deep breath when the door opens. I'm ready to face whatever lies beyond. No matter what everyone in *mi familia* thinks, this is my destiny.

I slide into the backseat and recognize Diego Rodriguez sitting next to me, a *Guerrero* who was so high up he was always talked about but rarely seen. I nod and wonder what he's doing with Wes Devlin. I know some guys consider themselves hybrids and jump gang affiliations, but I'd never actually seen anyone so high up in an organization get away with it.

"Long time no see," Rodriguez says. Up front are two white guys who look like they're both bodybuilders or at least trained to kick ass. They're definitely here to protect someone, and that someone definitely isn't me.

"Where's Devlin?" I ask.

"You'll meet him soon enough."

I look out the window to see if I can tell where we're headed, but it's no use. I'm totally lost and at the mercy of these three guys. I wonder what Kiara would do if she knew I was in a car with a bunch of thugs. She'd probably tell me I shouldn't have gone in the car in the first place. I'm not letting my guard down for one minute, that's for sure.

Thinking about letting my guard down makes me think of Kiara. Last night as I had her in my arms and felt her soft skin beneath my fingers, I totally lost control. Hell, I was ready to take anything she had to offer without caring about the consequences.

"We're here," Diego says, pullin' me out of my thoughts of Kiara and what might have been.

"Here" is a big house with a cement wall surrounding the estate. We're buzzed through. Diego directs me through the front door and leads me to an office big enough to intimidate any corporate CEO.

The blond guy sitting behind a dark wooden desk is obviously Devlin. He's wearing a dark suit with a light blue tie that matches his eyes. He motions for me to sit in one of the guest chairs in front of his desk. When I don't, the two overgrown guys from the car ride stand on either side of me.

I'm in dangerous territory, but I stand my ground. "Get your trained dogs away from me," I tell him. Devlin waves them away, and the two guys immediately back off and block the door to the room. I wonder how much he pays them to be his guard dogs.

Diego is still in the room, a silent second in command. Devlin leans back in his chair, assessing me. "So you're Carlos Fuentes, the one Diego here has been telling me so much about. He says you skipped out on the *Guerreros del barrio*. Bold move, Carlos, although I assume if you step one foot back in Mexico you're as good as dead."

"Is that what this is all about?" I ask. "If you've affiliated yourself with the *Guerreros* and they told you to get rid of me, why have Nick set me up?"

"Because we're not going to get rid of you, Fuentes," Diego chimes in. "We're going to use you."

Those words make me want to lash out and tell these guys that nobody is going to control me or use me, but I hold back. The more these guys talk, the more information I can get.

"Truth is, Fuentes," Diego says, "we're doin' you a favor by not bringin' you back to the *Guerreros* in pieces, and you're gonna do us a favor by being our bag boy."

Bag boy. He means I have to be their newest street dealer, and willingly take the fall if I get caught. The drugs in my locker were a test to see if I'd turn Nick in. If I did, I'd be pegged a snitch and probably be lying in the morgue right now. I proved I'm not a narc, so now I'm a valuable commodity. It reminds me of Brandon's video game, although this game is lethal.

Devlin leans forward. "Let's just put it this way, Fuentes. You work with us, you've got nothing to worry about. Besides that, you'll be a rich kid." He pulls out an envelope from the desk drawer and slides it over to me. "Take a look."

I pick up the envelope. Inside are a bunch of one hundred–dollar bills—more than I've ever held in my hands before. I set the envelope back on his desk.

"Take it, it's yours," Devlin says. "Consider it a taste of what you can earn with me in one week."

"So the Devlin family has aligned with the *Guerreros*? When did that happen?"

"I align with whoever and whatever gets me to my ultimate goal."

"What's your goal, world domination?" I joke.

Devlin doesn't laugh. "Right now it's to bring in shipments I've got coming in from Mexico and make sure they don't get misplaced, if you know what I mean. Rodriguez here thinks you've got what it takes. Listen, I'm not the head of a street gang that fights for territory, the color of your skin, or your damn nationality. I'm a businessman, running a business. I could give a shit if you're black, white, Asian, or Mexican. Hell, I've got more Russians working for me than the Kremlin. As long as you benefit my business, I want you working for me."

"And if I don't want in?" I ask.

Devlin looks to Rodriguez.

"Your *mamá* lives in Atencingo, doesn't she?" Rodriguez asks casually as he steps forward. "And your little brother, too. I think his name is Luis. Cute kid. I've had a guy watching them for weeks now. One word from me and bullets will fly. They'll be dead before they even know what hit 'em."

I lunge toward Rodriguez, not caring that he's most likely packing. Nobody gets away with threatening my family. He's shielding his face with his hands, but I'm fast and get a piece of him before the two big guys grab my arms and pull me away. "If you hurt *mi familia*, I'll rip your fuckin' heart out with my own two hands," I warn as I struggle to free myself.

Rodriguez cups his cheek where I clocked him. "Don't let him go," he orders, then swears at me in a mixture of English and Spanish. "You're *loco*, you know that?"

"*Sí. Muy loco*," I tell him as one of the guys makes the mistake of loosening his hold to get a better grip on me. I kick him away and send him crashing into a painting on the wall. When it cracks and smashes to the ground upon impact, I turn to see what other damage I can do to show I'm not someone who'll shrink back in fear if my family is threatened.

Two more guys storm into the room. Shit. I'm tough and can kick some ass, but five against one is bad odds. Not counting Devlin, who is sitting in his big leather chair watching the rest of us duke it out as if we're doing it solely for his amusement.

I manage to break free, then hold my own for a few minutes before two of the guys rush me and slam me into the wall. I'm dazed from the impact when another guy starts pounding on me. It might be Rodriguez, or it might be one of the four other guys. At this point it's all a blur.

I struggle against them, but each punch to my stomach is taking its toll and hurts like hell. When a fist connects with my jaw once, then twice, then three times, I taste blood. I've become their damn punching bag.

I gather all my energy, ignore the intense pain, and break free. Lunging forward, I connect hard with one of them. I won't go down without a fight, even one I have no chance of winning.

My advantage is short-lived. I'm pulled off the guy and shoved to the carpeted floor. If I get up maybe I can do more damage, but I'm being pummeled and kicked from all directions and feel my energy fading fast. A solid, painful kick to my back tells me one of the guys wears steel-toed boots. With my last ounce of energy, I grab the leg of whoever is kicking me. He tumbles forward, but it doesn't matter. I've got nothing left. No fight, no energy . . . just piercing pain with every move I make. The only thing I can do is pray to pass out soon . . . or die. At this point, either one would be welcome.

When I stop fighting, Devlin yells for them to stop. "Get him up," he orders.

I'm forced into the chair facing Devlin, who's still looking like a powerful CEO in his unwrinkled suit. My shirt is ripped in several places and has blood splattered all over it.

Devlin jerks back my head. "Consider this a jumping out of the *Guerreros del barrio* and a jumping in to the Devlin family. You're a Devlin now. I know you won't disappoint me."

I don't answer. Hell, I don't even know if I could respond even if I wanted to. I do know that I'm not a Devlin and will never be a Devlin.

"I appreciate your spirit, but don't mess up my house or fight with my guys again or you're a dead man." He walks out of the room, but not before ordering his guys to clean up his office before he gets back.

I'm hauled out of the chair. The next thing I know, I'm being shoved into the backseat of the SUV.

"Don't fight me or Devlin," Rodriguez says as we drive back. "We've got big plans, and I need you. Devlin's guys don't have the Mexican connections we have. That makes us valuable."

I'm not feeling too valuable right now. My head feels like it's about to explode. "Stop the car," Rodriguez orders when we're a few houses away from the Westfords'. He opens the door and drags me out. "Make sure you take care of that girl who you're livin' with. I wouldn't want anythin' to happen to her." He gets back in the car and tosses the envelope of money at my feet. "You should be as good as new in a week. I'll contact you then," he says, and drives off.

I can hardly stand, but I force myself to the front door of the Westfords' house. I bet I look the same as I feel: like complete shit. Once inside, I try to sneak upstairs so nobody sees what a bloody mess I am, careful to keep my shirt against my mouth so I don't drip blood on the carpet.

I head straight for the bathroom. Problem is, Kiara is walking out of it just as I try to enter it.

She takes one look at me, gasps, and covers her mouth with her hand. "Carlos! Oh my God, what happened?"

"You still recognize me with a busted-up face. That's a good sign, right?"

42

Kiara

My heart pounds wildly in fear and shock as Carlos moves past me and leans over the sink.

"Close the door," he says, moaning in pain as he spits blood into the sink. "I don't want your parents to see me."

I lock the door and rush to him. "What happened?"

"I got my ass kicked."

"That's obvious." I grab a navy towel off the rack and wet it in the sink. "By who?"

"You don't want to know." He rinses out his mouth, then looks at himself in the mirror. His lip is cut and still bleeding, and his left eye is swollen. By the way he's leaning on the sink I can just imagine how the rest of him feels.

"I think you need to go to the hospital," I tell him. "And call the police."

He turns to me and winces, the movement obviously painful. "No hospital. No police," he says, moaning each word. "I'll be better in the mornin'."

"You don't believe that." When he winces again, I feel his pain as if it's my own. "Sit," I say, pointing to the edge of the tub. "I'll help you."

Carlos must really be drained emotionally as well as physically, because he sits on the edge of the tub and stays still while I wet the towel again and gently wipe the blood off the lips that only last night were smiling when I kissed him. They're not smiling now.

I carefully dab at his open cuts, painfully aware of how close we are. He stills my hand as I move the towel across his swollen face. "Thanks," he says as I look into his sad eyes.

I need to break the intensity of his gaze, so I wet the towel in the sink, and wring it out. "I just hope the other guy looks worse."

He lets out a small laugh. "There were five other guys. They all look better than me, although I held my own for a while. You would've been proud."

"I doubt that. Did you start it?"

"I don't remember."

Five guys? I'm afraid to ask more details, because just looking at his injuries is making my stomach queasy. But I want to know what happened to him. An envelope is resting on the sink. I pick it up and notice money peeking out of the top. Hundred-dollar bills. A bunch of them. I hold out the envelope to Carlos. "Is this yours?" I ask tentatively.

"Sort of."

A million different scenarios about how Carlos got the money start swimming around in my head. None of them are good, but now isn't the time to drill him about how or why he's carrying a load of cash. He's hurt, and I might have to insist on bringing him to the hospital.

I hold up a finger in front of me. "Follow my finger with your eyes. I want to make sure you don't have a concussion."

I pay close attention to his pupils as he tracks my moving finger.

He seems fine, but he's following my orders without any argument, and that scares me. I'd feel much better if he'd get checked by a professional.

"Take off your shirt," I tell him. I search my medicine cabinet for Tylenol.

"Why, you want to fool around again?"

"Not funny, Carlos."

"You're right. But I've got to warn you. If I lift my arm over my head I might pass out. My side is killin' me."

Knowing his shirt is already ripped and ruined, I pull out scissors from one of the bathroom drawers and cut a line down the front.

"After you're done, can I return the favor?" he jokes.

I'm trying to act like we're just friends, but he keeps throwing me curveballs and it's confusing me. "I thought you didn't want to get involved."

"I don't. I want to numb the pain, and figure that seein' you naked right about now might help."

"Here," I say, shoving Tylenol and a paper cup filled with tap water into his hand.

"Got anythin' stronger?"

"No, but I'm sure if you let me take you to the hospital they'll give you something stronger."

Without answering, he throws his head back and swallows the pills. I peel off his cut shirt and try not to gasp again as I examine his injuries. I noticed a few old scars on his body before, but the damage done today to his back and chest is downright nasty.

"I've been in fights before," he says as if that's supposed to make me feel better.

"Maybe you should avoid them altogether," I suggest as I gently wipe down his back and chest. "You've got cuts and bruises on your back," I tell him. The sight of each mark makes me want to cry for him.

"I know. I can feel every one."

When I'm done wiping off all the blood, I step back. He tries to smile, but his lip is so swollen it's lopsided. "Do I look better?"

I shake my head. "You can't hide this from my parents, you know. One look at you and they'll be asking questions."

"I don't want to think about that. Not now, at least." He stands up, grabs his stomach, and growls in pain. "I'm goin' to bed. Check on me in the mornin' to see if I'm still alive." Carlos grabs his T-shirt and envelope before heading to his room, then collapses on the bed. When he looks up and realizes I've followed him, he says, "Did I thank you?"

"A few times."

"Good. 'Cause I meant it and I hardly ever say it."

I pull the covers over his aching body. "I know."

I start to walk out of the room, but I hear him start to panic and his breathing gets labored. He reaches out to me. "Don't go. Please."

I sit next to him on the bed, wondering if he's afraid of being abandoned. He slings his arm around my thigh and rests his forehead against my knee. "I have to protect you," he says softly.

"From who?"

"*El Diablo*."

"*El Diablo*? Who's that?" I ask.

"It's complicated."

What does that mean? "Try to rest," I tell him.

"I can't. My entire body hurts."

"I know." I gently rub the arm that's slung around me until his breathing slows. "I wish I could help you," I whisper.

"You are," he murmurs against my knee. "Just don't leave me, okay? Everyone leaves me."

As soon as I can sneak out of his room, I'm going to call Alex and tell him and my dad what happened. I imagine Carlos won't be thankful then. He'll likely be downright pissed.

43

CARLOS

I'm holding on to Kiara, feeling a desperate need to protect her. If I could only move without feeling like crap, I wouldn't be lulled to sleep with her fingers stroking my arm. While I welcome sleep, I don't want Kiara out of my sight. Rodriguez could hurt her, and I can't let that happen. As long as Kiara is safe, *está bien*. I need to warn Luis and *Mamá*, too. I just need to sleep off this pain . . . for a few minutes. Kiara's fingers trailing lines up and down my arm is soothing away the sharpness of the pain. I close my eyes. If I fall asleep for a few minutes, it's okay.

The sound of the door creaking makes me open my eyes. I suddenly realize that Kiara's not sitting beside me anymore. Not that I actually expected her to watch over me while I slept. I attempt to sit up, but I'm so damn stiff every bone, muscle, and joint in my body is protesting. Giving up, I stay on my side, under the blanket, hoping it's Kiara in the room and not her parents . . . or worse, Brandon. If the kid jumps on me, the result might be ugly.

I close my eyes. "Kiara?"

"Yeah."

"Please tell me you're alone."

"I can't."

Damn. I sink my head deeper into the pillow in a weak attempt at hiding the evidence on my face.

"Carlos, tell me what's going on. Now," Westford demands in a clipped and very military-like voice. Usually he's so easygoing and calm . . . not now, though.

"I got beat up," I tell him. "I'll be fine in a couple of days."

"Can you walk?"

"Yeah, but please don't make me prove it right now. Maybe later. Maybe tomorrow."

Westford pulls off the covers and curses. I didn't think the guy had it in him.

"I wish you wouldn't have done that," I tell him. I don't have a shirt on, and he's seeing the evidence firsthand. I look up at Kiara, standing beside the bed. "You betrayed me. I told you not to tell them."

"You need help," she says. "You can't do this alone."

Westford crouches down so he's face-to-face with me. "We're going to the hospital."

"Not a chance," I tell him.

I hear more footsteps in the room. "How is he?" my brother asks.

"Did you call the entire cavalry, or just half of it?" I ask Kiara.

My brother takes one look at me and shakes his head. He rubs his face, full of frustration and anger and responsibility. It's not his fault, it's mine. Whether I had a choice or not, I got myself into this and I'll get myself out. Right now I wish everyone would just leave me alone, because I don't want to talk about who was involved in the fight and why it happened in the first place.

"I'm fine. Or at least I will be," I tell him.

The Professor, with such a concerned look on his face you'd think the guy was upset about his own son, says to Alex, "He won't go to the hospital."

"He can't," Alex tells him.

"That's *insane*, Alex. What kind of people don't go to the hospital when they need medical attention?"

"Our kind," I tell him.

"I don't like it. I don't like it one bit. We can't just sit here and do nothing. Look at him, Alex. He's practically in a fetal position. We've got to do something." I hear Westford pace back and forth on the carpet. "Okay. I've got a friend, Charles, who's a doctor. I can call and see if he'll come over and take a look at Carlos's injuries." Westford kneels down to me. "But if he says you need to go to the hospital," he says, shaking his finger at me, "you're going, whether or not I have to drag you out of the house kicking and screaming."

Speaking of kicking and screaming . . . "Where's Brandon?" I ask. I don't want the kid seeing me until the swelling goes down.

"After Kiara told us what was going on, Colleen took him to her mother's house. He'll stay there for a few days."

Their entire life is in chaos because of me. It's bad enough I'm eating their food and taking up space in their house. Now their kid is banished because I'm a fuckup. "Sorry," I tell him.

"Don't worry about it. Kiara, I'm going to call Charles. Why don't we give Carlos and his brother some privacy." Oh, hell. That's the last thing I want.

When the door closes, Alex stands over the bed. "You look like shit, brother."

"Thanks." I look at his bloodshot eyes and wonder if he cried when he found out I was beaten down. I've never actually seen Alex cry in person though we've been through some tough times. "So do you."

"It was Devlin's guys, huh? Kiara told me you said it was *El Diablo*."

"They're the ones who set me up at school. Last night I got jumped in—against my will. They said I'm a Devlin now."

"That's bullshit."

Even though it hurts to move, I can't help but let out a short laugh. "Tell that to Devlin." On second thought . . . "I'm kiddin'. Stay the hell away from Devlin. You're out of all this. Keep it that way. I mean it."

I start to get up so I can make sure Alex is listening to me. He's my brother, my blood. He annoys the hell out of me most of the time, but when it comes right down to it I want to see him graduate from college and have little annoying mini-Alexes and mini-Brittanys running around in the future. This thing with Devlin . . . I just can't guarantee I can get out of it. I wince and hold my breath as I struggle to sit up, wishing I could suck it up and pretend I'm not in pain. I hate feeling weak and having everyone else watch me struggle.

Alex coughs a few times, then turns away so he doesn't have to watch me struggle more. "I can't believe this is happenin' again." He clears his throat, then turns to me. "What did Devlin say? He's got to want you for some specific reason."

The more he knows, the deeper he'll get into this mess. I can't allow that to happen. "I'll figure it out."

"The hell you will. I'm not leavin' here until you tell me everythin' you know."

"I guess you're gonna be here a while. Better make yourself comfortable."

Westford knocks and walks back in. "I called my friend Charles. He's on his way."

Mrs. W. joins us a second later, a tray in her hand. "You poor dear," she says, then immediately puts down the tray and rushes over to me. She examines my busted lip and bruises. "How did this happen?"

"You don't want details, Mrs. W."

"I hate fighting. It doesn't solve anything." She sets the tray in my lap. "It's chicken soup," she explains. "My grandmother told me it heals everything."

I'm not hungry, but Mrs. W. is so proud of the chicken soup I take a spoonful just to get her to stop looking at me so anxiously.

"So?" she asks.

Surprisingly, the warm, salty broth with noodles goes down easily. "It's great," I tell her.

They're all watching me like mother hens. I was fine with Kiara but I'm vulnerable right now and I don't want anyone else around. Well, besides Kiara. Where is she?

When the doctor arrives, he spends a half hour going over all my injuries. "You really got yourself in a doozy of a fight, Carlos." He turns to Westford. "Dick, he's going to be just fine. No concussion, no deep contusions. He's got badly bruised ribs. I can't be certain he doesn't have internal bleeding, but his color is good. Keep him home from school for a couple of days and he should start feeling better. I'll be back on Wednesday to check on him."

After everyone heads downstairs for dinner, Kiara slips back into my room and stands at the edge of the bed, looking down at me. "I'm not sorry I told them what happened to you. You're not as invincible as you thought. And another thing . . ." She bends down so she's eye to eye with me. "Now that I know you're going to be okay, I've decided not to have sympathy for you. If you were dealing drugs, you'd better come clean. I know that money in the envelope you stuck in your pillowcase didn't come from selling my magnet cookies."

"I liked you better when you were sympathetic," I tell her. "And you give yourself too much credit. I couldn't give your damn cookies away, let alone sell 'em. And I'm not sellin' drugs."

"Tell me where you got the money."

"It's complicated."

She rolls her eyes. "Everything with you is complicated, Carlos. I want to help you."

"You just said you don't have sympathy. Why help me then?"

"It's selfish, really. I can't stand watching my fake boyfriend in pain."

"So this is about you, not me?" I ask her, amused.

"Yeah. And just so you know, you ruined Homecoming for me."

"How?"

"If you haven't noticed the posters around school, it's next weekend. If you can't walk, there's no way you'll be able to dance by Saturday night."

44

Kiara

On Wednesday, Carlos insists on going to school. He says he's feeling better, although I can tell he's moving slower than usual and is still in pain. He's got a black eye and his lip is still swollen, but it just makes him look tougher and rougher. Most of the students at Flatiron are staring and pointing as we walk through the halls. Every time Carlos notices someone staring, he drapes his arm around me. Playing the role of his girlfriend isn't fun when all we're doing is being stared at. But we're together, and I feed off his strength in the face of all the gossip.

At lunch, I'm sitting with Tuck when Carlos walks up to us. "Eww," Tuck says. "My eyes are almost tearing from looking at your nasty eye. Do us all a favor and wear a mask or something. Or a blindfold."

Before I can kick Tuck under the table, Carlos takes the back of Tuck's chair and tilts it. "Beat it, fucker."

"It's Tucker," Tuck says, sliding off the chair but doing his best to hold on.

"Whatever. I need to talk to Kiara, alone."

"Stop fighting, you two," I tell them. "Carlos, you can't just order Tuck to leave."

"Not even if I'm going to ask you to Homecoming?"

I bite my bottom lip. He's definitely not serious. He can't be. There's no way he can take me to Homecoming when just three days ago he was barely able to move. I see him fighting the urge to wince every time he has to bend to get books from his locker or sit in a chair. He told me the doctor said he should move so he doesn't get stiff, but he's not superhuman, even though I think he wants to be.

Tuck motions to the floor. "Are you gonna get on one knee? 'Cause everyone is already staring at you guys. I could take a pic on my cell and send it to the yearbook committee."

"Tuck," I say, looking up at my best friend. "Beat it."

"Okay, okay. I'll go eat by Jake Somers. Who knows, maybe I'll be inspired by Carlos and gather up the nerve to ask him to Homecoming."

Carlos shakes his head. "I can't believe I ever thought you were datin' him." When Tuck is gone, Carlos pulls up a chair next to me. I notice he holds his breath as he bends to sit down. He's doing a good job of trying to hide his pain, and I don't think anyone else notices. But I do. He reaches in his pocket and pulls out a Homecoming ticket. "Will you go to Homecoming with me?"

He's focused only on me, not caring who may or may not be watching us. I, on the other hand, feel all eyes on me as if they're darts. "Why ask now, in the middle of lunch?"

"I just bought the ticket five minutes ago. Let's just say I was anxious to make sure you'd still go with me."

Ever since he got beat up, he's been really vulnerable and insecure. It makes me nervous, because I never know if he's going to end up pushing me away again. I can get used to this Carlos, the one who isn't afraid to tell me how much he wants to be with me. But it also makes me emotional, and the more emotional I get, the harder it is to control my stuttering. "You can hardly m-m-move, Carlos. You d-d-don't have to do this."

"I want to do it." He shrugs. "Besides, I can't wait to see you in a dress and heels."

"W-w-what are you going to wear?" I ask him. "A suit and tie?"

He shoves the ticket back in his pocket. "I was thinkin' more like jeans and a T-shirt."

Jeans? T-shirt? Besides being totally inappropriate for the homecoming dance . . . "We won't match. I can't pin a boutonniere on a T-shirt."

"Boutonniere? What the hell is that, and why would I want you to pin it to me?"

"Look it up in the dictionary," I tell him.

"As long as you're at it, *amigo*," Tuck says as he creeps up behind Carlos, "you might want to look up the word 'corsage.'"

45

CARLOS

cor·sage (kôr-säzh,-säj) *n.* A small arrangement of flowers
worn on the wrist or pinned to the shoulder.

That's what the dictionary says. REACH has a small room they call a
library with a bunch of self-help books. I got lucky and found a dictionary, and the first thing I did when I got here was open it. I'm sure
Kiara would be surprised that I did look it up. So now I'm wondering
how I'm gonna find something decent to wear for Homecoming.
Equally frustrating is what to do about getting one of these corsages.

Before Berger starts our little therapy session or whatever politi-
cally correct name they've come up with to call our group of fuckups
this week, Zana and Justin come up to me.

"What happened to you?" Justin asks. "Get run over by a truck
numerous times?"

Zana, wearing another skirt so short it might get her sent home
from school, bites into one of the brownies set out for us. "Rumor has
it you got jumped by some gang members fighting for territory." She
says it softly, so Berger can't hear.

"You're both wrong." I slide into a chair and hope Berger doesn't grill me about the fight. Hell, I finally got Alex to stop grilling me. I told him to back off, and promised to tell him if Devlin or his guys contact me again.

Again, I don't believe in promises. Why are people such suckers?

When Keno walks in late, I notice immediately he's ignoring me. Normally I wouldn't even notice, but everyone else is staring at me wide-eyed as if my face has been taken over by an alien life-form. Glad they weren't with me on Sunday. I look a helluva lot better now.

Berger walks into the room, takes one look at me, and walks back out. Sure enough, after a minute Kinney and Morrisey appear.

Morrisey points to me. "Carlos, come with us."

Both Kinney and Morrisey escort me to a little room off to the side. It's like a room at a doctor's office, complete with those needle disposal boxes hangin' on the wall. There's one difference, though. A toilet is in the corner, with a small privacy curtain hanging off the ceiling.

Morrisey points at my face. "Your guardian called you out on Monday and Tuesday. He said you were in a fight. Wanna tell us about it?"

"Not really."

Kinney steps forward. "Okay, Carlos, here's the drill. From the look of you, we suspect you've been under the influence in the past week. Fights usually go along with drinking and drugs. We're giving you a urine test. Go wash your hands in the sink over there."

I want to roll my eyes and tell them that getting your ass kicked doesn't mean you're a druggie, but instead I just shrug. "Whatever," I say, after I wash my hands. "Just give me a cup so I can get it over with."

"If you test positive, you're expelled," Morrisey says as he opens one of the cabinets and pulls out a urine cup. "You know the rules."

I reach for the cup, but Kinney holds his hand up. "Let me explain what you need to do. You'll have to strip down to your underwear in our presence, then go behind that curtain and urinate in a cup."

I toss my shirt on one of the chairs, then shrug out of my jeans. I hold my arms out wide and turn around. "Happy now?" I ask them. "I don't got any contraband on me."

Morrisey hands me the cup. "You have four minutes or less. And don't flush the toilet, or we're going to do this all over again."

I go behind the curtain with the cup in hand and piss. I've got to admit, it's humiliating having Morrisey and Kinney listening to me piss, although this is just routine for them.

When I'm done and dressed, I'm instructed to wash again and head back to the group. They won't have the results until tomorrow, so I'm off the hook until then. When I walk into the room, everyone is staring at me except for Keno. They obviously know the routine and probably figured out I'd just been tested.

"Welcome back," Berger says. "You've obviously had a rough week. We missed you."

"I was kind of laid up."

"Want to tell us about it? Whatever gets shared in this room, stays in this room. Right, guys?"

Everyone nods, but I notice Keno mumble under his breath and still avoid eye contact with me. He knows somethin', and I need to find out what. Problem is getting him alone, 'cause after every meeting he books out of here.

"Let someone else talk," I tell her.

"He's dating Kiara Westford," Zana chimes in. "I saw him with his arm around her in the hallway at school. And my friend Gina saw them at lunch together and heard him ask her to Homecoming."

That's the last time I'm doin' anything in public. "Don't you ever mind your own business?" I ask Zana. "Seriously, don't you have anythin' better to do than gossip with your stupid friends?"

"Fuck you, Carlos."

"Enough. Zana, we don't talk like that in here. I won't tolerate profanity. I'm giving you a warning." Berger takes her pen and writes shit down in her notebook. "Carlos, tell me about Homecoming."

"There's nothin' to tell. I'm goin' with a girl, that's all."

"Is she someone special?"

I look over at Keno. If he knows Devlin's crew, he might give them info. Is Berger that naive to believe what's said in our little group therapy sessions is actually gonna stay in our group therapy sessions? As soon as we're out of here, I guarantee Zana is on her cell sharing with her stupid friends every bit of info she can squeeze out of us.

"Kiara and I are . . . complicated," I tell the group.

Complicated. That seems to be the theme of my life lately. The rest of the group session is concentrated on Carmela, who complains that her dad is so old-fashioned he's forbidden her to schedule a trip to California with friends for winter break. Carmela should have parents like the Westfords, who believe everyone should set their own path and make their own mistakes (until you get beat up, then they're all over you and won't leave you alone). They're the opposite of Carmela's parents.

When we're let out of REACH, I follow Keno as he leaves the building. "Keno," I call to him, but he keeps walking. I curse under my breath, then jog to catch up with him before he gets into his car. "What's your fuckin' problem?"

"I don't got one. Now get out of my way."

I stay between him and his car. "You work for Devlin, don't you?"

Keno looks to his right and left, as if he suspects someone's watchin' us talk. "Get the hell away from me."

"No way, man. You know somethin'—that means you and me are best friends. I'm gonna ride your ass until you give up any info you have on me or Devlin."

"You're a *pendejo*."

"I've been called worse, man. Don't test me."

He looks a little nervous. "Then get in the car, before someone sees us."

"The last time someone told me to do that, I got my ass kicked by five *pendejos*."

"Just do it. Or we're not talkin'."

I have the urge to jump through the window, but then realize only Kiara's car has a stuck door. Keno drives out of the lot. Alex is waiting for me at McConnell's. I have no doubt he'll end up sending the cavalry if I'm not there, so I call him.

"Where are you?" my brother asks.

"With a . . . friend." He's not really a friend, but there's no need to send up a red flag. "I'll meet you later," I say, then hang up before he can give me any shit.

Keno doesn't say anythin' until he parks at a small apartment complex out of town. "Follow me," he says, then leads me into the building.

Inside, he greets his ma and sisters in Spanish. He introduces me, then we head to the back of the apartment. His small bedroom feels oddly familiar. I could probably spot a Mexican teen's bedroom from a mile away. The creamy white walls have family photos pushpinned to the wall. The Mexican flag attached to the wall and the green, white, and red stickers on the desk gives me a sense of comfort, even though I know I have to be on alert around Keno. I'm just not sure what his game is.

Keno pulls out a pack of cigarettes. "Want a smoke?"

"No." Never was my thing, even though I was brought up by a bunch of smokers. *Mi'amá* smokes, and so did Alex until he started dating the beauty queen. Right about now if he offered me a Vicodin or two I'd probably take it. I've pretty much been in bed since Sunday night and my body is still stiff.

Keno shrugs and lights up. "Morrisey gave you a drug test today, huh?"

I guess we're gonna bullshit around before we get to the real reason he brought me here. "Yep."

"Think you'll pass?"

"I'm not worried." I lean on the window ledge and watch as Keno sits in his desk chair and blows out smoke. The guy doesn't look like he has a care in the world, and right about now I'm jealous.

"Berger just about had a coronary when she saw you today."

"You can speak in Spanish to me, you know."

"Yeah, well, if I speak Spanish my ma will know what I'm sayin'. It's better when she's clueless."

I nod. It's always better when parents are clueless. Unfortunately, I had to call my uncle Julio yesterday and give him a heads-up on what's been goin' on. He promised he would make sure Luis and *mi'amá* had protection, and would try not to alarm them unnecessarily. He wasn't too happy with me for gettin' messed up with Devlin, but he pretty much expects me to be a fuckup, so he wasn't surprised.

Makes me want to prove I'm not totally useless, but that's not likely to happen. Being a fuckup is what I've done best my entire life. It's comforting to know that Kiara and her parents believe everyone can wipe the slate clean at any point.

"So you're datin' that Kiara chick, huh?" He blows out smoke. "Is she hot?"

"Smokin'," I say, knowing that Keno has no clue who she is since he doesn't go to Flatiron. Thoughts of Kiara in her DON'T BE A WIENER, CLIMB A 14'ER shirt run through my head. I've got to admit, Kiara's not the type I'm usually attracted to, and I'm certain Keno wouldn't be attracted to her, but lately I can't think of anything sexier than a girl who knows how to solder wires together and bake stupid-ass cookie magnets. I need to stop thinkin' about her so much, but I don't want to. Not yet. Maybe after Homecoming. Besides, I have to keep her close to protect her from Rodriguez and Devlin's guys.

Speaking of Devlin . . . "No more fuckin' around, Keno. Tell me what you know."

"I know you're part of the Devlin crew. It's all around—"

"All around where?"

"The Six Point *Renegados*, otherwise known as R6." He pulls up his shirt and shows off a black six-point star with a big blue *R* in the middle of it. "You're in deep shit, *ese*. Devlin is crazy, and the R6 don't like him closin' in on our territory. The R6 controlled things around here until Devlin messed it all up. A war is about to go down, and Devlin is recruitin' guys who know how to fight. All he's got now is a bunch of loser kids as bag boys who smoke 'bout as much as they sell. He needs warriors. Carlos, one look at you and anyone can see you're a warrior, a *guerrero*."

"He told me he wanted me to be his bag boy."

"Don't believe it. He wants you to be whatever he wants, whenever he wants. If he's got shipments from Mexico, he wants Mexicans in the mix. He knows we don't trust *gringos*. If he wants a soldier to fight a street battle, he's got you in his back pocket."

Keno is watching me, gauging my reaction to that news. Thing is, I pretty much knew it all along except for the R6 info. Great, I've been recruited for a drug war that has nothing to do with anything except money.

"Why are you telling me this?" I ask him. "What's in it for you?"

Keno leans forward, takes a drag, and blows smoke out in one long stream. He looks up at me, all serious. "I'm gettin' out."

"Out?"

"*Sí*. Out. Like disappearin', where nobody can find me. I'm sick of the same ol' *mierda*, Carlos. Hell, maybe the REACH bullshit is sinkin' in. Every time Berger says we're in charge of our futures, I think *lady, you've got no clue*. But what if I did have control over my future, Carlos? What if I left and started over?"

"And did what?"

He laughs. "Whatever I want, man. Shit, maybe I could get a job and somehow, someday, get my GED and go to college. Maybe get married and have a couple of kids who don't remember their dad bein' a gangbanger. I've always wanted to be a judge. You know, change the system and make it work so teens wouldn't end up stuck like me. I wrote it down on Kinney's REACH goal sheet. You probably think it's a stupid goal to be a judge after I got arrested for drug possession—"

"It's not stupid," I say, interrupting him. "I think it's cool."

"Really?" He waves the smoke away, and for the first time I sense his anticipation and fear wrapped together in one. "Wanna come with? I'm leavin' at the end of the month, on Halloween."

"That's three weeks away." Leaving Colorado would mean ditching Devlin and givin' my brother and the Westfords their normal lives back. They wouldn't have to deal with me or my bullshit. And Kiara could get on with her life, a life that was going to be without me anyway. Soon she'll realize the reality—I've got less than nothing to offer her. The last thing I need is to watch her date other guys. If she gets back with Michael I'll go nuts. I'd be delusional to think this thing we have could be permanent.

I nod to Keno. "You're right, I have to leave. But I've got to go back to Mexico first and make sure my family is safe. After I leave here, they're the only thing I have left."

46

Kiara

When I told my mom I was going to the homecoming dance with Carlos, she wasn't surprised. She said she'd take me to the mall to find a dress on Friday. It took me a while, but I finally found a long, black satin sleeveless dress at a vintage store. It hugs every curve in my body. It's totally out of my comfort zone to wear something so tight and with a huge slit down the side, but when I put it on it makes me feel pretty and confident. It reminds me of Audrey Hepburn in *Breakfast at Tiffany's*.

When I brought home the dress, I quickly snuck up to my room and hung it in my closet. I don't want Carlos to see it until I put it on for the dance.

Saturday morning the entire family, including Carlos, gets up and goes to the football game. Flatiron wins 21–13, so everyone is pumped and excited. After the game, Carlos says he has stuff to do before the dance. I go with my mom to buy shoes.

She picks up a pair of black flats with little buckles on the sides. "How about these? They look comfy."

I shake my head. "I'm not looking for comfy."

I walk around the store, making sure to pass up any heels that

Carlos would consider "granny" width. I set my sights on black satin pumps with a three-and-a-half-inch skinny heel and a vintage-looking ankle clasp. They're perfect. I don't know if I'll be able to walk in them, but they'll match my dress and look good. "How about these?" I ask my mom.

Her eyes go wide. "You sure? They'll make you taller than your father."

My mom doesn't own a pair of pumps with two-inch heels, let alone any that are over three inches.

"I love them," I tell her.

"Then try them on. It's for your special day."

Fifteen minutes later I walk out with the shoes, excited to have found the perfect pair to go with the perfect dress. I want tonight to be perfect, too. I hope Carlos isn't feeling pressured, even though I pretty much coerced him into asking me. Hopefully we can have fun and forget what happened last weekend. I don't expect us to do much dancing since he's still healing, but that's okay. I'll be happy just being there with him, whether or not we're a real couple.

"We have to pick up the boutonniere," my mom says as we get in the car.

"I already picked it up this morning."

"Good. I've got my camera ready. Dad's got the camcorder charging . . . we're all set. We'll send the pictures to Carlos's mother on Monday, so she doesn't feel like she missed out."

After we get home, I stay in my room with the door closed, practicing how to walk in my new shoes. I feel like I'm lurching forward every time I take a step. It takes me an hour before I get the hang of it. Tuck comes over and makes me more nervous when he brings me a box full of gifts for the evening.

"Open it," Tuck says, handing me the box.

I lift open the top and peek inside. I pull out a black lace garter. "You don't wear a garter for Homecoming."

"This one is specially made for Homecoming. Look, it's got a little fake-gold football charm hanging off it." I toss it on my bed, then pull out the next item. Rose-tinted lip gloss.

Tuck shrugs as I open it. "Personally it grosses me out, but I hear straight guys like it when girls have shiny lips. There's some eyeliner and mascara in there, too. The lady at the store said they're the best ones to get."

While I'm taking out each item, I stop and look at Tuck. "Why did you buy me all this stuff?"

He shrugs. "I just . . . didn't want you to miss out. Whether you want to admit it to me or not, you like him. I know I give the guy a hard time, but maybe you see something in him the rest of us don't see."

Tuck is the most awesome best friend. "You're so sweet," I say, just as I'm emptying out the box of breath mints and . . . two condoms. I hold them up. "You didn't buy me condoms."

"You're right, I didn't. I took them from the health-service office at school. They just hand 'em out if you want one . . . or two. You might want to ask him if he's allergic to latex, though. If he is, you're SOL."

I think about having sex with Carlos and my face feels hot. "I'm not planning on having sex tonight." I toss the square packages on the bed, but Tuck picks them back up.

"That's why you need the condoms, stupid. If you're not planning on it and it happens, you won't be prepared and then you'll end up pregnant or diseased. Do me a favor and stick 'em in your purse or shove 'em inside your Spanx."

I wrap my arms around Tuck and kiss him on the cheek. "I love you for caring about me so much. I'm sorry Jake said no when you asked him to Homecoming."

Tuck laughs. "I didn't tell you the latest."

"What's the latest?"

"Jake called about an hour ago. He doesn't want to go to Homecoming . . . but he wants to hang out tonight."

"That's great. I thought he was straight, by the way."

"What's wrong with you? For someone who's best friends with a homo, you've got no gaydar. Jake Somers is as gay as I am, no question about it. I've got to be honest, Kiara. I'm so nervous and anxious and excited I hope I don't screw this up. I've secretly liked Jake for a while now." Tuck walks over to my desk drawer and takes out the Rules of Attraction notebook. He tears out each page and rips it into little pieces.

"What are you d-d-doing?"

"Ripping up my Rules of Attraction. I've figured something out."

"What?"

Tuck tosses the ripped paper in my garbage. "There are no rules to attraction. Jake is nothing like who I wanted. He doesn't have the same interests I have, he hates Ultimate, and he reads and analyzes poetry in his spare time just for fun. I can't stop thinking about him. He said he wants to hang out tonight. What does *hanging out* mean?"

"I'm still trying to figure that one out myself." I reach for one of the condom packages and toss it to him. "You better take one, just in case."

47

CARLOS

"I told you one day you'd call me," Brittany says as we walk through the mall.

I called her yesterday and asked her to meet me after the Flatiron football game today. I need her help, because she's the only one I know who's hoity-toity enough to be an expert on all this Homecoming crap.

"Don't brag about it," I tell her. "I'm surprised Alex didn't insist on comin' with us. You two are joined at the hip."

She keeps her concentration on the racks of suits, picking out some for me to try on. "Let's not talk about Alex."

"Why not, did you two have a fight?" I joke, not believin' for a minute my brother would argue with his girlfriend.

Brittany blinks a couple of times, as if holding back tears. "Actually, we broke up yesterday."

"You're not serious."

"I'm dead serious, and I don't want to talk about it. Go try on those suits before I start bawling in the middle of the store. It won't be pretty." She shoves the suits at me and shoos me off to the dressing room. When I look back, she's taken a tissue out of her purse and is wiping her eyes with it.

What the hell? No wonder my brother hasn't wanted to talk to me much and hasn't drilled me about Devlin since Sunday night. What did he do to screw things up with Brittany, the girl he said was responsible for changing his life?

Thanks to Devlin's envelope full of cash, I buy the suit Brittany says makes me look like a *GQ* model. Then we pick up the corsage I ordered yesterday when I found a florist who would create one for Kiara on short notice. When we're back in the car, I figure it's safe to ask Brittany about the supposed breakup. If she cries now, nobody will see she's got mascara runnin' down her face.

I can't hold it in any longer. My curiosity is killin' me. "You and my brother are sickeningly perfect together, so what's the problem?"

"Ask your brother."

"I don't happen to be with him right now, I'm with you. Unless you want me to call him . . ." I pull out the cell from my pocket.

"No!" she cries. "Don't you dare call him. I don't want to see him, hear him, or have anything to do with him right now."

Oh, crap, this is serious. She's not foolin' around, so I better think of something quick. "Drive me to the body shop. I'm borrowin' Alex's new car tonight."

"You can use my car," she says, not batting an eye.

Oh, hell. I've got to come up with an excuse as to why I need my brother's new car instead of a hot Beemer convertible. "Kiara likes vintage cars. She'll be disappointed if I come in a Beemer when she's expectin' a Monte Carlo. She's not normal, you know. And she gets upset easily. I wouldn't want to make her cry and stutter on Homecoming."

"Are you going to feed me more bullshit until I drop you at McConnell's?"

"Pretty much."

At a stoplight, Brittany sighs and takes a deep breath. "Fine, I'll take you. But don't expect me to get out of the car or talk to *him*."

"But if I'm takin' *his* car, *he'll* need a ride home. Can you take him, so I can get ready for the dance?" My brother and Brittany together make me nauseous, but the thought of them apart and miserable is just . . . *no está bien*, not good. I give them a hard time, but deep down I envy their relationship. When they're together, the world could fall apart around them and they'd never notice or care as long as they have each other.

"Don't push it, Carlos," Brittany says. "I'm dropping you off, then leaving. But I'll give you a piece of advice for tonight, and then I'll shut up. Rein in your attitude and ego tonight and treat Kiara like you would a princess. Make her feel special."

"You think I've got a big ego and an attitude problem?" I ask her.

She lets out a short laugh. "I don't *think* you do, Carlos. I *know* it. Unfortunately, it's a Fuentes flaw."

"I'd call it an asset. It's what makes us Fuentes brothers irresistible."

"Yeah, whatever," she says. "It's what ruins your relationships. If you want Kiara to have great memories of tonight, just remember what I said and rein it in."

"Did I ever tell you that Alex loves you so much he got your name tattooed all over his body? Hell, he even got your name branded into the back of his neck."

"They say 'LB,' Carlos. The initials for Latino Blood."

"No, no, no. You've got it all wrong. He wants everyone to think that, but in reality it means Lover of Brittany. LB, get it?"

"Nice try, Carlos. Totally not true, but a nice try nonetheless."

True to her word, Brittany drops me off at the shop and speeds away. Her tires screech on the parking lot, something I'm sure my brother taught her to do. It's just more proof they should be together.

In the shop, my brother has his head under the hood of a Cadillac. I wonder if he's oblivious that his recent ex-girlfriend/love of his life just sped away.

"What are you doin' here?" Alex asks me as he wipes his hands on a shop cloth. "I thought you were half dead."

"You'd be surprised how far away half dead is from fully dead, Alex. Actually I feel like shit, but am doin' a helluva good job fakin' it."

"Uh-huh." I notice he's got a black bandanna on, something I haven't seen him wear since he was in the Latino Blood. It's not a good sign. He looks like a rebel, too much like me. I know firsthand when you take the time to look like a rebel, actin' like one isn't far behind. "I've got a bunch of work to do, and you've got a dance to get to, so if you don't mind—"

"Why did you break up with Brittany?"

"Is that what she told you?" Alex says, his eyebrows crinkling in frustration and anger. Man, he's pissed right now. From the ragged look of him, I don't think he's slept well lately.

"Keep your pants on, bro," I tell him. "She didn't say anythin'. She told me to ask you what happened."

"We broke up. You were right, Carlos. Brit and I are too different. We come from different worlds and it was never gonna work out."

When he ducks his head under the hood again, I pull him back. *"Usted es estupido."*

"You callin' me stupid? I'm not the one who *unintentionally* got jumped in to a gang last Sunday." He shakes his head. "Talk about stupid."

"I'll tell you what, Alex. You tell me why you and the beauty queen broke up, and I'll tell you everythin' I know 'bout Devlin."

Alex sighs, the action deflating his anger a bit. I know he wants to protect me and our family above all else. He knows next week I'm gonna be called to action by Devlin. He can't resist being involved in trying to help get me out of this.

"Her parents are comin' to town to visit her sister Shelley in two weeks," Alex says. "She wants to tell them we've been secretly dating seriously since we started college. They know how it ended between us back in Chicago. I was a total asshole to her, then I left." He presses his palms to his eyes and moans. "Look at me, Carlos. I'm still the same guy they wouldn't let her date back in Chicago. They think I'm the scum of the earth, and they're probably right. Brittany wants me to fuckin' go to dinner with them, as if they'll just accept that the girl they groomed to be a princess ended up with the guy they'll always see as the poor, dirty Mexican from the slums."

I can't believe it. My own brother, the one who bravely fought his own gang and wasn't afraid to get shot for it, is shittin' in his pants at the prospect of standing up for himself and their relationship in front of Brittany's parents. "You're afraid," I tell him.

"Am not. I just don't need the bullshit."

The bullshit is that my brother is scared. He's afraid of Brittany agreeing with her parents once and for all and dumping his ass. Alex can't take her rejection, so he's pushing her away and rejecting her before she can do it to him. I know, because that's the story of my own life.

"Brittany wants to stick up for your relationship," I say as I eye Alex's vintage Monte Carlo at the corner of the shop. "Why don't you? Because you're a coward, bro. Have a little faith in your *novia*. If you don't, you'll risk losin' her for good."

"Her parents will never think I'm good enough for her. I'll always feel like the lower-class *pendejo* who took advantage of their daughter."

I'm lucky Kiara's parents are the opposite. They're content when their kids are happy, no matter what. They try and influence us, but they don't judge anyone. At first I thought it was an act, that nobody could just accept me even when I try to push them away. I think the Westfords really do accept people for who they are, flaws and all.

"If you think you're the lower-class *pendejo*, then you are. Problem is, Brittany doesn't see different social classes or think of your bank account when she's with you. It's kind of sickenin', but she actually loves you no matter what. Maybe you guys *should* break up, 'cause she deserves a dude who'll stick up for his relationship at all costs."

"Fuck you," Alex says. "You don't know crap about relationships. Since when have you even had one?"

"I'm in one now."

"It's fake. Even Kiara admitted it."

"Yeah, well, it's better than what you've got, which is nothin'." I walk over to the blue Monte Carlo. "Just so you know, I was hopin' to borrow your car tonight. Not for me, but for Kiara. I know you think she's cool, and I can't very well use her car to take her on an official date."

"I was plannin' on headin' over to the Westfords' before the dance. They invited me."

"Save yourself the trouble," I say.

"Fine. But bring it back after the dance, 'cause I was plannin' on workin' on it tomorrow." After I toss the suit and corsage in the backseat, Alex says, "I thought you hated me and Brittany together."

"I just like to give you shit, Alex. That's what younger brothers are for, aren't they?" I shrug. "She might not be a *chica Mexicana*, but she's the best your ass is ever gonna get. Might as well seal the deal and marry the girl."

"With what, half a degree and a vintage car to offer?"

I shrug. "If that's all you got, I'm sure she'll take it. Hell, it's a helluva lot more than I got, and more than our parents had when they got married. Even worse, 'cause *mi'amá* was pregnant with your ugly ass."

"Speakin' of ugly, have you looked in the mirror lately?"

"Yeah. It's funny, Alex. Even with a busted lip and black eye, I'm still better lookin' than you."

"Yeah, right. Wait," Alex says. "You still never told me about Devlin."

"Oh, yeah." I start the car and rev the engine. "I'll tell you tomorrow. Maybe."

When I get to the Westfords', Brandon is in my room sitting on my bed with his his arms crossed. The kid is doing his best to put on a mean face that might actually intimidate someone in ten or so years.

"What's up, *cachorro*?"

"I'm mad at you."

Man, I'm gettin' heat from all sides today. "Take a number and get in line, kid."

He huffs like a car with a bad exhaust. "You said we were partners in crime. That if I did something, you wouldn't tattle. And if you did something, I wouldn't tattle."

"So?"

"You're a tattletale. Now Daddy won't let me play games on the computer unless he's watching, like I'm a baby. It's all your fault."

"Sorry. Life isn't fair."

"Why not?"

If life was fair, my father wouldn't have died when I was four. If life was fair, I wouldn't have to worry about Devlin. If life was fair, I'd have a real chance with Kiara. Life pretty much sucks. "Don't know. But if you figure it out, *cachorro*, let me know."

I expect him to throw a fit, but he doesn't. He jumps off my bed and heads for the door. "I'm still mad at you."

"You'll get over it. Now beat it. I've got to take a shower and get ready. I'm runnin' late."

"I'll get over it faster and leave you alone if you can sneak me some candy from the cabinet above the refrigerator. It's my mom's secret hiding place." He motions for me to bend down so he can tell me a secret. "She keeps *unhealthy* snacks in it," he whispers. "You know, the *good* kind." The more he talks about it, the more excited he gets.

Damn. I have less than an hour before I have to be Kiara's date, but I don't want to let the kid down. "All right, Racer. You ready to go on a secret mission to find the treasure?"

Brandon rubs his hands together, obviously pleased with himself for manipulating me. The kid does have talent in the persuasion department, I'll give him that much.

"Follow me." I peek my head out the door, then wave him over. I hide a laugh as he tiptoes toward me. Sometimes this kid acts like a six-year-old, and sometimes he acts like someone who has more sense than some adults I know.

We step down the stairs in silence. Before we reach the kitchen, someone walks out of Westford's office. It's Kiara, wearing a long black dress that hugs her delicious curves from her chest to her thighs.

Her hair is not only flowing down the front of her chest, the ends have been carefully and perfectly curled. One of her long, lean legs peeks out from the insanely sexy slit on the side.

I'm stunned.

I'm speechless.

My eyes roam over her, enjoying the view. I know I'll remember this moment for the rest of my life. When I look down at her sexy open-toe pumps with a higher heel than I ever imagined her wearing, my heart skips a beat. I'm afraid to blink for fear she's a figment of my imagination and will disappear.

"W-w-well, w-w-what d-d-do you think?"

Brandon gives her a loud, "Shh," and puts a finger over his mouth. "We're on a secret mission," he whispers loudly, oblivious that his sister has transformed into a goddess. "Don't tell Mom or Dad."

"I won't," she whispers. "What are you on a mission for?"

"Candy. The *unhealthy* kind. Come on!"

I look back at Kiara, wishing we were alone right now. *Really* wishing we were alone right now. "Brandon, go check where your dad is so we know the coast is clear," I tell him. I need a few minutes alone with his sister.

"Okay," he says, slithering out of the hall. "Be right back."

I've got less than a minute alone with her. I shove my hands in my pockets, to prevent me from showing my nervous, shaking hands. She rewards me with a half smile, then looks at the ground.

I look up at the ceiling, wishing I could get some advice, or at least a sign from my dad. I take another look at Kiara. Oh, man. She's staring right at me now, waiting for me to say something. Before I can come up with a meaningful or funny remark, Brandon comes back. "He's in his den. Let's do it before he catches us."

I choked. I've got to get Brandon out of here. We all head for the kitchen. I reach up and open the small cabinet door above the refrigerator. Sure enough, there's a big basket filled with contraband.

Brandon tugs on the bottom of my shirt. "Show me, show me."

I put the basket on the table. Brandon steps on a kitchen chair and checks out the loot. "Here," he says, shoving a chocolate bar in my hand. "They have nuts. I don't like nuts."

In the end, Brandon swipes one milk chocolate bar and two pieces of licorice. Satisfied with his treasure, he hops off the chair.

I put the basket back in the secret hiding place that everyone knows about. When I turn back around, Brandon is already breaking off a piece of chocolate and shoving it in his mouth.

"Kiara, why do you look like a girl?" Brandon asks with a mouthful of chocolate.

"I'm going on a date. With Carlos."

"Are you gonna French-kiss him?"

Kiara gives him a scolding look. "Brandon! That's totally not an appropriate thing to ask. Who told you about that?"

"The fourth graders on the bus."

"What did the fourth graders say it was?"

He gives her an exasperated look. "You know . . ."

"Tell me," she says. "Maybe I don't know."

I have firsthand knowledge that she does know what French kissing is, but I'm not giving her secret away.

"It's when you lick the other person's tongue," he whispers.

Damn, the kid knows more than I did at his age. First he's a cyber drug dealer, now he's talking about French kissing. Kiara looks to me, but I hold my hands up. While I'd like nothing better than to French-kiss her right now, I can wait until later. "He's not my kid."

"You can get a lot of germs that way," he says as he munches away and contemplates the consequences of French kissing.

"Absolutely," Kiara agrees. "Right, Carlos?"

"Right. Germs. Lots of 'em." I don't tell him that some girls' germs are worth getting.

"I'm never gonna do it," he declares.

"Nobody's ever gonna want to do it with you, *cachorro*, if you don't wipe your mouth after you eat chocolate. You're disgustin'."

As Kiara reaches for a napkin and wipes Brandon's face, he looks up at her curiously. "You never answered my question. Are you and Carlos going to French-kiss?"

48

Kiara

"Brandon, stop asking that or I'm telling Mom you just snuck chocolate without her permission." I lean over and kiss his now-clean cheek. "But I still love you."

"Meanie," Brandon says, but I know he isn't upset, because he bounces out of the kitchen with a spring in his step.

We're alone at last. Carlos comes up from behind me and gently swipes my hair to the side, exposing my neck. "*Eres hermosa*," he whispers into my ear. Just the sound of the Spanish words makes my insides feel like Jell-O.

I twirl around and face him. "Thanks. I needed to hear that."

"I should go take a shower and get dressed, but I don't want to stop lookin' at you."

I push him away from me, even though I'm actually giddy because he can't stop staring. "Go. I'm not missing my first high school dance."

Forty-five minutes later, I'm still standing in heels afraid to sit down and wrinkle my dress. My mom insisted on painting my fingernails pink, so I resist picking at them even though I can't help fidgeting.

We're in the backyard, where my mom and dad are snapping picture after picture of me standing next to the house, next to a potted plant, next to my car, with Brandon, and the fence and . . .

Carlos opens the sliding glass door and steps onto the patio. A black suit and white button-down shirt have replaced his ever-present T-shirt and ripped jeans. Just looking at him all dressed up *for me* makes my heart beat faster and my tongue feel thick and heavy. Especially when I see him holding a corsage in his hand.

"Oh, you look so handsome. You're sweet to take Kiara to Homecoming," my mom says. "She's always wanted to go."

"It's not a problem," Carlos says.

I don't interrupt and tell my mom that he asked me because we shook on it. I'm pretty sure if we hadn't made a deal we wouldn't be standing here in the nicest clothes we own.

"Here," Carlos says, holding out the corsage full of purple-and-white flowers with yellow centers.

"Put it on her, Carlos," my mom says excitedly as she holds up her camera.

My dad makes my mom put the camera down. "Colleen, let's go inside. I think we should give them a few minutes alone."

When my parents give us privacy, Carlos slips the corsage on my wrist. "I know it doesn't match your dress," he says shyly. "And it's not roses like I'm sure you were expectin'. They're Mexican asters. Every time you look at it tonight, I wanted it to remind you of me."

"They're p-p-perfect," I say, bringing the purple and white flowers to my nose so I can breathe in their sweet scent.

On the patio table is the boutonniere I bought him. It's a simple white rose with green leaves. I pick it up and hold it out to him. "I'm supposed to p-p-pin it to your lapel."

He moves closer. My hands are shaking as I take the big pin and try to put it on right. "Here, I'll just do it," he says as he watches me struggle to push the pin through the green florist tape on the bottom of the boutonniere. Our fingers touch and I can hardly breathe.

After we suffer through a few pictures with my parents, clouds start forming overhead. "It's supposed to rain tonight," my mom says, then orders me to bring my taupe raincoat that doesn't match my dress but repels water. Carlos seems excited to drive me in Alex's car. He knew I'd think it was cool that we have matching cars.

We drive up to the school parking lot ten minutes later, which is packed. But before we get to the doors, out of nowhere Nick Glass and two other big guys block our path. It's obvious they're not here to dance . . . they're here to cause trouble.

I grab on to Carlos's arm, scared that he'll get into another fight.

"It's okay," he assures me softly. "Trust me, *chica.*"

"This is my territory," Nick says, stepping closer. "I'm not sharin' it."

"I don't want it," Carlos tells him.

"What's the problem here?" Ram says, walking up to us with a girl who I don't recognize. Ram and Carlos have become friends in school, and it's nice to know someone is willing to stick his neck out for Carlos even though it's Homecoming.

"We're cool, right, Nick?" Carlos asks.

Nick looks from Carlos to Ram and back. Nick's friends aren't from Flatiron High. They look like guys who aren't afraid to fight, but in the end Nick steps back and lets us through.

Carlos grabs my hand and pushes past them without fear.

"If you need me, Carlos, I'm here," Ram tells him as we reach the front door to the school.

"Same to you, man," Carlos responds, then squeezes my hand. "If you want to go somewhere else, Kiara, I'm totally game."

I shake my head. "A deal's a deal. I want the photographer to take a picture, so I can pin it to my corkboard over my desk as a reminder of my first school dance. Just promise me, no fights."

"Okay, *chica*. But after the picture, if you want to go somewhere else, just let me know."

"Where would we go?" I ask him.

He looks around at the streamers and the posters and the students yelling and dancing to the loud music. He pulls me closer. "Somewhere quiet, where we can be alone. I don't really feel like sharin' you tonight."

The thing is, I don't feel like sharing him, either.

The photographer has us pose for pictures before we enter the gymnasium. Actually, he poses us, treating us like mannequins in a department store.

"Want a drink?" Carlos asks, his arm around my waist pulling me close so I can hear him over the loud, pounding music.

I shake my head, taking in the scene. Most of the girls are wearing really short dresses with frilly skirts that fly up when they twirl and dance. I look out of place in my long, black, form-fitting vintage dress.

"Food?" he asks. "There's pizza."

"Not yet." I watch the other students dancing. Most of them are dancing in groups, jumping up and down to the loud music. Madison isn't here. Lacey isn't, either. Knowing that I won't be the subject of their rude remarks tonight makes me let down my guard.

He grabs my hand and leads me to the far corner of the gymnasium. "Let's dance."

"You're not one hundred percent yet. Let's wait until there's a slow dance. I don't want you to hurt yourself."

Not listening to me, Carlos starts dancing. He doesn't act like he's in pain. In fact, he acts like he's been street dancing his entire life. The blaring music has a fast beat. Most guys I know don't have rhythm, but Carlos does. He's amazing. I want to step back and just watch him move his body to the beat.

"Show me what you got," he says at one point. He's got a mischievous gleam in his eye as he cocks an eyebrow. "I dare you, *chica*."

49

CARLOS

Kiara can dance like a pro. Man, one little dare and the girl moves to the music as if she owns it. I dance with her, our movements suddenly coming together. We're finding our own rhythm together, dancing to each song without stopping. Kiara takes me away from thoughts of Devlin and the Brittany/Alex drama that's going on.

Right in the middle of a fast song, the DJ mixes it up. A painfully slow song about love and loss echoes through the gymnasium. Kiara looks at me, unsure of how we're gonna do this.

I take her hands and wrap them around my neck. Damn, she smells great . . . like fresh raspberries you can inhale forever. When I pull her so her body is pressed up against mine, all I want to do is steal her away and never give her back. I'm trying to pretend Devlin doesn't exist and that I'm not leaving her for good at the end of the month. I want to savor today, 'cause my future is one big mess right now.

"What are you thinking about?" she asks me.

"Leavin' here," I say, telling her the truth. She doesn't know I'm actually talking about leaving Colorado, but that's okay. If she knew what my plans were, she'd probably call Alex and her parents and arrange an intervention. Hell, she'd probably invite Tuck, too, while she was at it.

With her arms still wrapped around my neck, she looks up at me. I lean down and kiss her gently on her soft, shiny lips, not caring that the teachers are watching. The entire student body has been warned about the possibility of being kicked out of the dance for PDA.

"We c-c-can't kiss," Kiara says, leaning away.

"Then let's go somewhere where we can." My hand slides down her back and rests on the curve right above her ass.

"Hey, Carlos!" Ram yells as he and his date walk up to us after we've danced and eaten and are ready to bounce. "We're gonna head out and hang at my parents' lake house. Want to come?"

I look over at my date. She nods.

"You sure?" I ask.

"Yeah."

It's raining, so we hurry to the car. I follow Ram and a few other cars out of the parking lot. A half hour later we all turn off the main road and head up a long driveway to a small house on a private lake.

"You sure you're okay with us bein' here?" I ask her. She hasn't said much since we left the dance.

"Yeah. I d-d-don't want the night to be over."

Me either. After tonight, reality will start to set in. We follow three other couples inside the house, running because now it's pouring. It's not a big house, but it's got huge windows with lake views. I'm sure if it wasn't dark outside we'd actually be able to see the lake. Now all we see is the rain pelting the windows.

Ram has the refrigerator stocked with cans of beer. "It's all ours," Ram says as he tosses one to each person. "And there's more in the garage, if we want it."

Kiara is holding the can of beer Ram tossed her. It's still unopened. "Are you going to drink?" she asks me.

"Maybe."

She holds out her hand. "Then give me the keys. I don't want you driving if you're drinking," she says softly so the other couples can't hear.

"By the way," Ram yells out, "everyone who drinks here needs to crash here. House rules."

I look around. It seems as if the other couples are ready to shack up. "Wait here," I tell Kiara, then run outside to the car and pull out the cell that I stashed on the dash. Five minutes later, I come back in the house. Despite her self-proclaimed shyness, Kiara is doing just fine. Ram has her talking about the benefits of diesel fuel and I'm tempted to say, "That's my girl." But she's not really my girl. At least, she won't be soon. Tonight she is, though.

I pull Kiara aside. "We're crashin' here," I tell her. "I just called your parents. They said it was okay."

"How did you get them to agree to us sleeping out?"

"I told them we'd been drinkin'. Ends up they'd rather have us crash here than drive drunk."

"But I wasn't planning on drinking at all."

I flash her a mischievous grin. "What they don't know won't kill them, *chica*."

While the rest of the party finds their own private places to crash for the night, I grab a bunch of blankets Ram pulled out of the closet and lead Kiara outside.

"Where are we going?" she asks.

"I saw a dock by the lake. I know it's cold out, and rainin' . . . but it's covered and private." I take off my suit jacket and give it to her. "Here."

She slides her arms through the holes and holds it closed. I like her wearing my jacket, as if somehow she's mine and nobody else's.

"Wait!" Kiara says, grabbing me by the wrist. "Give me your keys."

Oh, hell. This is it. This is where she tells me that she's not mine—and that she's still in love with Michael and wants to leave. Or that she just wanted me to take her to Homecoming and I got the wrong idea. While I had only one beer and am still painfully sober, I don't want to take her back home. I want this night to last as long as possible.

"I need my purse," she explains. "I left it in the car."

Oh. Her purse. I stand in the rain, looking dumbfounded at the girl who makes me want to hold on to her and never let go, as if she's my security blanket. My emotions are scaring the hell out of me. On the way to the dock we stop off at the car. She pulls out her purse and clutches it while we walk through the grass.

"My heels are sinking," she tells me.

I hand her the blankets and pick her up.

"Don't drop me," she says, trying to juggle the blankets on her lap while holding on to my neck for dear life.

"Trust me." That's the second time tonight I told her to trust me. Truth is that she shouldn't, because after tonight all bets are off. But I don't want to think about tomorrow. Tonight needs to last me a lifetime. Tonight . . . tonight she can trust me, and I can trust her.

I set her down on the covered dock. It's dark, and the black clouds are covering the light of the moon. The top blanket is wet, so I'm glad

I grabbed a bunch. I take them from her and set the dry blankets on the wood dock, giving us a padded place to sleep.

I just don't know if sleep is all we'll be doing tonight. "Kiara?" I say.

"Y-y-yeah?" she says, her word echoing in the darkness.

"Come lie with me."

50

Kiara

My heart flutters and I get a flush of excitement at his words. "It's d-d-dark. I can't see anything."

"Follow my voice, *chica*. I won't let you fall."

I reach out in the darkness as if I'm blind, all the while shivering from nervousness or the cold rain. I can't tell which one is making me shake more. When our hands connect through the black night, he guides me to the blankets. I place my purse with the condom in it beside the blanket, then awkwardly hitch up my dress so I can sit in front of him.

He wraps his strong, muscular arms around me. "You're shakin'," he says, pulling me back against his chest.

"I c-c-can't help it."

"Are you cold? I can find more blankets if you—"

"No, don't leave. S-s-stay with me." I turn so my arms are wrapped around his waist. I'm nuzzling into his body heat, not letting him go. "I'm just n-n-nervous."

He strokes my hair, now wet from the rain. "Me, too."

"Carlos?"

"Yeah?"

Since I can't see him, I reach up and feel his clean-shaven jaw.
"Tell me something about your childhood that you remember. Something g-g-good."

It takes him a long time to respond. Doesn't he remember anything happy about his life in Chicago?

"Alex and I always got in trouble after school when my ma was workin'. Alex was supposed to be in charge of everythin', but the last thing a thirteen-year-old kid wanted to do was schoolwork right when we got home. We'd have these contests we called the Fuentes Olympics and create the most ridiculous events."

"Like what?"

"Alex had this stupid idea to cut off the tops of my mom's panty hose and put tennis balls inside each leg. He called them the Panty Discus. We'd fling them around and around like windmills, then throw 'em as hard as we could. Sometimes the farthest would win, and sometimes the highest." He chuckles. "We were such idiots we'd stick them back in my ma's drawer and think she'd never suspect it was us who mutilated them."

"Was she tough with you?"

"Let's just say my ass still hurts from that day, and it was seven years ago."

"Ouch."

"Yeah. Alex and I spent a lot of time together back then. Once I wanted to be a pirate, so I went in my ma's room, took her jewelry box, and buried it in the woods by our house. Most of it was fake jewelry and stupid free pins she had to wear at work. I came home and drew a map with a big red *X* where I'd hidden the box, then told Alex to find it."

"Did he?"

"No." He gives a short laugh. "And neither could I."

"Did your mom freak?"

"Freak is an understatement, *chica*. Every day after school I went to the woods to dig up her jewelry, but never could find it. Worst part is that her weddin' ring was in the box . . . she never wore it because after *mi papá* died she didn't want to risk losin' it."

"Oh my God. That's horrible."

"Yeah. It wasn't funny at the time, that's for sure. But one day I'll find that box, if someone else hasn't gotten to it first. Okay, your turn. What did you do to piss off the almighty Professor and the Queen Mother of Organic Teas?"

"I once hid my dad's car keys so he wouldn't go to work," I tell him.

"Not bad enough. Give me somethin' else."

"I used to pretend to be sick so I could stay home from school."

"Please, I was the champion at that. Don't you got anythin' really bad? Or have you been a Goody Two-shoes your entire life?"

"When I was mad at my parents, I used to spike their toothpaste with Tabasco sauce."

"Now that's what I'm talkin' about. Nice."

"But my parents never hit me; they don't believe in it. I got a lot of time-outs during my rebellious stage when I was twelve, though."

He laughs. "I live in a permanent rebellious stage." His fingers graze my knee and slowly move higher. When they reach the garter, he touches the lace. "What's this?"

"A garter. You're supposed to take it off and keep it as a memento. K-k-kinda like a trophy for going far sexually with a girl. It's stupid, really. And kind of d-d-degrading if I think about it too m-m-much."

"I know what it is," he says, amusement evident in his voice. "I just wanted to hear your explanation." He slides it off me slowly, his lips following the path of the garter. "I like it," he says as he slides my shoes off. The garter follows.

"Do you feel rebellious now?" I ask him.

"*Sí*. Very rebellious."

"Remember when you told me you and I were gonna get in trouble one of these days?"

"Yeah."

"I think that day is here." I reach up with shaking hands and start unbuttoning his shirt. I slide his shirt open and place slow kisses down his solid, bare chest. I move my kisses lower and lower as I open more buttons. "Want to get in trouble with me, Carlos?"

51

CARLOS

Get in trouble with her? Hell, the first minute I laid eyes on her at Flat-iron High I was in trouble. Now I'm lost in the sensation of her soft, warm lips on my skin. I let her take control of this. I'm holding back, even though my body is screamin' for more. Brittany told me to rein in my ego and attitude tonight. Problem is, I don't have a handle on either one right now.

Her wet tongue reaches out and grazes my left nipple. "Is that o-o-okay?" she asks.

No girl has ever done that to me. Hell, I don't know if I'd ever let any other girl do that to me. But this isn't just any other girl; this is Kiara. I have a feeling she could do whatever the hell she wanted right now and I'd be fine with it. "Yeah. Feels damn good, *chica*. I can't wait to return the favor."

My breathing is ragged as I try to urge the rest of my body to calm down as her mouth moves to the other side of my chest.

I need to feel her against me. I never claimed to be patient. "Hey," I say, lifting her chin. I kiss her softly, wanting nothing more than to have her lying beside me right now. "It's my turn."

I slide my jacket off her shoulders and toss it out of our way. My fingers move up the zipper on her back, stopping when I reach the top. When I pull the slide lower and lower, exposing skin I wish I could see but can only imagine, Kiara unbuttons my pants and reaches inside to feel me over my shorts.

"What are you doin'?" I ask her.

"Sorry," she says quickly, pulling her hand back. "I n-n-needed to do s-s-something with my hands and wanted to know if I was t-t-turning you on."

I laugh. Leave it to Kiara to go searchin' in my pants for answers. "Did you feel the evidence?" I ask, amused.

"Yes," she whispers. "You're turned on."

"Just so you know . . ." I take her hand and place it over me again. "Just thinkin' about you makes me hard."

I can sense her smile, even though I can't see it. I imagine her eyelashes are framing her chameleon eyes, which have probably turned a light shade of gray.

I slide her dress down her shoulders and don't stop until it's completely off her.

"Your turn," she whispers, pulling away as I reach out to touch her.

I shrug out of everythin' but my underwear, then pull her under the covers with me. "You cold?" I ask, noticing a slight shake of her hands when she reaches up and memorizes my face with her fingers.

"No."

I lean over her and kiss her. "Give me your germs," I tell her, making fun of Brandon's take on French kissing.

"Only if you'll give me yours," she says against my lips. She opens her mouth to me and we slide our tongues together, the slippery wetness making me even harder—if that was even possible.

We move together, our bodies grinding against each other for what seems like an eternity. I reach inside her panties, feeling her at the same time her hands are wrapped around me.

"I brought a condom," I tell her when I slide her panties down. We're both hot and sweaty, and I can't resist her anymore.

"I did, too," she whispers against my neck. "But we might not be able to use it."

"Why not?" I expect her to tell me this was all a mistake, that she really didn't mean to get me all hot and bothered just to tell me I'm not worthy enough to take her virginity, but it's the truth.

She clears her throat. "It all d-d-depends on whether or not you're allergic to l-l-latex."

Latex? I've never been asked that question. Maybe it's because every other girl I've been with expected me to bring protection, or didn't expect me to use it at all. "*Chica*, I'm not allergic to anythin'."

"Good," she says, reaching for her purse and pulling out a condom package. "You want me to put it on you?"

She can't see the side of my mouth quirk up. I'm not the virgin here, and yet tonight has been full of firsts for me. "You sure you can figure it out?"

I hear the rip of the package opening. "Do I hear a challenge?" she whispers, then leans forward and says against my lips, "Oh, Carlos. You know I can't resist a challenge."

52

Kiara

"Wake up, *chica*."

The sound of Carlos's voice and the gentle touch of his fingers on my naked shoulder makes me stir. My legs are intertwined with his, my head is nestled in the crook of his arm, and memories of what we did a few hours ago are bringing bittersweet feelings to the surface.

I open my eyes. It's still dark, and we're both completely naked under the covers. "Hi," I say, my voice groggy and tired.

"Hey. We need to go."

"Why? Can't we just stay here longer?"

He clears his throat and rolls away, the movement bringing the cold night air rushing to my skin. "I forgot I've got to bring Alex's car back tonight."

"Oh," I say dumbly. "Okay." It's obvious he's freaking out and regretting what we did. I get it. I don't know what triggered it just now, but I get it.

"Get dressed," he says, no emotion in his voice.

When he hands me his jacket after we're both dressed, I don't take it from him. "I have my raincoat," I tell him.

"You left it back in the car, Kiara. Wear this. It'll protect you from the rain."

"I don't need it," I say, then walk out into the rain in my dress and bare feet. I need his love. I need his honesty. Handing me his jacket is superficial protection anyway. The jacket is wet, inside and out.

In the car, after he shoves the blankets in the trunk and mumbles something about having to go to the Laundromat to clean them, we drive through the dark, empty streets in silence. The only sound is the rain tapping against the windows. I wish rain wouldn't remind me of tears so much.

"Are you angry with me?" I ask him as I put my raincoat on so he doesn't see my arms shaking.

"Nope."

"Then s-s-stop acting like it. Tonight was perfect for me. Please don't ruin it."

He pulls into my driveway and parks next to my car. The rain is coming down harder now.

"Wait a few minutes until it lets up," he says as I gather my shoes and purse.

"How are you getting back home after you drop off the car?"

"I'll just crash at my brother's place," he says.

I watch the droplets of rain make tracks down the car window, then disappear. I can't stay here for much longer without getting emotional. "Just so you know, I don't regret tonight. Not one bit."

He looks right at me. The outside lights shine on his beautiful, strong face. "Listen, I need to figure things out. Everything is so—"

"Complicated," I say, finishing his sentence. "Let me m-m-make this easy for you, then. I'm not stupid to think things have changed just b-b-because we had sex. You made it p-p-perfectly clear from the

beginning you weren't looking for a girlfriend. There, now I uncompli-
cated everything. You're free and clear."

"Kiara—"

I can't stand to hear him tell me what a mistake tonight was,
despite my declaration that it didn't have to mean anything. I get out
of the car, but instead of running through the rain, I head straight for
my car. I need to be in a place where I can think and cry without anyone hearing me. Right now, my car is my sanctuary. If Carlos would
just drive off, I could cry in peace.

He opens his window and motions for me to open mine. When I
do, he tries to say something. His voice barely carries through the
sound of the rain coming down hard between us.

I lean out the car window. "What?"

He leans out his window, meeting me halfway. We're both wet and
soaked, but neither of us seems to care. "Don't run away from me
when I need to tell you somethin' important."

"What?" I say, hoping he doesn't notice the tears running down
my face, and praying they're getting mixed up with the rain.

"Tonight was . . . well, it was perfect for me, too. You've turned
my world upside down. I've fallen in love with you, *chica*, and it scares
the fuckin' shit outta me. I've been shakin' all night, because I knew it.
I've tried to deny it, to make you think I wanted you as a fake girlfriend, but that was a lie."

"I love you, Kiara," he says before his lips move forward and meet
mine.

53

CARLOS

"What are you doin' here?" Alex asks me when I arrive at his place at five a.m.

"I'm movin' back in," I say, pushing past him. At least until Keno and I disappear at the end of the month.

"You're supposed to be at the Westfords'."

"I can't stay there anymore," I tell him.

"Why not?"

"I was kind of hopin' you wouldn't ask that."

My brother winces as he asks, "Did you do somethin' illegal?"

I shrug. "Maybe in some states. Listen, Alex, I got nowhere else to go. I guess I can always go live on the streets with the other kids whose brothers have kicked 'em out . . ."

"Don't give me that bullshit, Carlos. You know you can't stay here. Judge's orders."

Judge's orders or not, I can't take advantage of Westford. He's one of the good guys that I used to think only existed in movies. "I screwed the Professor's daughter," I blurt out. "So can I stay here, or not?"

"Please tell me you're jokin'."

"I can't. It was Homecoming, Alex. And before you give me a lecture on right and wrong, remember that you screwed Brittany for the first time as a bet—on the floor of our cousin's auto-body shop—on Halloween, no less."

Alex rubs his temples with his fingers. "You don't know anythin' about that night, Carlos, so don't act like you do." He sits on his bed and puts his head in his hands. "I'm sorry for askin', but I've got to know . . . did you use a condom?"

"I'm not an idiot."

Alex looks up and cocks a brow.

"Okay," I say. "I admit I'm an idiot. But I still used a condom."

"At least you did one thing right. You can stay tonight," Alex says as he tosses me a pillow and blanket from the closet.

Alex returned the air mattress, so I have to sleep on the floor. Ten minutes later, when the lights are off and I'm staring up at the shadows on the ceiling, I ask, "When did you first fall for Brittany? Did you know it all along, or did somethin' specific happen?"

He doesn't answer at first, so I think he's sleeping. But then a long sigh fills the silence. "It was in Peterson's chemistry class . . . when she told me she hated me. Now stop yappin' and go to sleep."

I turn on my side and go over the entire night in my head, starting with the moment I saw Kiara with that black dress on. The girl literally took my breath away. "Alex?"

"What?" he asks, annoyed.

"I told her I loved her."

"Did you mean it?"

I wasn't kiddin' when I said the girl had turned my life upside down. What kind of girl wears baggy shirts every day, has a gay best friend, stutters when she's nervous, tapes shower schedules on the bathroom mirror, makes stupid cookie magnets just to piss me off, works on cars like a guy, and gets excited about the challenge of puttin' on a condom? The girl is fuckin' nuts. "I'm in deep shit, Alex, 'cause I think I'd like nothin' better than to wake up with her every mornin'."

"You're right, Carlos. You *are* in deep shit."

"How am I gonna get out of this thing with Devlin?"

"I don't know. I'm as clueless as you at this point, but I know who might be able to help us."

"Who?"

"I'll tell you in the mornin'. In the meantime, shut up and let me sleep."

My cell phone goes off, the beeping sound echoing loudly through-out the small apartment.

"Who the hell is callin' you at this hour?" Alex demands to know. "Is it Devlin?"

I read the text and laugh. "No. It's a text from your ex-girlfriend."

Alex practically jumps out of bed and snatches my phone from me. "What did she say? Why is she textin' you?"

"Keep your pants on, bro. She asked me how my date was, and I texted her back before I came to your place. I didn't know she was gonna respond right away."

"She wants to know if I'm as miserable as she is," Alex says, read-ing Brittany's text.

The glow of the screen on his face reveals it all. He's still hope-lessly and disgustingly in love with Brittany. I'd make fun of him if I didn't think I had the same look on my face when I woke up with Kiara's naked body pressed against mine and I realized that I'd rather die than live one day without her. I haven't known her long at all, but just lookin' at her feels so right. Being with her feels like . . . home. It may not make sense to anyone else, but it does to me.

"Yo, Alex, just text back that you're a complete mess, and that you'll do anythin' to get her back . . . even if it means havin' dinner with her stupid parents and kissin' her pearly white ass for the next seventy or so years."

"What do you know about relationships, or pearly white asses? Forget it. I don't want to know the answer to that question." He walks into the bathroom with my phone and closes the door.

As long as he's not in the room, I might as well take advantage of his empty bed. He'll be in the bathroom awhile, texting his ex-girlfriend until she's his girlfriend again. I guess it didn't hurt that I was sure to text her just before I came here, knowing she's probably awake and as miserable as my brother is.

Back at the dock when I stroked Kiara's long hair as she fell asleep in my arms, a paralyzing fear washed over me. I realized that what I had with Destiny wasn't anything compared to what I have with Kiara. It scared me, and I panicked. I just needed to get away from her to process everything, because being near her makes me fantasize about a future with Kiara instead of focusing on reality—that I'm leaving Colorado at the end of the month. As Keno said, there's really no other choice.

The next thing I know, Alex is shaking me. "Get up," he orders.

"I need a few more hours of sleep," I tell him.

"You can't," he says. "It's already noon. And you got a message."

Brittany again. Those two better get back together so I have one less thing to worry about. "I told you to text her and let her know you'll do anythin' to get her back."

"The message wasn't from Brit."

I open one eye. "From Kiara?"

He shrugs. "You did get *one* text from Kiara."

I bolt upright, the sudden movement giving me a nasty head rush. "What did she want?"

"She wanted to know if you were okay. I texted her back and said you slept here last night, and you were still sleeping. But you got a voice mail message from Devlin. He wants to meet with you tonight."

I rub the knot of tension forming on the back of my neck. "Well, I guess that's it, then. No use thinkin' he forgot about me. He spent a lot of energy recruitin' me. I don't see a way out, Alex."

"There's always a way out." He tosses me a towel. "Take a shower and get dressed. You can wear my clothes. Hurry up, we don't have much time."

Alex drives me to the Boulder campus. I follow him into one of the buildings, but freeze when we get to a door marked RICHARD WESTFORD, PROFESSOR OF PSYCHOLOGY.

"Why are we here?" I ask my brother.

"Because he can help us." Alex knocks on the Professor's door.

"Come in," he says. Westford looks up when we enter his office. "Hey, boys. I trust you and Kiara had a good time last night. Colleen told me she was still sleeping this morning when I left the house, so I didn't have a chance to ask her."

"It was fun," I mumble. "Kiara is—"

"A handful sometimes, I know. She definitely keeps us on our toes."

"I was gonna say amazin'," I tell him. "Your daughter is amazin'."

"I can't take all the credit. Colleen has done an incredible job raising the kids. Kiara just needed to come out of her shell a bit. It was nice of you to take her. I know she really appreciated it. Now, I'm sure

Alex didn't want to meet me here just to shoot the breeze. What's on your minds?"

"Tell him what you told me," Alex orders.

"Why?"

" 'Cause he's hard-core."

I take a look at the balding Westford. Hard-core, my ass. Maybe he used to be, but not now. He's a shrink now, and no longer a soldier.

"Just do it," Alex says, getting impatient.

I'm out of options, so I might as well tell him. Maybe Westford can come up with somethin' I haven't thought of. Unlikely, but it's worth a try.

"You know when I got beat up and I told you I got jumped near the mall?"

He nods.

"I lied. Truth is . . ." I look over at Alex, who's urging me on. "I got recruited by this guy named Devlin."

"I know who Devlin is," the Professor says. "I never met the guy, but I've heard about him. He's into drug smuggling." His eyes narrow, and I detect a little bit of that hard-core personality trying to shine through. "You'd better not be dealing drugs for Devlin."

"That's my problem," I tell the Professor. "It's either I deal drugs, or he kills me. At this point I'd rather deal drugs than die."

"You're not doing either," Westford says.

"Devlin's a businessman who only cares about the bottom line."

"Bottom line, huh?" Westford leans back in his chair, those wheels in his brain working overtime. The chair tips so far back he has to quickly grab on to his desk so he doesn't tumble backward. The Professor is hard-core, all right. All the way down to his designer penny loafers.

"Any suggestions?" Alex asks. "We're out of ideas."

Westford holds up a finger. "I might be able to help. When are you supposed to meet with him?"

"Tonight."

"I'm going with you," Westford says.

"Me too," Alex chimes in.

"Oh, goodie. We're startin' our own little *renegados* gang." I give a short laugh. "You can't just walk up to Devlin."

"Watch me," Westford says. "No matter what it takes, we'll get you out."

Is this guy kiddin' me? He's not my flesh and blood. He should think of me as a burden and liability instead of someone worth fighting for.

"Why are you doin' this?" I ask him.

"Because my family cares about you. Listen, Carlos, I think it's about time I tell you about my past so you know where I'm coming from."

Oh, I gotta hear this.

I lean back in the chair, ready to get a long drawn-out sob story about how his parents were mean to him because they didn't buy him the exact toy he'd asked for on his sixth birthday. Or the fact that a kid in high school beat him up for his lunch money. Maybe he was upset because his parents bought him a used car instead of a brand-new one when he turned sixteen. Does the Professor expect me to actually feel sorry for him? I can beat him in the sob-story department, hands down.

Westford shifts in his desk chair uncomfortably, then lets out a long breath. "My parents and brother died in a car accident when I was eleven." Whoa. I wasn't expectin' that. "We were driving home one night, it was snowing, and my dad lost control of the car."

Wait. "You were in the car, too?"

He nods. "I remember him swerving, then the car spinning." He hesitates. "Then the truck colliding with the car. I can still hear my mom's screams as she saw the big headlights aiming right at her, and my brother looking to me as if I could somehow help."

He clears his throat and swallows, and my cockiness over winning the game of "whose childhood was worse" starts to fade quickly.

"After the impact, when my body stopped jerking around like a rag doll, I opened my eyes and saw blood splattered all over the car. I wasn't even sure if it was mine or my parents' . . . or my brother's." His eyes are glassy now, but he doesn't shed a tear. "It was like he was in pieces, Carlos. Even though I thought I would die if I moved because of the pain I was in, I needed to save him. I needed to save all of them. I held the gash in my brother's side together for as long as I could, the hot, fresh blood streaming all over my hands. The paramedics had to pry my hands off him, because I wouldn't let go. I couldn't let him die. He was just seven, a year older than Brandon."

"They all died except you?"

He nods. "I didn't have relatives who could take me in, so I spent the next seven years bouncing from foster home to foster home." He stares right into my eyes. "Actually, I got kicked out of most of them."

"For what?"

"You name it. Fighting, drugs, running away . . . basically, I was in need of some understanding and guidance, but nobody was willing or had the time to straighten me out. Eventually I turned eighteen and was put out on the streets. I found my way to Boulder, where there were plenty of kids like me. But living on the streets was dirty, and I was alone and had no money. One day I was begging for money and this man sneered at me and said, 'Does your mother know where you are and what you're doing with your life?' At that moment I thought about it. If my mother up in heaven was looking down at me, she'd be pissed as hell at me for not trying to make something better out of myself.

"But I realized that no amount of fighting would bring back my family," he continues. "No amount of drugs would completely erase the look in my brother's eyes begging me to help him. And I could never run away from that image, because running away just made things worse. I refocused that energy in the military."

"I don't want you to risk your life for me, Professor. It's bad enough I want to date your daughter."

"We'll have that discussion another time. Now let's focus on the problem we've got right now. When are you supposed to meet with Devlin?" Westford asks. Determination is radiating off the guy.

We agree to meet at seven and put some sort of plan in motion. What that actual plan is, I have no clue. Hopefully by seven o'clock to-night Westford will figure it out. Truth is, it's a relief to finally put my life in the hands of someone I trust.

54

Kiara

My mom is making pancakes for breakfast on Monday morning. "What are you still doing home?" I ask.

"I've got some employees opening the store." She smiles warmly, that sweet smile that always made me feel better when I had to stay home sick in grade school. "It'll be nice see you and Brandon and get you off to school for a change."

"Have you or Dad talked to Carlos?" I ask for about the trillionth time since yesterday. Both of my parents have been acting strange since my dad came home from work yesterday. He locked himself in his office with my mom for hours. The two of them have seemed on edge since then, and I can't figure out why.

Carlos told me he was going to Alex's place, right before he told me he loved me. I wish he was here so he could assure me everything will be okay between us, but I know he needed to get away and figure things out in his own head.

The problem is, I never eased his biggest fear. He needs to know I'm not going to suddenly give up on him or give up on us. I wish I could have talked to him before school today, but that didn't happen. He hasn't been back since he dropped me off early Sunday morning.

I watch my mom as she vigorously mixes the pancake batter faster in her bowl. "I'm not sure."

"What does that mean?"

"It means I don't want to talk about it."

I walk over and put my hand on her arm, stopping her from mixing. "What's going on, Mom? You have to tell me." I swallow, hard. I won't stand back and have the boy I love live in misery because he loves me back. It's not worth it. I would give him up if it meant making him happy. "I need to know."

When she looks at me, her eyes are watery. Something is definitely up. "Your father said he's taking care of it. I've trusted him for the past twenty years. I'm not going to stop now."

"Does it have to do with Carlos? Does it have to do with him getting beat up? Is he in danger?"

My mom puts her hand on my cheek. "Kiara, honey, go to school. I'm sorry I'm a little tense this morning. It will all be over soon."

"What's going to be over, Mom?" I ask in a panic. "Just t-t-tell me."

She stands back, obviously contemplating the consequences of spilling whatever secret she's holding. "Your father said he's handling it. He had a long talk with Tom and David yesterday, his buddies from the military who work in the DEA's office."

"I feel sick," I say.

"It will be fine, Kiara. Now get ready for school, and don't say one word about this to anyone."

"Is breakfast ready?" my brother asks as he walks in the kitchen.

My mom goes back to mixing. "Almost. We're having whole-wheat pancakes."

Brandon gives her his famous pouty face, the one nobody in our house can resist. I wonder if that look will ever get old. Knowing Brandon, he'll still be using it when he's fifty. "Can you put chocolate chips in them? Pleeeeease."

My mom sighs, then kisses his big cheeks. "Okay, but put on your shoes so you're not late for the bus."

As she ladles the batter into the hot pan, I walk into my dad's office. I know it's terrible of me, and it's totally inappropriate, but I sit in front of my dad's computer and browse his history. First on the Internet and then in each of his document folders. If there's some clue to what's going on, I need to know. And since nobody will tell me, I have no choice but to snoop around and investigate, myself.

Unfortunately for my dad, but fortunately for me, he didn't erase his history. I pull up everything he's worked on in the past twenty-four hours. I look at a letter he wrote to his boss about introducing a new curriculum, an outline of the test he's working on for his class, and a spreadsheet with a bunch of numbers on it.

I study the spreadsheet. It's a financial one . . . detailing one of their bank accounts. The last entry is from today—a debit for fifty thousand dollars—leaving my parents with a balance of five thousand dollars. In the description line is one word: CASH.

My dad is taking fifty thousand dollars out of his bank account today. Somehow that money is connected to Carlos getting beat up, I just know it.

"Kiara, the pancakes are ready!" my mom yells from the kitchen.

Obviously she's not going to tell me why my dad is taking a

whopping fifty thousand dollars out of their bank account. I play innocent, eating my pancakes with a fake carefree smile on my face.

As soon as we're finished with breakfast, my mom rushes Brandon
outside to his bus. I quickly sneak back onto my dad's computer because
I have one more idea: I go to the maps website my dad usually uses and
click on his recent searches.

Sure enough, the last two searches are addresses unfamiliar to me.
One is near Eldorado Springs and the other is in Brush, a town that's
about an hour and a half away from my house. I know there are a lot of
drug problems there, and my heart sinks. What's going on? I quickly
scribble down the addresses, then close the computer and try to look
innocent when my mom comes back in the house.

At school, I open my locker and find two roses lying on top of
my books, one red and one yellow. They're bound together by a black-
beaded rosary and a note. There's no doubt in my mind they're from
Carlos.

I kneel in front of my locker and read the note, written on a torn
piece of notebook paper.

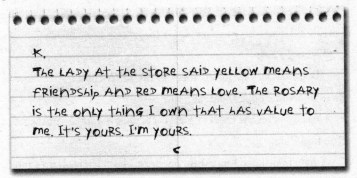

> K.
> The lady at the store said yellow means
> friendship and red means love. The rosary
> is the only thing I own that has value to
> me. It's yours. I'm yours.
> C

"Is that Kiara Westford?" Tuck says, coming up to me. "The one
who doesn't call me back?"

I clutch the flowers, rosary, and note to my chest. "Hi. Sorry, things have been crazy."

His eyebrows furrow. "What are you holding?"

"Stuff."

"From the Mexican stud?"

I look down at the beautiful flowers. "He's in t-t-trouble, Tuck. My dad's with him, and my mom is acting weird, and I need to help somehow. I can't just be left in the dark, when they're all in d-d-danger. I feel so useless. I just . . . don't know what to d-d-do." I don't even realize it at first, but I'm rubbing the rosary beads with my fingers.

Tuck pulls me into one of the empty classrooms. "What kind of trouble? Stop shaking, you're scaring me."

"I c-c-can't help it. I think it has to do with Carlos and some drug dealers. I'm freaking out because my dad thinks he's Rambo and can fix this. The DEA might be involved, too. I have a feeling he's in over his head, Tuck. I don't even know who this drug dealer guy is, except that after Carlos got beat up he referred to him as The Devil, in Spanish—*El Diablo*."

"*El Diablo?*" Tuck shakes his head. "Doesn't mean anything to me. You know who you should talk to?"

"Who?" I ask.

"Ram Garcia. His mom works in the DEA's office. She came to talk to us a while back about her job."

I kiss Tuck on the cheek. "You're a genius, Tuck!" I say, then run off to find Ram.

A half hour later I'm sitting opposite Mrs. Garcia, Ram's mom. She's wearing a navy pantsuit and a crisp, white shirt, looking very much like a DEA agent. When Ram gave me her number, I snuck out to my car and called her. I told her everything I know. I've never ditched school before, but then again, I've never been so worried about my dad and Carlos before.

Mrs. Garcia just got off the phone with my mom. "She's on her way," she tells me. "But you're going to have to stay here for a few hours. I can't let you leave this building."

"I don't get it," I tell her. "Why?"

"Because you know the address in Brush. Your knowledge could put a lot of people in danger." Mrs. Garcia sighs, then leans forward on her desk, piled high with manila file folders. "To be quite blunt, Kiara, your father, Carlos, and Alex have stumbled into something we've been working on for months."

"Please tell me they're not in danger," I beg, my heart pounding faster and faster.

"We've got word to our undercover special agents working inside the gang that your father and the Fuentes brothers are to be protected. They're as safe as they can be on the brink of a DEA drug raid, and your father will take all necessary precautions."

"How do you know that?"

"Your father has worked with us before on some criminal profiling and undercover ops," she says. "He's keeping the operation a secret from Carlos and Alex for their protection. The less they know, the better."

What? My dad has worked with the DEA? For how long? He never mentioned anything before. I always see him as my dad, not some guy who does undercover work with the U.S. Drug Enforcement Agency. All I knew was that he had friends from the military who he kept in touch with and went out with occasionally.

Mrs. Garcia can probably see the confusion written all over my face, because she leaves her desk and crouches in front of me. "Your father was in some heavy-duty combat missions with some of our agents. He's well respected, and he knows what he's doing." She looks at her watch. "All I can tell you is that we've got them under constant surveillance, and our agents working on the inside are highly trained."

"I don't care that they're highly trained." Tears well up in my eyes, and I think about all the things I want to say to Carlos that I've held back and all the times I should have told my dad how much I appreciate him. "I want a one hundred percent guarantee that they'll all be fine." I tell Mrs. Garcia.

She pats my knee. "Unfortunately, there are no guarantees in life."

55

CARLOS

I look over at my brother, his knuckles white as he grips the wheel of his car. The Professor spent all day going over the different scenarios, just in case Devlin or any one of his guys decided to go back on their word and start shooting at us.

When we met last night, the Professor arrived at Alex's place in a black turtleneck and black pants, as if he were Zorro. I think the poor guy misses whatever covert military operations he used to be involved in, because his raw excitement couldn't be more obvious.

Don't ask me how Westford came up with the idea of making a deal with Devlin. I spent an hour arguing with him, telling him there was no way in hell I'd let him pay tens of thousands of dollars of his own money to get me out of trouble. I argued until my throat was sore, but Westford insisted. He said he'd negotiate with Devlin with or without my consent.

Before he made the deal with Devlin, Westford and I sat down for a long talk. He was willing to offer to buy Devlin off for whatever it took . . . on one condition.

I'd have to enter the military or go to college.

That was it. The Professor was willin' to take a shitload of cash out of his own bank account to buy my way out of Devlin's chains, with rules attached. "It's like slavery," I told him this afternoon as we went over the plan in detail.

"Cut the crap, Carlos. Is it a deal or not?" he'd said.

I shook hands with him, but to my surprise he pulled me forward into a bear hug and said he was proud of me. It feels weird to have a guy who knows the truth about who I am and what I've done still care about my future and want me to succeed.

Devlin gave the Professor twenty-four hours to come up with fifty thousand dollars to buy me out, but only after I showed up at some secret location in Brush and proved to have a united front with Rodriguez in front of allies of the *Guerreros*. I guess some big deal is about to happen, but the Mexican suppliers don't trust Devlin. I wonder if the street war with the R6 has already started.

We're in the car on the way to meet with Devlin and Rodriguez in Brush. Westford has the cash in a duffel between his feet. I'm in the backseat, looking at the two guys who've become my posse. My heart is beating strong and hard at the prospect of bringin' my brother and the Professor. I was supposed to be in this alone, without draggin' anyone down with me. Devlin is my problem, and they've made him theirs.

I remember when Kiara brushed her fingers over one of my tattoos. *La rebelde*. I'm not that big of a rebel if I need an old man and my big brother as my posse. And while havin' them with me doesn't sit well in my gut, I admit I don't know what the hell I'd do without 'em.

"There's still time for both of you to back out. I can go in there alone."

"That's not happenin'," Alex says. "I'm comin' with you, no matter what."

Westford pats the duffel filled with money. "I'm ready for this."

"That's a helluva lot of money, Professor. You sure you want to part with it? You can wipe your hands clean of me and keep the money. I wouldn't even blame you."

He shakes his head. "I'm not backing out now."

"If one of us feels that somethin' is off, get out fast," I tell them. "Devlin makes sure he's got numbers on his side."

Alex drives slowly through Brush. The streets remind me of Fairfield, our town back in Illinois. We didn't live on the richest side of town. Some people refused to drive through the south side for fear of being carjacked, but it was home to us.

A bunch of guys our age are standing on the corner, eyeing Alex's unfamiliar car suspiciously. If we look like we know what we're doing and have a purpose, we'll be just fine. If we act like we have no clue where we are or how to get where we want to go, then we're toast.

As Alex drives down a winding driveway and ends up in front of what looks like an abandoned warehouse, chills race up and down my spine. Why did Devlin insist on us meeting him here?

"You ready to do this?" Alex says as he puts the car in park.

"No," I say. Both Westford and Alex turn back to look at me. "I just wanted to say thanks," I mutter. "But you think Devlin'll take your money and run, or shoot us dead and take the money anyway?"

Westford opens the car door. "Only one way to find out."

We all pile out of the car, our senses heightened and on alert. As much as I made fun of Westford for wearing all black again today, he does look like a badass. An *old*, balding badass, but a badass nonetheless.

"There's a guy on the roof, two more at two o'clock, and ten o'clock," Westford tells us.

What was his nickname in the military, Eagle Eye?

A guy is standing at the entrance, waiting for us. He's probably in his twenties, but he's got blond hair so bleached it's almost white. "We're expecting you," he says in a gruff voice.

"Good," I say, taking the reins and stepping inside first. If anyone starts shooting, I'll be the target, and Alex and Westford might still be able to get away. As the white-haired guy pats us down for any weapons, Westford is clutching that sack of money as if it's too painful to part with. Poor Westford. He's totally out of his league. "You know I don't want you to do this, right?" I ask him.

"Don't argue," Westford says. " 'Cause that would be a waste of time and get you nowhere."

The white-haired guy leads us to a small office off to the side. "Wait here," he orders.

Here we are, two Fuentes brothers and one ex-military guy clutching a duffel bag filled with fifty thousand dollars of freedom money.

Rodriguez comes in the room and sits on the desk. "So what do you have, Carlos?"

"Money. For Devlin," I say. I guess The Big Guy didn't show up.

"I was told you had a benefactor to buy you out. You know people in high places, huh?" he says, eyeing the Professor.

"Sort of."

He holds out his hand. "Give it to me."

Westford grips the duffel tighter. "No. Devlin and I made the deal together, and we're going to see it through together."

Rodriguez gets in his face. "Let's get one thing straight, Grandpa.

You've got no leverage here. In fact, you should be kissin' my ass or you might find yours on the ground with a hole in it . . . or two."

"Oh, but I do have leverage," Westford says. "Because my wife has a letter she's been instructed to give to the police if we all don't come home safely. Believe me, a well-respected professor won't easily be forgotten. You and Devlin will be hunted down."

Westford doesn't release the death grip on the duffel.

A frustrated Rodriguez leaves us again. I wonder if next time he'll just shoot us and take the money for himself.

"What, do you think Devlin's gonna give you a receipt for it?" I ask the Professor. "I don't think you get a tax break for payin' someone off."

He shakes his head. "Even in the face of danger, you're still a smart-ass. Do you ever give it up?"

"Nope. It's just part of my charm."

"How do you know Devlin's even here?" Alex asks.

The Professor doesn't bat an eye. "If there's a guy on the roof and two more monitoring the comings and goings, the Boss is here. Trust me."

Sure enough, Devlin himself comes sauntering in a half hour later. He obviously made us wait on purpose, to make sure we knew who was in charge. Devlin glances at the duffel. "How much is in there?" he asks.

"The amount we agreed on . . . fifty thousand."

Devlin walks around the room, eyeing us skeptically. "I checked you out, Professor Westford."

For half a second, Westford looks nervous. He masks that nervousness an instant later. I don't know if my brother or Devlin noticed, but I sure did. "And what did you find out?" Westford asks.

"That's the strange part about it," Devlin says. "Not much. Makes me think you've got some kind of intelligence connections. Maybe you came here just to set me up."

I can't help but laugh. The Professor doesn't have intelligence connections. Maybe in his glory days he was some covert special-ops soldier, but now he's just Kiara and Brandon's dad. The guy gets a hard-on for Family Fun Night, for God's sake.

"The only connections I have are with the psychology department at the university."

"Good, 'cause if I find out you have any connections with the cops, you and these kids will regret you ever met me. Rodriguez told me your wife has a letter for the cops to ensure your safety. I don't like threats, Professor. Open the duffel."

Westford opens it and takes out the money. When Devlin is convinced all the money is there and isn't marked, he orders me to pick it up and hand it to him.

"Now we've got one more piece of business," Devlin says, gesturing to me. "You and Rodriguez are going to be meeting some very important friends of mine. In Mexico."

What? No way.

"That wasn't part of the deal," Westford says.

"Well, I'm changing the deal," Devlin says. "I have the money, a gun, and the power. You've got nothing."

As soon as he says it, the ground starts shaking as if we're in the middle of an earthquake.

"It's a bust," someone yells through the door. Devlin's men have all scattered, giving up their duties to protect their boss to save their own skins.

DEA agents in blue jackets burst in the warehouse, guns at the ready. They order everyone to the ground.

Devlin's eyes are crazy-wild as he pulls a .45 from his waistband and aims it at the Professor.

"No!" I scream, then lunge forward to knock the gun out of Devlin's hand. Nobody is gonna kill Westford, even if that means I end up in the morgue. I hear the gun go off and feel like my thigh is on fire. Blood drips down my leg and lands on the cement floor. It's surreal and I'm afraid to look at my leg. I don't know how bad it is, only that it feels like a thousand bees have clung to my thigh with their stingers. Alex rushes Devlin, but Devlin is too quick. He turns the gun on my brother, and a deathly panic washes over me. I scramble toward Devlin to stop him, but Westford holds me back just as the white-haired guy bursts into the room with a Glock. "Police! Put the gun down!" he orders.

What the—

In a flash, Devlin turns his gun on the guy and they exchange gunfire. I hold my breath but let it out when Devlin is down, clutching his chest. His eyes are open and blood is streaming on the floor under him. The biting pain at the prospect of losing my brother or Westford at the hands of Devlin makes me squeeze my eyes shut.

When I open them, I see a glimpse of Rodriguez out of the corner of my eye. He's got a gun pointed to the white-haired undercover agent. I try to warn the agent, but to my surprise Westford grabs Devlin's gun and shoots Rodriguez as if he's a trained sharpshooter.

Westford barks orders to one of the DEA agents as he and Alex carry me out of the warehouse.

"Are you DEA?" I ask Westford through gritted teeth, because my damn leg stings like a mother.

"Not exactly. Let's just say I still have friends in high places."

"Does this mean you get to keep the fifty Gs?"

"Yep. I guess that means our deal is off. You don't have to go to college or the military."

Two paramedics rush over with a gurney. They strap me down, but I reach for the Professor before they can wheel me away. "Just so you know, I'm goin' to enlist."

"I'm proud of you. But why?"

I groan against the pain but manage to give him a half smile. "I want to make sure Kiara's got a boyfriend who has more to offer than a hot bod and a face that could make angels weep."

"Do you *ever* lose the ego?" Westford asks me.

"Yeah." When his daughter kisses me, my ego flies out the window.

56

Kiara

I stroke Carlos's arm and let him squeeze my hand as we're waiting to hear what the doctor has to say about his leg. A stoic Alex also hasn't left Carlos's side since we arrived at the hospital. He's scared, and it looks like he blames himself for not preventing his younger brother from getting hurt. But it's all finally over.

My dad found out that Carlos's mom and brother were threatened, so with their permission he's arranged for them to come to Colorado. He's also helping them get temporary housing, which is great.

"My dad says you'll live," I tell Carlos as I lean forward and kiss him on his forehead.

"Is that a good thing?"

Okay, Kiara, it's time to spill it, I tell myself. *It's now or never.* I lean close to him, so only he can hear me. "I . . . I think I need you, Carlos. The forever kind of need." I look up. Carlos's eyes are locked on mine. I want this, I want him. More than that, I really do need him. We need each other. The closer I get to him, the more I feed off the energy and strength radiating from him.

I can tell he wants to say something, to fill the silence like he usually does, but he holds himself back. Our eyes are still locked, and I won't look away. Not this time.

I slowly reach out a shaky hand and touch the center of his chest over his shirt, wanting to take his pain away. He's breathing heavier now, and I can feel his heart beating against my palm.

He cups my cheek in his hand, his thumb gently stroking my skin. I close my eyes and lean into his touch, melting in the warmth of his hand.

"You're dangerous," he says.

"Why?"

"Because you make me believe in the impossible."

After Carlos's surgery, my entire family is surrounding his hospital bed. There's a knock at the door. Brittany walks in tentatively.

"Thanks for calling me, Kiara," she says.

Carlos told me to call right before his surgery, after he told me about Alex and Brittany breaking up. "No problem. I'm glad you're here."

"So am I," Carlos says. "But I'm on morphine, so you might want to get that in writing." Alex is about to walk out of the room, but when he reaches the door Carlos blurts out, "Alex, wait."

Alex clears his throat. "What?"

"I know I'm gonna regret sayin' this, but you and Brittany can't break up."

"We already did," Alex says, then looks at Brittany. "Right, Brit?"

"Whatever *you* want, Alex," she says, frustrated.

"No." He walks up to her. "*You* wanted to break up. *Mamacita*, don't put the blame on me."

"*You* want to keep our relationship a secret from my parents. *I* don't. I want to scream to the world that we're together."

"He's afraid, Brittany," Carlos says.

"About what?"

Alex reaches out and tucks her blond hair behind her ear. "That your parents will make you realize you deserve better."

"Alex, you make me happy, you make me strive to work hard. I get caught up in your future dreams and am desperate to be part of it. Whether you like it or not, you're a part of me. Nobody can change that." She looks up at him, tears streaming down her face. "Trust me."

He cups her cheek and swipes her tears away. Without a word, I hear Alex choke up as he pulls her close and doesn't let go.

A half hour later, Alex, Brittany, and my parents have escaped to the hospital cafeteria. Tuck walks in with a big vase filled with hot pink carnations and a balloon attached that reads FIFTY PERCENT OF ALL DOCTORS GRADUATE IN THE BOTTOM HALF OF THEIR CLASS—HOPE YOUR SURGERY WENT WELL!

"Hey, *amigo!*" he says.

"Oh, hell." Carlos snorts in fake annoyance. It makes me feel good to know he hasn't lost his fighting spirit after what happened today. "Who invited you?"

Tuck sets the vase down on the window ledge and smiles wide. "Oh, come on. Don't be such a grump. I'm here to cheer you up."

"By bringin' me pink flowers?" Carlos says, gesturing to the vase.

"Actually, the flowers are for Kiara because she has to deal with you." He pulls out the balloon and ties the string to the hospital-bed handrail. "Consider me your candy stripper . . . I mean striper."

Carlos shakes his head. "Kiara, tell me he didn't just call himself a stripper."

"Be nice," I tell Carlos. "Tuck drove all the way here because he cares about you."

"Let's just say you've grown on me," Tuck admits, then brushes his long hair out of his face. "Besides, if I didn't have you to annoy, my life wouldn't be the same. Face it, *amigo* . . . you complete me."

"You're *loco*."

"And you're a homophobe, but with Kiara's and my guidance you've got potential to be a decent and tolerant human being." Tuck's cell starts ringing. He pulls it out of his pocket and announces, "It's Jake. I'll be right back." He disappears into the hallway, leaving me and Carlos alone. Well, we're not entirely alone. Brandon is in the chair in the corner of the room, busy playing one of his video games.

Carlos grabs my wrist and pulls me onto the bed with him. "Before today, I was plannin' on leavin' Colorado," he tells me. "I figured it was better if I wasn't a burden to your parents or Alex anymore."

"And now?" I ask nervously. I need to hear him say he wants to stay here for good.

"I can't leave. Did your dad tell you my ma and Luis are comin' here?"

"Yeah."

"That's not the only reason I'm stayin', *chica*. I can't leave you any more than I could walk out that door right now while my leg is busted up. I was just thinkin' . . . should we tell your parents now or later?"

"Tell them what?" I ask, eyes wide.

He kisses me softly, then says proudly, "That we're in a serious, monogamous, committed relationship."

"We are?"

"*Sí*. And when I get out of here, I'm gonna fix the door to your car."

"Not if I fix it first," I tell him.

He bites his bottom lip and looks at me as if I just turned him on. "Is that a challenge I hear in your voice, *chica*?"

I take his hand and weave my fingers through his. "Yeah."

He pulls me closer to him. "You're not the only one in this relationship who loves a challenge," he says. "And just so you know for the future, I like my double-chocolate chip cookies warm and soft in the middle . . . and without magnets glued to them."

"Me, too. When you decide to bake me some, let me know."

He laughs, then leans his head toward mine.

"Are you guys about to French-kiss?" Brandon blurts out.

"Yeah. So close your eyes," Carlos says, then pulls the blanket over us, giving us as much privacy as we can get right now. "I'll never leave you again," he whispers against my lips.

"Good. I'm never letting you leave." I lean back a little. "And I'm never leaving you either. Remember that, okay?"

"I will."

"So does this mean you're going to learn to mountain climb with me?"

"I'll do anythin' with you, Kiara," he says. "Didn't you read the note I put in your locker? I'm yours."

"And I'm yours," I tell him. "Forever and always and then some."

EPiLOGue

Twenty-Six Years Later

Carlos Fuentes watches as his wife of twenty years tallies up the day's receipts. Business was good at McConnell's Auto Body, which they bought when he got out of the service. Even during the slow years they'd gotten by just fine. His wife always appreciated the simple things in life, even when they could afford more. Hell, hiking near The Dome made her smile more than anything else—that hike had become a weekly ritual for them.

Now skiing or snowboarding, that was another thing altogether. Carlos took Kiara and their kids to the resorts in the winter, but he watched from a distance as Kiara taught all three of their girls to ski, then snowboard. They especially liked it when their uncle Luis came along, because he was the only Fuentes brother who was crazy enough to race them down the black-diamond slopes.

Carlos wipes his hands on a shop cloth after changing the oil on his old friend Ram's car. "Kiara, we gotta talk about this kid your dad coerced me into letting stay with us."

"He's not a bad kid," Kiara says, looking up at her husband and giving him a reassuring smile. "He just needs some guidance, and a home. He reminds me of you a little bit."

"Are you kiddin'? Did you see how many piercings that delinquent has? I bet he's got 'em in places I don't even want to know about."

As if on cue, their oldest daughter, Cecilia, drives up to the garage door with the delinquent in the passenger seat beside her.

"His hair is too long. He looks like a *chica* who needs a shave," Carlos says.

"Shh, be nice," his wife reprimands.

"Where were you two?" Carlos questions accusingly as the two high school juniors simultaneously hop out of Cecilia's car.

Neither of them answers.

"Dylan, follow me. We need to have a man-to-man." Carlos catches the delinquent roll his eyes at him, but he follows Carlos into his private office in the corner of the body shop. Carlos closes the door and settles into the chair behind his desk while he motions for Dylan to sit in the guest chair opposite him.

"You've been stayin' with us a week already, but I've been so busy at the shop I haven't been able to go over house rules," Carlos says.

"Listen, old man," the kid says lazily, then leans back and plants his dirty shoes on Carlos's desk. "I don't follow rules."

Old man? Doesn't follow rules? Damn, this kid needs a good asskicking. Truth be told, Carlos did see a bit of his old, rebellious self in the kid. Dick was the best stand-in father Carlos could ever ask for back when he'd first come to Colorado . . . Hell, he'd called the Professor "Dad" even before he married Kiara, and couldn't imagine how his life would have turned out without her father's guidance.

Carlos pushes Dylan's feet off his desk, then thinks back to the time Kiara's dad recited a speech similar to the one about to come out of his mouth. "*Uno*, no drugs or alcohol. *Dos*, no profanity. I have three daughters and a wife, so keep it clean. *Tres*, curfew on weekdays is ten thirty; on weekends it's midnight. *Cuatro*, you're expected to clean up after yourself and help around the house when asked, just like our own children. *Cinco*, there's no TV unless you're done with homework. *Seis* . . ." He couldn't remember what his father-in-law's sixth rule was, but it didn't matter. Carlos had his own rule he wanted to make sure was stated loud and clear. "Dating Cecilia is out of the question, so don't even think about it. Any questions?"

"Yeah, one." The delinquent leans forward and looks Carlos straight in the eye with a mischievous smirk. "What happens when I break one of your fuckin' rules?"

ACKNOWLEDGMENTS

This book wouldn't be possible without Emily Easton, my editor, who waded through the many drafts of Carlos's story with me. I think you deserve sainthood for this one.

Dr. Olympia González gets a special thanks for spending time with me to help me flavor my book with Spanish and Mexican culture. I take full credit for any mistakes I've made, as they are purely my own, but I hope I've made you proud.

I'm so lucky to have Ruth Kaufman and Karen Harris as my friends and colleagues. Both of you helped me from the very beginning until the very end. I can't thank you two enough for being there when I needed you most.

I want to thank Alex Strong for being my inspiration for Tuck. I hope he's half as entertaining and witty as you are, Alex.

I also want to thank my agent, Kristin Nelson, for her never-ending support while I was writing this book. It meant so much to me to have a cheerleader cheering me on. You even went white-water rafting with me in Colorado when I went there for research, you poor dear. Talk about a full-service agent!

Other people who have helped with this book or have been wonderfully supportive friends (and family) are Nanci Martinez, Dayna Plusker, Marilyn Brant, Erika Danou-Hasan, Meko Miller, Randi Sak, Michelle Movitz, Amy Kahn, Joshua Kahn, Liane Freed, Jonathan Freed, Debbie Feiger, Nickey Sejzer, Marianne To, Melissa Hermann, Michelle Salisbury, and Sarah Gordon. Meeting with Jeremy, Maya, Sarah, Koby, Victor, and Savi was extremely helpful in giving me insights on what it's like to be a teen in Colorado. And I could never forget to thank Rob Adelman for his infinite wisdom.

I also want to thank my fans. They are the best part of writing novels, and I never get tired of reading fan mail they send and e-mail to me.

Last but never least, I want to thank Samantha, Brett, Moshe, and Fran. They definitely are my inspiration and have been so wonderful and patient while I was writing this book.

I love to hear from my readers. So don't forget to visit me at www.simoneelkeles.net!

Read all about Alex and Brittany's love story in . . .

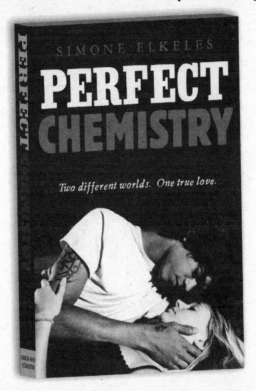

SIMONE ELKELES

PERFECT
CHEMISTRY

Two different worlds. One true love.

Brittany Ellis and Alex Fuentes couldn't be more different; she's the "perfect" cheerleader living a life of luxury and he's a gang member from the wrong side of town. But when they are forced together by a school project, sparks begin to fly and both Alex and Brittany realise that sometimes appearances can be deceptive.

Will their emerging feelings be enough to keep them together when the world is determined to tear them apart?